Kyril Bonfiglioli was born in Eastbourne in 1928 of an English mother and Italo-Slovene father, and after studying at Oxford University and spending five years in the army, took up a career as an art dealer, the same career as his eccentric creation, Charlie Mortdecai. He lived in Ireland and then in Jersey, where he died in 1985. Penguin publish all three Mortdecai novels (*Don't Point That Thing at Me*, *After You with the Pistol* and *Something Nasty in the Woodshed*) as well as *All the Tea in China*, a historical novel featuring a disreputable ancestor of Mortdecai, and *The Great Mortdecai Moustache Mystery*, which was left unfinished at his death and was completed by Craig Brown.

An accomplished fencer, a fair shot with most weapons and a serial marrier of beautiful women, Bonfiglioli claimed to be 'abstemious in all things except drink, food, tobacco and talking' and 'loved and respected by all who knew him slightly'.

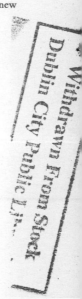
Withdrawn From Stock
Dublin City Public Lib...

After You With the Pistol

KYRIL BONFIGLIOLI

Brainse Ráth Maonuis
Rathmines Branch
Fón / Tel: 4973539

PENGUIN BOOKS

PENGUIN BOOKS

Published by the Penguin Group
Penguin Books Ltd, 80 Strand, London WC2R 0RL, England
Penguin Group (USA) Inc., 375 Hudson Street, New York, New York 10014, USA
Penguin Group (Canada), 90 Eglinton Avenue East, Suite 700, Toronto, Ontario, Canada M4P 2Y3
(a division of Pearson Penguin Canada Inc.)
Penguin Ireland, 25 St Stephen's Green, Dublin 2, Ireland (a division of Penguin Books Ltd)
Penguin Group (Australia), 707 Collins Street, Melbourne, Victoria 3008, Australia
(a division of Pearson Australia Group Pty Ltd)
Penguin Books India Pvt Ltd, 11 Community Centre, Panchsheel Park, New Delhi – 110 017, India
Penguin Group (NZ), 67 Apollo Drive, Rosedale, Auckland 0632, New Zealand
(a division of Pearson New Zealand Ltd)
Penguin Books (South Africa) (Pty) Ltd, Block D, Rosebank Office Park,
181 Jan Smuts Avenue, Parktown North, Gauteng 2193, South Africa

Penguin Books Ltd, Registered Offices: 80 Strand, London WC2R 0RL, England

www.penguin.com

First published by Secker and Warburg Ltd 1979
First published by Penguin Books in *The Mortdecai Trilogy* 2001
Reissued in this edition 2014
002

Copyright © the Estate of Kyril Bonfiglioli, 1979
All rights reserved

The moral right of the copyright holders has been asserted

Printed in Great Britain by Clays Ltd, St Ives plc

Except in the United States of America, this book is sold subject
to the condition that it shall not, by way of trade or otherwise, be lent,
re-sold, hired out, or otherwise circulated without the publisher's
prior consent in any form of binding or cover other than that in
which it is published and without a similar condition including this
condition being imposed on the subsequent purchaser

ISBN: 978-0-241-97031-7

www.greenpenguin.co.uk

MIX
Paper from
responsible sources
FSC™ C018179
www.fsc.org

Penguin Books is committed to a sustainable
future for our business, our readers and our planet.
This book is made from Forest Stewardship
Council™ certified paper.

All the characters in this book are fictitious: any similarity to real people or corpses is both accidental and disgusting.

The epigraphs are all by Alfred, Lord Tennyson except one which is a palpable forgery. The forgery is signed, after a fashion.

Disclaimer

There is not a word of truth in this book. I have neither met nor heard of anyone who resembles any character in it, I am glad to say. They are all figments of my heated imagination, every one of them. This is particularly true of the fictional narrator, whose only resemblance to me is around the waist-line.

I apologize for what he says about the art-trade. Why, some of my best friends, etc.

There is, I believe, a very sophisticated cop-shop South of the Thames but I have never seen it except in the mind's eye, which is where I should like to keep it. The only pub I know called The Bunch of Grapes is in Gracie Fields' deathless aspidistra song. I believe that there was once a shop in the East End called Mycock's Electrical but I know of no pig-abattoirs of that name.

The lavatory inspection-panel ruse for smuggling heroin was, indeed, once used but it has long been 'blown' or I would not have related it. It is almost as old-fashioned as using motor-car tyres, cameras from Kowloon, hollowed-out boomerangs from Bendigo (New South Wales), 'pregnant' ladies from Amsterdam, long-playing records pressed out of ganja resin, or even dusty carpets from Kashmir which need a little attention from a certain dry-cleaner in London's dockland before they are delivered to the consignee. The same is true of other naughty techniques described: pray do not let them tempt you to embark upon a life of crime. You may be a hare but 'Old Bill' is a most capable tortoise.

I apologize to Air France: its hostesses are all excellent linguists. Many of them can even understand my French.

Leabharlanna Poibli Chathair Bhaile Átha Cliath

Dublin City Public Libraries

1 Mortdecai prepares to meet his Maker

Come into the garden, Maud,
I am here at the gate alone . . .

Maud

Yes, well, there it was. That was that. I'd had my life.

So I drank the last of the whisky, looked a loving last once more on the naked Duchess and shed perhaps – I forget – a tear of self-pity, that last of luxuries, before climbing stiffly to my feet. The heavy, friendly old Smith & Wesson pistol was loaded in all chambers with the murderous soft lead target ammunition. I pulled the hammer back a little, which allows the cylinder to spin. I span it, listening to the quick, fat chuckle of the ratchet.

Then I sat down again.

I had left it just that few minutes too late and there had been just too small a jolt of Scotch in the tail of the bottle. Had there been even one more fluid ounce, I could have gone roaring out of my smelly cavern like some old grizzly bear, but now sobriety had me by the throat. You see, I had begun to consider just where the bullets would smash into my well-nourished body; what bones would be shattered, what spillikins of the said bones would be sent splintering through which of my delicate organs, how *long* this mangling would last before generous Death brushed pain aside and passed his hand over my eyelids, closing them forever.

1

No, wait, sorry. Hang about a bit. It has just occurred to me that you might be a trifle puzzled as to why Charlie Mortdecai – I – should have been preparing for death in a smelly cavern, chaperoned only by a naked Duchess, a large revolver and an empty whisky-bottle. I realize that some might find these circumstances unusual, perhaps even bizarre.

This, then, is what happened before you came in. Nude readers begin here. There's this chap Me, you see – the Hon. Charlie Mortdecai – I was actually christened Charlie – who is, or rather am, a nice, rich, cowardly, fun-loving art-dealer who dabbles in crime to take his mind off his haemorrhoids. Then there's this fantastic painting by Goya of 'The Duchess of Wellington' who, at the time of being painted, had absent-mindedly forgotten to put her knickers back on. Or, indeed, anything else. Having so much respect for other people's property that I sometimes feel bound to care for it myself, I had nicked the painting from the Prado, Madrid, and exported it personally to a millionaire art-lover in New Mexico. I found the art-lover freshly murdered, and his randy-eyed young widow casting about for a replacement. All went wrong, as all these things do, and, as my sense of fun started to fray at the cuffs, I shortened my lines of communication – as the generals used to say – and made tracks for England, home and beauty, in the order named.

All sorts of people were by that time disliking Mortdecai warmly, and in an almost-final hot pursuit I was obliged to kick in the head of my trusty thug Jock, who was about to die even more unpleasantly in the quicksands of Morecambe Bay, Lancashire. I – Mortdecai – holed up in a disused red-oxide mine on Warton Crag (still in Lancashire), found that my enemies had traced me thither, and realized that my life was over. I was in a pretty shabby mental and physical state by then and resolved to get as drunk as I could, then to come roaring out of my stinking lair and kill at least Martland, chief of my persecutors.

Right? Any questions? There I was, then, preparing to go out and meet the kind of messy death I had too often seen happen to other people. I couldn't see myself in the rôle at all.

Ah, yes, *but*. What else? Where was your actual alternative?

I upturned the bottle and collected three more drops, or it may have been four.

'Pull yourself together, Mortdecai,' I told myself sternly. 'Nothing in life became you like the leaving of it. It is a far, far better thing that you do now. You are ready and ripe for death. You'll *like* it up there.'

'Up?' I thought. '*Up* there? Must you joke at a time like this?'

Then I looked again at the painted Duchess, her canvas propped against the wall of the mine-shaft, smiling like a whole choir of Mona Lisas, voluptuously sexless, erotic only on a level that I could never reach. Although God knows I have tried.

'Oh, very well,' I told her.

I crawled to the entrance of the little mine. There was no sound outside, no movement, but they were there, all right. There was nowhere else they would be.

I emerged.

An enormous light burst out but, unaccountably, it was pointed not at me but in the opposite direction. It illumined not me but a pallid, startled Martland. Well, at least I could fulfil that part of my programme. He peered down the beam at me, making urgent little movements with his hands.

'Martland,' I said. I had never heard myself use that voice before but I knew that there was no need for more than the one word.

He opened his mouth. It seemed difficult for him. Perhaps he was going to remind me that we had been at school together. I couldn't find it in my heart to shoot anyone looking as soppy as he did, but my trigger-finger had a life of its own. The pistol jumped hard in my hand and a puff of dust bounced out of his trousers just below the belt-buckle.

I gazed at the spot, entranced. There wasn't any blood; you couldn't even see a hole. Martland looked puzzled, vexed even. He sat down hard on his bottom and looked at me, cross and disappointed. Then he started dying and it was rather dreadful and went on and on and made me feel even more ill than I was and I couldn't bear it and I shot him again and again but I couldn't seem to make him stop dying.

Whoever was working the searchlight finally tore himself away from the spectacle and nailed me with the beam. I clicked the revolver three or four times – empty as Mortdecai now – three or four times up into the glaring eye of the light, threw it as hard as I could, missed again.

3

'Mr Mortdecai,' said a polite American voice.

I whipped around, eyes tearing at the darkness, my gut hungry for the coming of the bullets.

'No, Mr Mortdecai,' the voice went on, 'please compose yourself. Nobody's killing anyone else tonight. Everything's going to be all right. I mean, *really* all right.'

You cannot imagine how disappointing it is to be all braced for death and then to find, at the very moment of truth, that they're not frying tonight. I sort of suddenly found myself sitting down and weeping noisily; the sobs tore through my breast like the bullets that hadn't.

They gave me a flask of whisky and I was sick again and again but at last I kept some down and then there was a dull, silencer *plop* from Martland's direction and the noises of his dying stopped and then the woman got me to my feet and helped me down the slope and across the road and up into Fleagarth Wood and to their tent. She was very strong and smelled of old fur coats. I was asleep as I hit the groundsheet.

2 Mortdecai finds that his Maker does not want to meet him

> . . . when the steam
> Floats up from those dim fields about the homes
> Of happy men that have the power to die . . .
>
> *Tithonus*

The woman woke me up a few moments later. The moments must have been hours, actually, for a dank and dirty dawn was oozing into the tent. I squealed angrily and burrowed back down into the sleeping-bag: it smelled of nasty policewomen but I loved it – there were no people there. She coaxed me awake with a finger-and-thumb-nail in the ear-lobe: she must have found that in the works of Lord Baden-Powell. (Don't you often wonder what B.P. would have done for a living if he had lived in these times? *Oxfam?* Peace Corps?)

She had won her Camp Cookery Badge, that was clear, for the mug of tea wheedled into my quaking fingers was of no tenderfoot quality. I, personally, have no quarrel with Evaporated Milk: it lends a heartening, lusty thickness to cheap tea which, once in a while, I find most gratifying.

Then she made me wash and shave (she lent me a tiny razor with a pink plastic handle: it was called 'Miaouw' – why?) and then she showed me where the Elsan was and then we went, *hand in hand*, down through the wood to where a huge American camper-van was parked just off the road. We climbed in. Two other people were there already. One was on a stretcher, covered all over with a blanket. Well, Martland, obviously. I didn't have any feelings about that. Not then. Later, perhaps. The other was the American, gabbling gibberish into a wireless set which was quacking back at him. He was, it fuzzily seemed to me, patiently telling someone to get into touch with someone else who would authorize yet another someone to blah-blah. He was very polite to the quacker. At last he went through the 'Roger and out' nonsense, switched off all the little knobs and turned around, giving me a smile which was quite unwarranted, considering how early in the day it was. He proved to be a man called Colonel Blucher, whom I had met before. We had never actually hit each other.

'Good morning, Mr Mortdecai,' he said, still smiling in that unwarranted way.

'Oink,' I said. There was, clearly, something pretty wrong with me still, for I had meant to be a trifle civiller than that, but 'Oink' was what came out.

He blinked a little but took no offence.

'I'm very, very sorry to have to rouse you so early, Mr Mortdecai, for I recall that you are not an early riser. You must be very tired still?'

I was more articulate this time.

'Oinkle oink,' I said courteously. It was the strangest feeling: the words were perfectly clear in my head but all I could produce were these farmyard imitations. Distraught, I sat down heavily and put my head in my hands. A sort of juicy noise underneath me and a sort of knobbly softness made me realize that I was sitting on Martland. I jumped up again, squeaking. Blucher was looking worried so, naturally, I tried to hit him, didn't I? I mean, it seemed a sensible thing to do at the time. But my wild swing only threw me flat on my face and I started to cry again. I wanted my mummy badly, but I knew she wouldn't be coming: she never did, you know, even when she was alive. She was one of those Mums who believe that Christopher Robin kills all known germs. A kind of literary Harpic.

Blucher came and put his arm around me and helped me to my feet and I fancy I probably started to scream a bit – for I thought it was Jock come back from his grave in the quagmire – so he took something out of his hip-pocket and, with a look of infinite compassion on his face, slugged me carefully behind the ear. This was much better.

'Roger and out,' I thought gratefully as the lovely blackness encompassed me.

3 Mortdecai regains consciousness, if you can properly call it that

All things are taken from us, and become
Portions and parcels of the dreadful Past.

The Lotus-Eaters

To this day I still do not know where it was that I awoke nor, indeed, how long I had been separated from my cogitative faculties, bless them. But I think it must have been somewhere awful in the North-West of England, like Preston or Wigan or even Chorley, God forbid. The lapse of time must have been quite three or four weeks: I could tell by my toenails, which no one had thought to cut. They felt horrid. I felt cross.

'I have had a Nervous Breakdown,' I told myself crossly, 'the sort of thing that one's aunts have for Christmas.' I lay motionless for what seemed a long time. This was to deceive *them*, you see, whoever they were, and to give me time to think about it all. I soon became aware that there were no *them* in the room and that what I wanted was a great, burly drink to help me think. I decided, too, that since they had kept me alive they must want something from me and that a drink would not be an unreasonable *quid pro quo* for whatever it was, if you follow me. (You will observe that the very recollection of that time interferes with my well-known lucidity.)

Another thinking-bout persuaded me that the way to get such a drink was to summon whatever chalk-faced, black-uniformed,

8

Kafkaesque she-policewoman was standing guard over me. I could find no bell to ring so I heaved myself out of bed and sat down absurdly on the floor, weeping with puny rage.

My getting out of bed must have triggered some sort of alarum, for the swing-doors swung or swang and an apparition appeared. I examined it narrowly. It was clearly the photographic negative of a chalk-faced, black-uniformed police-woman.

'You are clearly a photographic negative,' I cried accusingly. 'Be off with you!' Her face, you see, was of the deepest black and her uniform of the brightest white: all wrong. She giggled, showing, paradoxically, about forty-eight large *white* teeth.

'No, mahn,' she retorted, 'negative. Ah'm not under-developed, jest underprivileged.' I looked again; she spoke truth. As she scooped me up and lifted me into bed (oh the shame of it) I was even more convinced, for my nose was flattened by one of her magnificent 100-Watt headlamps. Despite my effete condition (oh, all right, I know that's not the right word but you know perfectly well what I mean) I felt the old Adam surging about freely in my loins – and I don't mean the gardener. I desired more than anything else in the world to go out and slay a dragon or two for her: the thought was so beautiful that I began to weep again.

She brought me a drink; rather a thin one but undeniably alcoholic. Enoch Powell had lost my vote for good. I cried a little more, rather relishing it. The tears, I mean, not the drink, which tasted like milk from a dead sow. It was probably Bourbon or something of that sort.

Much later she came in again, smiling enormously, and stood with her back to the open door.

'Now – here's Doctor Farbstein to see you,' she chortled richly, as though it was all a huge joke. A great, jolly, bearded chap brushed past her splendid bosom (I swear they *twanged*) and came and sat on my bed. He was full of fun.

'Go away,' I piped feebly, 'I am an anti-Semite.'

'You should have thought of that before they circumcised you,' he roared merrily. A stray beam of sunshine (perhaps we weren't in North-West England after all) struck splinters of gold from his brave Assyrian beard; Kingsley Amis would have recognized them instantly for beads of breakfast egg but I am a romantic, as you must have realized by now, even if you have still not read my previous adventures.

'You have been quite ill, you know,' he said, keeping his face straight and trying to sound grave and concerned.

'I am *still* quite ill,' I retorted with dignity, 'and my toenails are a disgrace to the National Health Service. How long have I been in this pre-Lysol *guet-apens*, this quasi-medical Lubyanka?'

'Oh, ages and ages it seems,' he replied cheerily. 'Every now and then they tell me you're stirring and I pop in and shoot you full of paraldehyde to stop you chasing the nurses and then I forget you for days on end. "Letting Nature take its kindly course" is what we call it.'

'And what have I been eating, pray?'

'Well, nothing much, really, I fancy. Nurse Quickly tells me that the dust lies thick on your bed-pan.'

'Faugh!' I said. I realized then that I was indeed on the mend, for it takes a strong man to say 'faugh' properly and with the proper curl of the upper lip.

But I realized, too, that this was a man who was a match for me unless I could soon put him down. I summoned up my most aristocratic glare.

'If you are indeed a doctor, as your ah sunburned accomplice claims,' I grated, 'perhaps you will have the goodness to tell me who your employers are.'

He leaned low over my bed and smiled seraphically, his beard splitting to disclose a row of teeth which seemed to be a random selection from Bassett's celebrated Liquorice Allsorts.

'*SMERSH!*' he whispered. The garlic on his breath was like acetylene.

'Where have you been lunching?' I croaked.

'In Manchester,' he murmured happily. 'In one of the only two fine Armenian restaurants in Western Europe. The other, I am happy to say, is also in Manchester.'

'I shall have some Armenian food sent in,' I said, 'and with no further delay or shilly-shallying. See to it that there is lots of *houmous*. And whom do you really work for?'

'You would be horribly sick. And I work for the Professor of Psychiatry in the University Hospital of North-East Manchester, if you want to know.'

10

'I don't care how sick I would be – it would provide employment for these nurses, who seem to be disgracefully underworked. And I don't believe a word of this North-East Manchester nonsense: only London is allowed to have points of the compass, everyone knows that. You are clearly one of these impostors, probably struck off the register for using an unsterilized button-hook.'

He leaned close to me again.

'Arseholes,' he murmured.

'That too, probably,' I rejoined.

We became rather friends at that point – was it what he would have called aversion-therapy? – and he agreed that he might see his way to sending in a little *houmous* and hot Armenian bread and perhaps a touch of that lovely sour-bean salad with a chick-pea or two sculling about in it. He also said that I might be allowed a visitor.

'Who would visit me?' I asked, shedding another ready tear.

'There's droves of them,' he leered, 'queues of juicy little *shicksas* wanking in the waiting-room; it's becoming quite a health-hazard.'

'Oh, bollocks,' I said.

'Suck 'em,' he replied. Salt of the earth, some of these doctors.

Having settled the amenities he became less human and got down to business.

'I won't bother to tell you what's the matter with you,' he said crisply, 'because you'd only ask me to spell it and I can't. You might call it traumatic massive neurasthenia if you were a country GP thirty years out of date. Someone of your age might well call it a nervous breakdown, which is how mentally inadequate people describe a syndrome of boring signs and symptoms exhibited by people who find that they have bitten off more than they can emotionally chew.'

I thought about that.

'The answer to that,' I said at last, 'is in the plural again.'

He thought about that.

'Now I come to think of it,' he said judicially, 'you could just be right. However, what matters is that I've had you under heavy sedation for a good long time and I think you're now pretty well all right – at any rate, as all right as you were before, ha ha. You may find yourself crying a little from time to time but it'll pass. I'm going to give you stimulants now – one of the methedrines – they'll soon sort you out. In the meantime, just go on using the Kleenex, ha ha, and cry as much as you like.'

My lower lip trembled.

'No, no!' he shouted, 'not now! Because here' – and with this he flung open the door like an exhibitionist's mackintosh – 'here is your visitor!'

It was Jock who stood in the doorway.

I felt the blood draining out of my brain; I think I may have shrieked. I know I fainted. When consciousness came back there was still Jock in the doorway, although I clearly – all too clearly – remembered having kicked his head in, weeks before, as he lay in the grip of that quagmire.

He was grinning uncertainly, as though unsure of his welcome; his head was bandaged, there was a black patch over one of his eyes and new gaps in his few, strong, yellow teeth.

'You all right, Mr Charlie?' he asked.

'Thanks Jock, yes.' Then I turned to Dr Farbstein.

'You disgusting bastard,' I snarled, 'you call yourself a doctor and spring things like this on your patients? What are you trying to do, kill me?'

He chuckled happily, making a noise like a cow defecating.

'Psychotherapy,' he said. 'Shock, terror, rage. Probably done you a power of good.'

'Hit him, Jock,' I pleaded. 'Hard.' Jock's face fell.

'He's all right, Mr Charlie. Honest. I been playing gin rummy with him every day. Won *pounds*.'

Farbstein slid out, doubtless on his way to spread a little more sunshine elsewhere. He was probably a very good doctor, if you like that kind of doctor. When I felt a little better I said 'Look, Jock . . .'

'Forget it Mr Charlie. You only done it because I asked you to. My mum would have done the same if she'd been there. Lucky you wasn't wearing boots, reely.'

I was a bit startled: I mean, I suppose Jock must have had a mummy at some stage but I couldn't quite visualize her, least of all in boots. I suddenly felt desperately tired and fell asleep.

When I awoke, Jock was perched decorously on the end of my bed, looking hungrily out of the window at what can only have been a giggle of passing nurses.

'Jock,' I said, 'how on earth did they . . .'

'Range Rover. They got a sort of winch on the axle; wound me out with it. Didn't half hurt. Dislocated me shoulder, cracked a couple of ribs and give me a double rupture in me actual groin. All sorted out now.'

'Is your eye, er, badly hurt?'

'It's gorn,' he said cheerfully. 'You put the leather smack into it and I was wearing me contack lenses. The nurses like me patch, romantic they call it. I'm not having no glass eye, bugger that, me uncle had one and swallowed it, never got it back.'

'Goodness,' I said feebly, 'how was that?'

'He put it in his mouth, see, to warm it up and make it so it would slip in the socket easy, then he hiccupped, having been on the piss the night before. Down it went. Cured the hiccups but he never saw the eye again.'

'I see.' How the other half lives; to be sure. There was a long and happy silence.

'*Never* got it back?' I wondered aloud.

'Nah. Me uncle even got the croaker to have a look up his bum but he said he couldn't see nothink. "Funny," says me uncle, "I can see you as clear as anythink, doctor." '

'Jock, you're a bloody liar,' I said.

'Mr Charlie?'

'Speaking.'

'You don't half owe me a lot of wages.'

'Sorry, Jock. You shall have them as soon as I am strong enough to lift a cheque-book. And, now I come to think of it, I've got a hefty Employer's Liability insurance policy on you; I think you get two thousand pounds for an eye. Out of my own pocket I shall buy you the finest glass eye that money can buy, even if I have to pay cash. Please wear it in the house; you can save the romantic black patch for your wenching expeditions.'

Jock lapsed into an awed silence: in his world people only get two thousand pounds by doing highly illegal things which earn you five years in the nick. I fell asleep again.

'Mr Charlie?' I opened a petulant eyelid

'Yes,' I said, 'this is still I.'

13

'You remember when you went to see that Colonel Blucher geezer at the American Embassy?'

'I remember vividly.'

'Well, he's here. Well, any road, he comes here every day almost. He's got them all jumping except Doctor Farbstein; I reckon Doctor Farbstein reckons he's a Kraut.'

'That figures.'

'Funny thing is,' he went on, 'he never asks me nothing – Blucher I mean – just asks are they looking after me and would I like a Monopoly set to play with the nurses with.'

I waited while he subsided into helpless giggles.

'Jock,' I said gently when he had finished. 'I know Colonel Blucher's here. As a matter of fact, he's right behind you, standing in the doorway.'

He was. So was a huge, black, automatic pistol, which was pointing unerringly at Jock's pelvis. (Very nice, very professional: the pelvic region doesn't move around nearly as much as the head and the thorax. A bullet there, smashing through bladder and privates and all the other butcher's offal we keep in our pelvic girdles, is just as certain as one between the eyes and, I'm told, a great deal more painful.)

Blucher ostentatiously flicked on the safety-catch and magicked the pistol away into the waistband of his trousers. That is a very good place to carry a pistol while you still have a waist-line; afterwards the bulge becomes a little ambiguous.

'Sorry about the dramatics, gentlemen,' he said, 'but I thought this might just be a good time to remind you that you are alive right now because I put in a request for you. I can change my mind at any time I feel I have to.'

Well, *really*! I cringed of course, but it was only partly funk: the rest was embarrassment at his lamentable bad taste.

'Are you aware,' I asked bravely, 'that you are occupying space which I have other uses for? Or rather, for which I have other uses?'

'I like P.G. Wodehouse too, sir,' he rejoined, 'but I would hesitate to use any kind of flippancy in the situation you find yourself in. Or rather, in which you find yourself.'

I gaped at the man. Perhaps he was human after all.

'What exactly do you want me to do?' I asked.

'Well, it's more *who*, really. Think of someone young and beautiful and fabulously rich.'

I thought. I thought briefly because I am not wholly stupid.

'Mrs Krampf,' I said.

'Right,' he said. 'Marry her. That's all.'

'All?'

'Well, practically all.'

'I need to go back to sleep,' I said. Back to sleep is where I went.

4 Mortdecai applies his razor-keen brain to the proposition

O Sorrow, wilt thou live with me
No casual mistress, but a wife.

In Memoriam

To tell the truth, that was not one of the times when I enjoyed a long and untroubled repose. Well, look, do you remember the last time *you* were told that you could continue living on the condition that you married a madly beautiful, sex-happy she-millionaire whom you were pretty sure had murdered her last husband in an almost undetectable way? Did *you* get in the wholesome eight hours of sleep?

The actual sequence of events was that I awoke, sat up and chewed fingernails, cigarettes and Scotch whisky – not necessarily in that order – for an hour or two. (I need scarcely tell you that Jock had smuggled me in a bottle of Messrs Haig and Haig's best and brightest.)

Those secret agents and chaps that you read about in the story-books would have had it all figured out to the last bloodstain in a moment, I don't doubt, but I had not their resilience, nor their youth. Perhaps, too, I was not, in those days, quite as clever as I am now. After a while I said 'bollox' and 'I dunno' and 'soddem' – in that order, this time – and went back to sleep after all. I don't really know why I troubled to wake up in the first place, for it was evident to the most casual eye that the old anti-Mortdecai conspiracy still had its hand on the wheel, its finger on the pulse and its thumb up to the knuckle-joint. 'Soddem' was without doubt the best phrase I had coined that day. I said it again. It seemed to help.

'I gotta get me bottle back,' mumbled Jock the next day, sitting on my bed and watching Nurse Quickly deal with my neglected toenails.

'Oh, I'd not worry about that, Jock. They're sending us off on a convalescent holiday to the Lake District tomorrow – a couple of lungfuls of mountain air and you'll be as full of fight as a lion. It's all these nurses that have been sapping your strength.' He shifted uneasily.

'I don't reckon you quite got the idea about "bottle", Mr Charlie. It isn't just guts, it's more like sort of relishing using your guts. You know, like sort of having a bit of a laugh when you're duffing someone up.'

'I think I see,' I said, shuddering thoughtfully and strumming one of Nurse Quickly's gorgeous breasts with a newly trimmed great toe. Without a flicker of expression she drove half an inch of scissor-point into my other foot. I didn't scream; I have a bit of bottle myself, you know.

A moment later, when she had completed my pedicure, Jock took the scissors gently from her and with one hand crumpled them up. Then he held out his spade-like hand, cupped. Nurse Quickly leaned forward until the breast previously referred to rested in his hand. He growled quietly; she made a sort of throaty noise as he started to squeeze. Disgusted, I dragged my foot with some difficulty out from between them and sulkily turned my back.

They left the room together, without a word, headed for the linen-cupboard if I know anything about hospitals.

'Youth, flaming youth,' I thought bitterly.

5   Mortdecai decides that there are plenty of fates nicer than death

'Tirra lirra' by the river
Sang Sir Lancelot.

The Lady of Shalott

Well, there we were, Blucher and Jock and me, sitting around a table on the terrace of an hotel under one of those Lake District mountains that people send you postcards of, sipping tea (!) and watching a party of idiots getting ready to walk up the mountain. It was a fine day for early November in Lakeland – in fact it was a fine day for anywhere in England, any time – but it was only about five hours before dusk and the climb they were planning takes a smart three hours each way. A Mountain Rescue Warden was pleading with them, almost tearfully, but they just looked at him with amused contempt, the way a female learner-driver looks at her instructor. (She *knows* that hand-signals are a lot of nonsense invented by men to baffle women; why, her mother has been driving for years and has never used a hand-signal and she's never been hurt. A few other people, yes, perhaps, but not her.)

The mountain-rescue chap finally raised both hands and dropped them in a gesture of finality. He turned away from the group and walked towards us, grinding his teeth audibly. Then he stopped, whirled around and *counted* them ostentatiously. That would have frightened me. They just giggled. As he walked towards us I made a sympathetic grimace and he paused at our table.

'Look at the buggers,' he grated. 'Wearing *sandals*! Just a lot of nasty accidents looking for somewhere to happen. Coom nine o'clock, me and my mates'll be scouring t'bloody mountain for the twist in t'dark, brecking wor necks. And I'll miss t'Midnight Movie, like as not.'

'Too bad,' I said, keeping my face straight.

'Why do you do it?' Blucher asked him.

'For *foon*,' he growled, and stalked away.

'Going to overhaul his equipment,' said Blucher wisely.

'Or beat his wife,' I said.

We went on sipping tea; that is to say, Blucher and I sipped while Jock sort of hoovered his up with a lovely, wristy motion of the upper lip. I don't much care about tea-drinking in the afternoon; in the morning the stuff Jock brings to me in bed is like that Nepenthe which the wife of Thone gave to Jove-born Helena, but in the p.m. it always makes me think of Ganges mud in which crocodiles have been coupling.

'Well, now,' said Blucher.

I put on my intelligent, receptive face, the one I wear when a heavy customer, pen poised over cheque-book, starts to tell me about his philosophy of art-collecting.

'Mr Mortdecai, why do you suppose I and my superiors have uh preserved you from uh death at very very great trouble and expense?'

'You told me: you want me to marry Johanna Krampf. I cannot begin to understand why. By the way, what did you do with Martland's er cadaver or mortal coil?'

'I understand it was fished out of the Thames at Wapping Old Stairs. The uh marine organisms had done a good job and the cause of death is recorded as "uncertain". Police suspect a vengeance homicide.'

'Goodness,' I said, 'their *minds*!'

He fidgeted fretfully. I was not asking the right questions. Chaps like him do not like to volunteer information, they like it to be wheedled out. I sighed.

'All right,' I said, 'why must I marry Mrs Krampf? Is she planning to overthrow the Constitution of the United States?'

'Charlie,' he said heavily.

'Please don't be formal,' I interrupted. 'My acquaintances call me Mr Mortdecai.'

'Mortdecai,' he compromised, 'if you have a fault it is a regrettable tendency towards flippancy. I am a humourless man and I recognize it – few ʰumourless people can – I do ask you to bear this in mind and to remember that I hold the strings of your life in my hand.'

'Like the Blind Fury with the Abhorrèd Shears,' I chirrupped. It was his turn to sigh.

'Ah, *shit*,' is what he sighed. 'Look, I perfectly realize that you are not afraid of death; in your own kooky way I believe you to be a pretty brave man. But death as an inevitability-concept-situation is very very far removed from the slow infliction of death by means of PAIN.' He sort of barked that last word. Then he collected himself, leaned over the table towards me and spoke gently, reasonably.

'Mortdecai, my Agency is concerned only with winning. We are not regular guys in any sense of the word; we have no code of behaviour which would stand the light of day, still less an in-depth investigation by the *Washington Post*. What we do have is a number of specialized operatives who are skilled in inflicting PAIN. Many of them have been doing it for years, they think about it all the time. I'm afraid that some of them kind of like it. Do I have to go on?'

I straightened up in my chair, looked bright, helpful, unflippant.

'You have my undivided attention,' I assured him. He looked meaningfully at Jock. I took the hint, suggested to Jock that we must be boring him and that the hotel swarmed with chambermaids whose bottoms needed pinching. He ambled off.

'Right,' said Blucher. 'Now. Mrs Krampf seems to be kind of crazy about you. I won't say I find that easy to understand, I guess it's a case of whatever turns you on. I don't have any clearcut idea right now of why we want you around her except that we know there must be something. Something big. A few months before her husband uh died, our uh accountancy branch, as we call it, had detected the clandestine movement of very large amounts of currency into and out of the Krampf empire. After his demise we looked for these movements to cease. They did not. In fact they increased. Understand, we're not talking about low-grade, bush-league money-shifting – that's for the IRS or Currency Control guys. We're talking about sums of money which could buy a Central

American republic – or two African ones – overnight and still leave you a little walking-about money. We don't have any idea what it's all about. So go marry Mrs Krampf and find out.'

'Okay,' I said briskly, colloquially, 'I'll cable her first thing tomorrow and slip her the good news.'

'You don't have to do that, Mortdecai. She's already here.'

'Here?' I squeaked, looking about me wildly, like any pregnant nun. 'What do you mean "here"?'

'I mean right here in this hotel. In your room, I guess. Try looking in your bed.'

I made a sort of imploring noise. He patted me on the shoulder in a scoutmasterly way.

'You ate a dozen and a half oysters at luncheon, Mortdecai. I *believe* in you. Go in there and win, boy.' I gave him a look of pure hatred and crept whimpering into the hotel and up to my room.

She was there all right but she wasn't in bed, thank goodness, nor even naked: she was wearing a thing which looked like a cream silk pillowcase with three holes cut in it – cost hundreds of pounds, probably – Mrs Spon would have priced it at a glance. It made her look a great deal more than naked. I fancy I blushed. She paused, poised, for a second or two, drinking me in like Wordsworth devouring a field of yellow – yes, yellow – daffodils. Then she rushed forward and into my arms with an impact which would have felled a lesser man.

'Oh, Charlie Charlie Charlie,' she cried, 'Charlie Charlie Charlie!'

'Yes yes yes,' I countered, 'there there there,' patting her awkwardly on her charming left buttock. (That is not to say that the other, or right, buttock was not equally delectable, I only single out the left for praise because it was the one under advisement at the time, you understand.)

She squirmed ecstatically in my arms and, to my great relief, I felt the dozen and a half oysters getting down to their task in the dormant Mortdecai glands. (Wonderfully selfless little chaps, oysters, I always think; they let you swallow them alive without a murmur of protest and then, instead of wreaking revenge like the surly radish, they issue this splendid aphrodisiac dividend. What beautiful lives they must lead, to be sure.)

'Well,' I thought, 'here goes,' and made an unequivocal move towards what J. Donne (1573–1631) calls 'the right true end of love' but to my amazement she pushed me away firmly and sort of wiggled her frock back into position.

'No, Charlie, not until we are married. What would you think of me?' I gaped in a disappointed way but I must admit to having felt a bit *reprieved*, if you take my meaning. You see, this gave me time to put myself into the hands of a capable trainer: a canter round the paddock every morning and a diet of beefsteak, oysters and Guinness would soon lift me out of the selling-plate class and put me into good, mid-season form.

'Charlie, dear, you are going to marry me, aren't you, hunh? Your lovely doctor said marriage would be very therapeutic for you.'

'Farbstein said that, did he?' I asked nastily.

'No, darling, who's Farbstein? I mean the cute American doctor who's here looking after you – Dr Blücher?' She pronounced it beautifully, in the accents of old Vienna.

'Ah, yes, Blücher. *Doctor* Blücher, yes, of course. "Cute" is the very word for him. But I think he'd not much like you to pronounce it that way, he'd think it sounded kind of Kraut: he likes to say it "Bloocher". To rhyme with "butcher",' I added thoughtfully.

'Thank you, dear. But you didn't answer my question,' she said, pouting prettily. (Pouting is one of those dying arts; Mrs Spon can do it, so can the boy who creates my shirts, but it's almost as rare nowadays as tittering and sniggering. There are, I believe, a few portly old gentlemen who can still *chuckle*.)

'Dearest Johanna, of *course* I mean to marry you and as soon as possible. Let us say next month. People will talk, of course . . .'

'Charlie, dear, I was thinking more of tomorrow, really. I have this crazy British Special Licence for it. No, it was easy; I just got the Chancellor from the US Embassy to take me to see one of your Archbishops, such a sweet, silly old guy. I said I guessed your religion was "atheist" and he said, well, so were most of his bishops so he wrote "Church of England" on the form. Was that all right, Charlie?'

'Fine.' I kept my face straight.

'And Charlie, I have a surprise for you, I hope you'll be pleased; I called up the Vicar in your own village – well, it's only maybe forty miles from here – and he was, well sort of hesitant at first about your church-attendance record, he said he couldn't recollect seeing you there since he confirmed you thirty years ago, but I told him how the Archbishop had officially written you down as a Church of Englander and anyway he finally came around and said, Okay, he'd stick his neck out.'

'He said *that*?'

'Well, no, what he said was something kind of sad and resigned in Latin or maybe Greek but you could tell that was what he meant.'

'Quite so.' I'd have given a lot to have heard that bit of Latin or maybe Greek, for our Vicar has a pretty wit.

'Oh, yes, and he said how about a best man and I said "Oh Golly" and he said he'd round up your brother Lord Mortdecai to do it. Isn't that lovely?'

'*Quite* lovely,' I said heavily.

'You're not cross, are you, Charlie? Are you? Oh, and he can't get the choir together on a weekday morning, he's real sorry about that; do you mind terribly?'

'I can bear it with fortitude.'

'Ah, but his wife has a gang of ladies who sing Bach and I told him yes, great.'

'Splendid,' I said, sincere at last.

'And the organist is going to play "Sheep May Safely Graze" before the ceremony and "*Amanti Costanti*" from *Le Nozze de Figaro* as we go out: how *about* that?'

'Johanna, you are brilliant, I love you excessively, I should have married you years ago.' I almost meant it.

Then she came and sat on my knee and we nuzzled and chewed each other's faces a goodish bit and murmured sweet nothings and so forth. Pleasant for a while but it becomes a trifle painful for the male half of the sketch, doesn't it?

Johanna said she wanted an early night and would have sandwiches sent up to her room, and as soon as I could stand up I escorted her thither.

'Not before time,' said the look on the face of a passing chambermaid.

Back in my room I sank wearily into a chair and lifted the telephone.

'Room service?' I said. 'How many oysters have you in the hotel?'

6 Mortdecai reaps his reward and gets reaped a bit himself

You must wake and call me early, call me early, mother dear;
. . . It seemed so hard at first, mother . . .
But still I think it can't be long before I find release;
And that good man, the clergyman, has told me words of peace.

The May Queen

The marriage which had been arranged, as the newspapers say, took place, as the newspapers say, the next day at noon. The Vicar preached ripely and briefly, the ladies' Bach Group sang like little cock-angels, the organist made his organ peal like Kraft-Ebbing's onion (sorry) and, of course, my brother almost made me puke. The fact that his morning clothes were clearly the work of that genius in Cork Street, whereas mine had been hired in Kendal from a firm which had once made a pair of spats for the Duke of Cambridge, had nothing to do with my disgust. It was his *unction*.

After the ceremony, to make quite sure that he had spoiled my day, he drew me aside and asked me, infinitely tactfully, whether I was quite sure that I could really afford to support a wife who dressed so well, and could he help. While asking this he flicked compassionate glances at the set of my alleged coat around the shoulders.

'Oh yes, I think I can manage, Robin, but thanks for the offer.'

'Then she must be the relict of Milton Q. Krampf, who died the other month in odd circumstances, hmh?'

'I fancy that was his name – why?'

'Nothing at all, dear boy, nothing at all. But do always remember that you have a home here, won't you.'

'Thank you, Robin,' I said, gnashing mentally. How can a chap as nice as me have a brother like that?

Then he wanted us all to go up to the Hall for champagne and things but I put my foot down; I had taken enough stick for one day and I certainly was not going to bare my buttocks for more. Why, he might even have unlocked his wife from wherever he keeps her, like something from *Jane Eyre*. 'Brrrr,' I thought.

So we went to the pub across the road and ordered an Old-Fashioned (Johanna), a split of Roederer (Robin), a Bourbon on the rocks (Blucher), a glass of milk (me) and a half of bitter (the Vicar). The congregation behind us – retired chaps, unemployed chaps and a few idle window-cleaners and coffin-makers – murmured 'rhubarb, rhubarb' while the landlady told us that she hadn't got any of that except the half of bitter. In the end we settled for brandy and soda all round except for the Vicar and the unemployed chaps. (Goodness, have you ever tasted cheap brandy? Don't, don't.) Robin insisted on paying, he loves to do things like that and he loves to count the change, it makes him happy.

Then I went to the lav and changed my clothes and gave the hireling garments to Blucher to return to the honest artisan in Kendal – I enjoyed making him do that. Soon afterwards we parted in a spaghetti-like tangle of insincere matiness – except for the Vicar, who was doing his Christian best to believe that we were all nice chaps – and went our separate ways.

My separate way was to be driven two-hundred-odd miles to London in what Johanna called 'a cute little British auto' – a Jensen Interceptor. She had no patience with the absurd British affectation of using the left-hand side of the road; I probably secreted more adrenalin in those four hours than Niki Lauda uses in a whole Grand Prix season.

White and quaking, I was decanted at Brown's Hotel, London, W1, where Johanna firmly sent me to bed for a nap with a huge pottle of brandy and soda. It was, of course, good brandy this time. Sleep, Nature's kindly nurse, ravelled up the sleeve of care until dinner-time, when I arose with my nerve-endings more or less adequately darned. We dined in the hotel, which spares me the trouble of saying how good the dinner was. The waiter, who to my certain knowledge has been there since 1938, murmured into my ear that he could recommend the mustard: a statement that has never failed to charm me. Indeed, those were the very words, spoken by that very waiter, which first opened my youthful eyes on the enchanted landscape of gastronomy, long, long ago. (Few men and almost no women understand about mustard, you must have noticed that. They think that mustard-powder and water mixed five minutes before dinner makes a condiment; you and I know that this is merely a poultice for sore feet.)

Then we went to the River Room or the Saddle Room or whichever night-club it was that year; my heart was not really in it. I moodily ordered a plate of radishes to throw at passing dancers of my acquaintance but my aim was poor and I desisted after a professional wrestler offered to tear my leg off and beat me with the wet end. Johanna was in tearing high spirits and laughed merrily; she almost charmed away my sense of doom and inadequacy.

Back at the hotel, she showed no signs of fatigue; what she did show me was a nightdress which could have gone through the mail as a postcard if there had been enough space on it to accommodate a postage-stamp.

Only a few of the oysters seemed to be pulling their weight but I was pretty good the first time.

My mental clock is amazingly good: at 10.31 I opened a petulant eye and croaked a complaint to Jock. Where, where, was the life-giving cup of tea, the balm which, at 10.30 precisely, brings the Mortdecais of this world back to some kind of membership of the human race? 'Jock!' I croaked again, desperately. A throaty, girlish voice beside me murmured that Jock wasn't around. I swivelled a bloodshot eyeball and focused it on my bride. She was wearing that absurd nightdress again – it seemed to have lost its shoulder-straps. She was sitting up, toying with *The Times* crossword; the garment in question only afforded modesty because her nipples were supporting it like a pair of chapel hat-pegs. I shut my eyes firmly.

'Charlie darling?'

'Grmblumblegroink,' I said, unconvincingly.

'Charlie dearest, can you think of a word of seven letters beginning with "m" and ending with a double "e" and meaning "an extra performance in the afternoon"?'

'Matinée,' I mumbled.

'But doesn't "*matin*" mean morning, Charlie?'

'Yes, well, the original meaning of matinée was "a way of amusing oneself in the morning",' I said learnedly. A moment later I could have bitten off my tongue.

Luckily, one intelligent, public-spirited oyster had been holding itself in reserve against just such a contingency.

It really is quite astonishing how sex affects the sexes. I mean, it usually leaves the chap tottering about and feeling like a disposable dish-rag in search of an incinerator, whereas the female half of the sketch tends to skip about uttering glad cries and exhibiting only those delightful smudges under the eyes which head-waiters would notice. Another by-product of the primal act in women is that they exhibit a frenetic desire to go shopping.

'Charlie, dear,' said Johanna, 'I think I shall go shopping. I hear you have a cute little street right here in London called Bond Street, right? Kind of a poor man's Rue de Rivoli?'

'More of a rich man's *Marché des Puces*,' I said, 'but you have the general idea. Almost any taxi-driver will know the way there; it's almost a furlong. Don't overtip. Have fun. I'll go to my bank, I think.'

That was where I went, on foot, for the good of my health. This journey involved passing through the more Chinese parts of Soho – for reasons which I shall presently make clear – and I chanced to glance through the window of a particularly well-set-up-looking restaurant. To my amazement, there sat Johanna, deep in conversation with a portly person who looked like an owner of such a place. She did not see me.

Now, you do not have to be a natural worrier to worry a little at the sight of your bride deep in conversation with Soho restaurant-owners when she has assured you that she is shopping in Bond Street, nor do you have to be a jealous or suspicious man to feel a stirring of curiosity as to what such a bride could possibly have to discuss with such a restaurant-owner. I mean, I had papers to prove that Johanna was my ever-loving wife; I had her word for it that she was in Bond Street, snapping up bargains in wild mink and such, and the restaurant-owner's best friend would have felt bound to admit that he, the restaurant-manager, was as Chinese as a restaurant-owner can be, even in Soho.

Pray do not for a moment think that I dislike Chinese chaps; some of my best friends are those who make life beautiful with spare-ribs cooked in oyster sauce, not to mention pieces of duck swaddled in pancakes. No, what disturbed me was a certain wrongness about this situation, a wrongness which imparted an all-too-familiar twitching pang in the soles of my feet. Johanna, you see, was not a liar in the way that ordinary wives are liars. Although my acquaintance with her so far had been brief and torrid, I had formed the opinion that she was too rich, too self-confident, too *clever* to resort to lying in day-to-day matters.

Why, then, was she not in Bond Street, as advertised, scribbling her signature on Travellers' Cheques and scooping up emerald parures and things?

What I did was what I always do when in doubt: I telephoned Jock.

'Jock,' I said, for this was his name, you see, 'Jock, are you still friends with that rough, ugly, deaf-and-dumb night watchman at those publishers in Soho Square?'

'Yeah,' he said succinctly.

'Then straddle your great motor-bike, Jock, scoop up this sturdy, deaf-and-dumb friend and drop him in Gerrard Street. He is to enter a restaurant called the No Tin Fuk and order a simple, nourishing repast. Give him some money for this because I am sure those publishers he works for keep him short of the readies. When in the restaurant he is to watch, guardedly, a beautiful blonde lady called Mrs M. – yes, the one I married the other day – and to use his skill at lip-reading. She will be talking to a portly Chinese gentleman; I long to know what she is saying.'

'Right, Mr Charlie.'

'Make all haste, Jock, please.'

'That's us you hear coming round the corner,' he said.

I replaced the receiver in a courteous position then trotted puzzledly off to my bank. This was not my real bank, where I keep my overdraft, it's what I call my Savings Bank. It isn't even a Savings Bank in any ordinary sense of the word: it is the long-established premises of the most learned print-seller in London, an ancient person who does not approve of me for reasons which I do not understand. Why I call him my Savings Bank is as follows: I have a large and lavishly-produced book called *The Complete Etchings of Rembrandt van Rijn*. Every etching R. van R. ever etched is reproduced in its exact size and so exquisitely that it is hard to believe that they are not the originals. Moreover, these illustrations are 'tipped in', which means that they are printed separately and just lightly gummed to the pages by one edge. Whenever I have a few pennies to spare in my pocket, pennies which I might not want to confuse the nice tax-man with, I trundle round to the said print-dealer and buy a Rembrandt etching from him. A real one, of course, for he sells no others. This purchase takes some little while because he is an honest man, you see, and honest men can afford to stick out for the real price. Unlike some I could name.

When I have bought such an etching I toddle home, rip out the appropriate illustration in the *Complete Etchings*, and lovingly replace it with the real one I have just bought. Your common burglar would not dream of nicking such a book but, as it stands today, it's worth about a quarter of a million in any large city in the world. Decent chaps like me scarcely ever have to flee for our lives but, if we must, it's nice to have our savings with us unobtrusively. Your common Customs Officer, bless him, is unlikely to spare a glance for a fat, dull art-book with little or no pornographic content, carried by a fat, dull art-dealer.

The ancient dealer, on this occasion, grudgingly admitted that he had a pretty fine second-state impression of 'The Three Trees' with thread margins, and gave me the sort of look which art-dealers give you when they are pretty sure that you cannot afford the work of art in question. I, however, was embarrassingly flush with money from my American caper and said disdainfully that what I really had in mind was an impression of the first state of that etching, on vellum. He reminded me that there was only one such example, which happens to be in Samuel Pepys's scrapbook in the Library of a place called Magdalene College, which is in a town called Cambridge, famed for its unsound scholarship and web-footed peasantry. Forty minutes later he handed over the etching and gave me a glass of better sherry than you would think, while I parted with a sheaf of great, vulgar currency-notes. Over his largest print-cabinet he has a mahogany tablet inscribed with the words of one of my favourite authors, Psalms xx, 14: '*It is naught, it is naught, sayeth the buyer: but when he is gone his way, then he boasteth.*' As I lurched out, grumbling, he directed my attention to this.

'There's an even better writer,' I snarled, 'called Psalms xxviii, 20, and *he* says *He that maketh haste to be rich shall not be innocent!*' I thought I had him there but he blandly asked me which of us I was referring to. You can't win, you see, you can't win. Ordinary art-dealers are human beings in their spare time but honest print-sellers are a race apart.

Here is what us scholars call an excursus. If you are an honest man the following page or two can be of no possible interest to you. You are an honest man? You are sure of that? Very well, turn to page 214, because this part is only about how people deploy sums of money which used to belong to other people.

Taking large slabs of money away from other people is, I am told, a simple action for anyone who is strong and brave and doesn't lose any sleep after hitting people on the head or breaking the law in other ways. Getting it into the fiscal system again in one's own favour is a different matter altogether. Take a few examples, starting from the bottom.

(A) Your simple villain whose only task in the caper was nicking a get-away car just before the event and wiping the fingerprints or 'dabs' off it afterwards. He gets perhaps £500 in used one-pound notes and, regardless of his superiors' warnings, splashes them about in his local pub, buying drinks for one and all. The boys in blue pick him up within 72 hours and kindly ask him to tell them the names of his superiors. He does not tell them, not out of honour-amongst-thieves but because his superiors have been too smart to let him know their names. This is unfortunate for the simple villain because the fuzz has to make quite sure that he does not know. He is often *tired* when he finally comes up before the magistrate.

(B) The slightly less simple villain with a sensible streak of cowardice who learns of the capture of villain (A) and, at dead of night, takes his £1000 in used notes, dumps them in the nearest public lavatory, telephone-kiosk or other evil-smelling place and, in the morning, resumes his honest trade of scrap-metal merchant or whatever.

(C) The mealy-mouthed person who did nothing but 'finger' the caper slits open his Softa-Slumba mattress and tucks his £25,000 therein while his wife is getting her blue-rinse at the hairdressers. After eight or nine months, when he thinks all is safe, he buys a bungalow and pays the deposit in cash. Two nice gentlemen from the Inland Revenue call in for a chat; they go away quite satisfied. While he is heaving sigh of relief, two other nice gentlemen in blue uniforms call in for a chat and suggest that he pack a toothbrush and a pair of pyjamas.

(D) Now we are among the Brass, the higher echelons of the piece of villainy under discussion. This villain, called (D), is old-fashioned; he believes that a numbered account in a Swiss bank is as safe as the Houses of Parliament. He hasn't heard about Guy Fawkes. He has heard about Interpol but he believes it is designed to protect chaps like him – chaps who have numbered accounts in Swiss banks. His trial is long, expensive and complicated. He gets a nice job in the prison library but *horrid* things happen to him in the showers.

(E) He thinks that he can run for it; he has two passports. His share is, perhaps, £150,000. His arithmetic is not good: that kind of money is very nice in, say, South Norwood, but it sort of dwindles as you scoot around the world at today's prices, especially if you feel bound to arrange for your ever-loving wife to meet you in Peru or places like that.

(F) Yes, well, (F) is nearly the smartest of the bunch. First he tucks away a handy little sum like £20,000 in a safe place in case he gets nicked. (£20,000 will get you out of any prison in the world, everyone knows that.) Then he takes the rest of his ill-gotten g's and, having bought a dinner-jacket far above his station in life, he joins one of those gaming-clubs where they sneer at you if you are seen with anything so plebeian as a £10 note. He buys a couple of hundred poundsworth of chips; plays at this table and that and, in the small hours of the morning, gives the lovely cashier-lady a handful of chips and bank-notes, say, £2000, telling her to credit his account. He gives her a tenner for herself and she assumes that he has won. He does this discreetly for months, sometimes seeming to lose but usually winning. Every once in a while the lovely cashier-lady tells him that he has an awful lot of money in his account and he lets a big cheque which he can prove to be gambling-winnings slide into his account at the bank. You can legalize about a hundred thousand a year in this way if you are careful.

(G) He is the man who organized the whole thing. (G) is very rich already. There are no problems for him; his holding-companies can make his one-third of a million vanish like a snowflake on a frying-pan. I'm sure there's a moral there somewhere.

If it comes to that, I daresay there's a better moral in my book of Rembrandt etchings.

Back in my slum on the fourth floor in Upper Brook Street (W1) (I know it's a duplex, but I still think it's robbery at £275 a week) I was happily tipping-in my new purchase into the *Complete Etchings* when Jock sidled in.

'Jock,' I said severely, 'I have repeatedly asked you not to sidle. I will not have this sidling. It smacks of the criminal classes. If you wish to better yourself you must learn to shimmer. What's the name of those naval-outfitter chaps at the Piccadilly end of Bond Street?'

'Gieves?'

'That's it. There you are, you see,' I said, completely vindicated. Jock is not good at these things. He waited until I had fully relished my vindication; then he uttered.

'I got what rows 'e wrote.' I stared at the fellow. He showed none of the outward signs of brain-disease but these signs would not necessarily have been apparent, you see, for it is well known in art-dealing circles that you could stuff Jock's brain into any hedgehog's navel without causing the little creature more than a moment's passing discomfort, while Jock, on his part, would not notice the loss until the next time he played dominoes.

'What rows who wrote?' I asked at length.

'Nah, *Rosie*,' he said, 'me deaf-and-dumb mate. It's his monniker.'

'Goodness, is he one of *those*? How awkward for him, with his disabilities. I mean, however does he lisp and titter in sign-language?'

'Nah. His whole monniker is Rosenstein or Rosinbloom or one of them Eyetalian names but he doesn't like you to use it because he hates foreigners.'

32

'I see. Well, let's have it.' He handed me a newspaper folded open at the Sports Page, around the margins of which Rosie had done his dictation. I gave him marks for camouflage: the only way a ruffianly publisher's nark can be seen reading or writing without arousing suspicion is when he is at work picking his daily loser, and figuring out what a pound each way at nine to four will bring in after tax.

This is what he had written. 'I cooden get sat were I cood see the Chink's moosh but I cood see the lady ok she has lovly lips –' I frowned here '– I cood read ever word she said.' I unfrowned. 'She said No Mr Lee i have explained befor I don't want a million pounds. I already have a million pounds. I want the use of your organization. I have the women and you have the organization. I want to sell no part of my end. You will do very well out of your part of the operation. I can finance my self. Now for the last time is it a deal or not. Good. Now I must go shopping. I hav to buy my husband a present to put him in a good mood for what I am goin to ask him to do about the womin.'

I read it again and again. Aghast is the only word for what I was. Of course I had no illusion about Johanna's saintliness – she was very rich, wasn't she? – but the White Slave Trade! The sheer brilliance and audacity of reviving that wonderfully old-fashioned way of turning an honest million dazzled me. Johanna was, clearly, even cleverer than I had thought. The only bit that gnawed at my conscience was the suggestion that I was to be involved. It has always been my policy that wives should be free, nay, encouraged to do their own things but that spouses should not be conscripted. Let wives give cocktail parties until the distillery runs dry, but do not ask me to be polite to their awful friends. Let them take up knitting or some such wholesome exercise, but do not expect me to hold the wool. Above all, let them dabble in a little lucrative illegality – but on no account ask C. Mortdecai to participate except in helping to spend the proceeds with his well-known good taste.

White-slaving, you see, is strictly against the law. That is well-known. I might get *caught*; think how my friends would chuckle. Goodness, how they would chuckle if, after all the dubious capers I have survived, I were to be 'sent up the stairs' for living off the immoral earnings of naughty ladies.

I don't know how the ordinary man in the street reacts to musing furiously for a few hours at having learned that his newly wedded wife is a big wheel in the white-slaving trade. Some would doubtless fish out a little pocket calculator and start figuring percentages. Others would pack a bag and run for their lives. I would have telephoned Col. Blucher and told him all, but he had refused to give me any procedure for getting in touch with him for the nonce; this would come later, he promised me, but in the meantime I was to 'play it by ear'. (He had translated this for me as: 'Feel for your own handholds, Mortdecai; it's only a very small mountain you have to climb. Just *kid* yourself that there's a guy above you with a rope. You'll make out. I guess.')

Since that telephone call was denied me I adopted Alternative Plan B, which involves taking a firm handhold upon a bottle of Scotch and reading a few pages of the adventures of people called Mulliner, as related by the late P.G. Wodehouse. It was, after a while, difficult to concentrate because the doorbell rang and rang as obsequious chaps delivered huge cardboard boxes full of Johanna's shopping-loot, but when she at last arrived in person I was mellowed by Mulliner tales and, I suppose, not a little soothed by the healing Scotch whisky. What I was not in was a honeymoon frame of mind.

She embraced me with all the innocent fervour of a bride who has never said anything to a Chinese restaurant-proprietor more compromising than a shy request for a doggy-bag. She ran in and out of the bedroom, ripping open valuable cardboard boxes and parading before me wearing their contents. I made suitable noises but my heart was not in it. To tell the truth, my conscience, with whom I had not been on speaking terms for twenty years, was murmuring that the boxes alone would have kept a starving stockbroker in cigars for a week. For her last trick she appeared in a piece of night-wear which made her previous night's garment look like something a retired headmistress might wear in the Arctic Circle. I cringed.

'Johanna,' I said as she sat on my knee.

'Mhm?'

I cleared my throat. 'Johanna darling, is there anything good on the television tonight?'

'No.'

'How can you be so sure?'

'There never is.'

'But shall we just look at the newspaper to make sure? I mean, we might be missing an old Gary Cooper or Humphrey Bogart or . . .'

'Tonight,' she said in a firm but loving voice, 'there is nothing whatever on the television. Unless . . .' she cast an appraising eye on the large, solidly-built television set '. . . well, I guess I could sort of lean over it? I mean, if you *really* want something on the TV?'

'Try not to be immodest, I beg of you,' I said in a distant, British sort of voice. 'What you are trying to say, evidently, is that since there is nothing on the television you would prefer to spend the evening at the cinema.'

'The movie-houses are all closed.' I couldn't tell her that she lied, could I? Nor could I explain, in so many words, that an hour or so watching *Naughty Knickers* or *Adventures of a Teenage Window-cleaner* might inflame me to the point where I could forget the terrifying wench-mongering trade in which she was about to involve me and summon up enough of the Old Adam to play the part of the lust-crazed bridegroom.

I made her two, or it might have been three, strong – hopefully soporific – drinks, then followed her to bed.

7 Mortdecai is given an order which no decent man would even consider for a moment

It was my duty to have loved the highest:
It surely was my profit had I known:
It would have been my pleasure had I seen.

Guinevere

Later that night, my confidence in the invigorating powers of the vitamins E and B12 once again ratified, I was sinking into a well-earned hoggish slumber when Johanna prodded me and said:

'Charlie, little stallion, I want you to do something . . .'

'Darling, we've only just . . . I mean, I'm not a young man, I've explained that before . . . perhaps in the morning, eh?'

'Silly, I didn't mean that; what do you think I am, a nymphomaniac or something?'

I mumbled something sort of reprieved and perhaps ungallant, nuzzling back sleepily between her warm, damp breasts.

'What I want you to do is something *quite* different.' I stirred; the words strained and sifted through the well-earned slumbrousness already referred to. Misgiving took me by the throat; I could almost feel my teeth rattle.

'Darling Johanna,' I said in as reasonable a voice as I could muster, 'wouldn't *tomorrow* night be a better time for anything, ah, *far-out* that you have in mind? I mean . . .' she giggled.

'Yes, Charlie dear, I know that you are no longer a young man – although you could fool most people.' I smirked. 'In the dark, of course,' she continued, spoiling it for me. 'No, I don't want you to tax your beautiful glands. Well, just the adrenalin ones maybe. I just want you to kill someone for me. OK.?'

'Kill someone?' I burbled sleepily. 'Certainly. Any time. Slay a dragon or two with pleasure, any time. Any time after breakfast, that is. Got to get my sleep now, d'you see.'

She shook my shoulder, which only made me nuzzle more firmly, more determined to sleep. Then she shook a much more vulnerable limb and I awoke indignantly.

'I say,' I said, 'don't do that! Might damage a chap. And where would you be then, eh? Make a nonsense of your honeymoon, you can see that, I'm sure. G'night.'

She sat up in bed in a peremptory fashion, taking most of the bedclothes with her. There was nothing to do but awake. I awoke. I shall not pretend that my mood was mild.

'My dear Johanna, this is neither the time nor the occasion for tantrums. All the world over, chaps and their charming bedmates are zizzing away for all they are worth, irrespective of colour or creed, coiling in the tissue-restoring eight or nine hours. You asked something of me which I agreed to accomplish tomorrow. Can't recall what it was but I'm delighted to fall in with your lightest wish. Tomorrow. Whatever it is.'

'Oh, Charlie, have you forgotten already? I simply asked you to kill someone for me. It doesn't seem much to ask one's bridegroom on one's honeymoon. However, if it's too much trouble . . .'

'Not at all; don't be petulant, darling. It'll be the work of a moment, work of a moment. Just give Jock the feller's name and address and he'll see to it the day after tomorrow. Goodnight again, sweetheart.'

'Charlie!'

'Oh well, all right, I suppose he could manage it *tomorrow* night but he'll have to scout about for a pistol with no history, you understand. I mean, I couldn't ask him to use his own Luger on this feller, could I? You see that, surely?'

'Charlie, the person to be killed isn't a, uh, feller. In fact you'd probably think it improper to call her a person, even.'

'You speak in riddles, Johanna of my heart,' I sighed. 'Who is this august "she" – the Queen of bloody England?'

She clapped her hands together, as pleased as a little girl.

'Oh Charlie, you guessed, you guessed!'

I distinctly remember saying 'good-morning' to Jock next morning.

'Good morning, Jock' were the words I selected, for they never fail to please.

'Morning, Mr Charlie,' he rejoined, setting the tea-tray down within reach of my quaking hand. 'Breakfast?' he asked.

'Buttered eggs, I think, please.'

'Right, Mr Charlie. Scrambled eggs.'

'Buttered eggs,' I repeated (but Jock will not yield on this point of language) 'and very runny. Do not agitate them too much, I detest the gravelly appearance: a well-buttered egg should appear as large, soft, creamy clots. Like Roedean schoolgirls, *you* know.'

'Toast?' was all the reaction I got out of him.

'Well, of course toast. Toast-making is one of your few talents; I may as well get the good of it while you still have possession of your faculties.'

You can't get through Jock's guard – his riposte was like a flash of lightning. 'And an Alka-Seltzer, I reckon?' he said. Game, set and match to him, as ever.

'Please salt the eggs for me,' I said by way of conceding defeat, 'I always overdo it and spoil them. And do please remember, the fine, white pepper for eggs, not the coarse-ground stuff from the Rubi.' (Cipriani of Harry's Bar in Venice once told me why waiters of the better sort call that huge pepper-grinder a 'Rubi': it is in honour of the late, celebrated Brazilian playboy Porfirio Rubirosa. I don't understand it myself because my mind is pure.)

Jock pretended not to be listening; this is an easy trick if you happen not to be listening and one quite unfair to an employer who is in the throes of struggling to the surface of wakefulness.

'Sod him,' I thought bitterly. Then I remembered.

'By the way, Jock,' I said casually . . . (If you happen to be a physician in General Practice, God forbid, you will be all too familiar with the 'By the way, Doctor' gambit. It works like this: a chap is concerned because his left testicle has turned bright green, so he goes to his croaker or physician and complains of headaches and constipation. Having collected his prescriptions he starts to exit and then, his hand on the doorknob, turns back and casually mumbles 'By the way, Doctor, it's probably nothing of interest but . . .')

'By the way, Jock,' I said casually, 'Mrs Mortdecai wants the Queen shot.'

'Awright, Mr Charlie. Did you say two eggs or three?'

'The *Queen*,' I insisted.

'Yeah, I heard you. You mean the old ponce what runs the drag-club down Twickenham way. I'll do him tomorrow night, no sweat. You'll have to give me a score to buy an old throwaway shooter, though, I'm not using me good Luger.'

'No, no, Jock. I refer to Her Majesty Queen Elizabeth the II, whom God preserve and upon whom the sun never sets, etcetera.'

He fell silent; anyone who didn't know him might well have thought that he was thinking.

'Jock,' I said sternly after a while, 'your glass eye is leaking. Pray take it out and wipe it.'

' 'Tisn't watering. It's crying,' he said in an ashamed but defiant voice.

'Eh?'

'Yeah, well, she's a lovely lady, isn't she? She never bought me no beer but she never did no one no harm, did she?'

I know how to deal with rhetorical questions; you don't answer them.

'Couldn't we just do the Earl of –'

'*No!*'

'– or Princess – I mean no one would . . .'

'The *Queen*,' I said firmly. 'For personal reasons, such as fear, cowardice, patriotism etcetera, I am as reluctant as you to perform this dastardly act but international politics says the deed must be done. So does my wife. Two eggs, please.'

'Two eggs,' he muttered, shambling out of the room.

How dearly I would have loved to sink back into innocent sleep but matters of great moment had me by the lug-hole and furthermore Jock sulks if I let my eggs grow cold. I ate them up, every scrap, although they were far from perfect. As I ate, I planned.

An hour later, carelessly clad and deliberately unshaven, I went off to consult my gunsmith. I don't mean my real gunsmith, of course; he is a bishop-like personage who presides over dim, hushed premises near St James's Palace and knows the difference between a gentleman and a person. The chap I was going to see is what you might call my other gunsmith, a chap of great dishonesty who sells illegal firearms to *persons* and whose only work-bench skills are fitting new barrels to pistols which have been in a little trouble and sawing off a few inches from shotgun barrels. He believes me to be a sort of Gentleman Jim The Country House Jewel Thief and I have not thought fit to correct this belief. He does not know my name, naturally. His only points of principle are to refuse credit, to refuse cheques and to refuse to sell firearms to Irishmen. This last is not because he dislikes the Irish or their politics, but for their own good. He is not convinced that they will hold the weapon the right way round, you see, and he likes his customers to come back.

He greeted me with his usual surliness: dealers in illegal firearms almost never smile, you must have noticed that. He was discreetly clad in a filthy singlet and underpants and the carrotty hair with which he is matted was dark with sweat. He had been making toffee-apples, you see, for this is his 'front', and the darkened, poky room into which he admitted me was fiercely hot and heavy with the stench of boiling sugar, rotten fruit and gun-oil. The murmur of wasps and blow-flies in the immemorial toffee-vats was quite terrifying to me. (As a child I once swallowed a wasp in a glass of lemonade; it stung me on the left tonsil and my mother feared – in a half-hearted but well-bred way – for my life. Nowadays I *stamp* on wasps when the conservation chaps aren't looking.)

'Hello, Ginge!' I cried.

'Oy, mate,' he replied.

'Look, Ginge, do you think we could go into another room? I'm wearing silk underclothes, you see, and they're horrid when one sweats.'

With ill grace he led me into a little, overstuffed back-parlour which was as icy as the workshop had been tropical. With unconscious grace he threw a stolen mink bolero around his shoulders and squatted on a horsehair-covered tuffet. I must say he did look droll but I didn't dare to snigger; he is very strong and rough and famous throughout the Borough of Poplar for hitting people in vulnerable parts on the smallest provocation.

'A friend of mine . . .' I began.

'Oh, ah,' he sneered.

'A friend of mine,' I repeated firmly, 'does a little commercial poaching – or culling – of deer in the Highlands of Scotland the Brave. He has a large standing order for venison from an hotel whose name I seem to forget. The police have taken his rifle away and are being stuffy about giving it back. He needs another. What have you got, Ginge?'

'Nuffink,' he said.

'He's a bit particular about his guns,' I went on. 'He likes something with a bit of class. And it's got to be a stopper, a high-velocity job, something with real clout.'

'I got nuffink like that.'

'And the ammunition must be fresh; no stale old ex-army rubbish.'

'I gotter go now, mate.'

'And, of course, a good telescopic sight.'

'Fuck off.'

So far, the dialogue was going well, the protocol was in the best tradition. Dealing with chaps like Ginge is extraordinarily like negotiating with a Soviet Trade Delegation. I fished out the flat half-bottle of whisky and tossed it to him. He drank from the bottle, dirty dog, and didn't pass it back. He belched, thrust a hand into his underpants and scratched thoughtfully.

'Got a Mannlicher,' he grunted after another swig. I made a sympathetic face and suggested a course of penicillin. He ignored that.

'Pre-war.'

'No.'

'Clip holds three.'

'Useless.'

'Belonged to a Count.'

'A *what*?'

'Count. What they call a Graf. Got a coat of arms on the lock-plate, all in gold and stuff.'

41

'Worse and worse.'

'And it ain't never been in no trouble. Guarantee.'

'You begin to half-interest me, Ginge.'

'Two hundred and eighty quid. Cash.'

I stood up. 'Next millionaire I meet I'll tell him about it. Cheers, Ginge.'

'Lovely Zeiss 'scope on it, × 2½.'

'× 2½!' I squeaked (you try squeaking the phrase '× 2½'). 'That's no use, is it?'

'Look,' he said, 'if you need more than that on 'scope you don't want a rifle, you want a bleeding anti-aircraft gun.'

I began to sulk in good earnest and he sensed it instantly; he has that sixth sense which stands Armenian carpet-dealers in such good stead. He stole out and returned with a slim, elegant leather case which he dumped into what I still like to call my lap. It contained the Mannlicher in three easily assembled parts; the sniperscope, a fitted torch for shooting crocodiles or mistresses by night, and two hundred pounds of pretty fresh 7.65 mm ammunition, not to mention a rosewood cleaning-rod, a silver oil-bottle, a crested silver sandwich-box, a roll of 4" × 2" flannelette and a tool-kit complete with the thing for picking Boy Scouts out of Girl Guides' knickers. It was quite beautiful; I longed to own it.

'You could get a fortune for this from an antique-dealer,' I yawned, 'but my friend wants something to shoot things with. No one has used a toy like this since Goering roamed the primeval swamps.'

'Two hundred and seventy-five quid,' he said, 'that's me last word.'

Twenty minutes, two bursts of ill temper and half a bottle of Scotch later, I left owning the rifle and having paid two hundred pounds, which we had both known all along was what I was going to pay.

'What's that old load of rubbish for then?' asked Jock surlily when I brought it home.

'It's what we're going to do that job with.'

'You can. I'm not,' he said.

'Jock!'

'I'm British. By the way, it's me night off, innit, and I'm off playing dominoes. There's some cold pork in the fridge. Madam's out, gorn to some pub called the Clarence House.'

I waved an icy, dismissive hand. Things were bad enough without having to bandy words with uppity servants who couldn't muster up enough loyalty to join their indulgent masters in so traditional an old English practice as a spot of regicide.

The cold pork in the fridge was wilting at the edges; it and I exchanged looks of mutual contempt, like two women wearing the same hat in the Royal Enclosure at Ascot. I changed into a slightly nattier suit and went off to Isow's, where I ate more than was good for me. One always does at Isow's, but it's worth it.

I retired early to the narrow bed in my dressing-room, for I needed to digest and furiously to muse and plan. I heard Johanna open the door a fraction – I made convincing zizzing-noises and she crept away. I heard the merest rattle and clink as she dropped her tiara into the jewel-box, then all was silence.

I continued to muse and plan. By the time I fell asleep I had formulated a tripartite plan:

(1) Obtain an impenetrable disguise.

(2) Select a sniper's post.

(3) Arrange an escape-route.

Something attempted, something done had earned a night's repose and a night's repose was what I got, broken only by those contented noises from the digestive tract familiar to all who have dined at Isow's. Well, I had some nasty dreams, too, but I have always maintained that relating one's dreams is the third most boring a man can do. I need not tell you what the other two are.

8 Mortdecai dips a terrified toe into the shark-infested waters of regicide

O purblind race of miserable men,
How many among us at this very hour
Do forge a lifelong trouble for ourselves,
By taking true for false, or false for true!

Geraint and Enid

The suit was dreadful, quite dreadful. Clearly, it had been made for
a colour-blind Roumanian pimp or perhaps ponce in the 1940s. The
checks of the blue-and-orange pattern were, it must be admitted,
not much larger than an ordinary packet of cigarettes: perhaps the
pimp or ponce had been aiming at an inconspicuous effect. There
were no dirty postcards in the pockets, nor any factory-reject french
letters: this reassured me that it had at least been to the dry-cleaners.
I bought it in a shop called GENTS' WARDROBES PURCHASED
and indeed its folds draped themselves from my shoulders in
just the manner of a plywood wardrobe. GENTS' WARDROBES
PURCHASED also sold me a pair of shoes to match, although
these, in their brown-and-white splendour, seemed to date from
an even earlier day – a fortune-hunting petty nobleman might well
have sported them in the *Salon Privé* at Monte in, say, 1936.

I glanced just once at myself in their fitting-room mirror: under
the bludgeonings of suit I may have winced but I swear I did not
cry aloud.

44

There seemed to be no end to the resources of GENTS' W.P. 'Vere,' I asked in my best Mittel-Europ accent, 'Vere could I buy a goot, strong, musical-instrument case for my musical instrument? I vould need vun of about *so* big' – even as I gestured, the hateful suit sliced cruelly into my armpits – 'ze kind dot ze Shicago gangsters used to carry dere sob-moshine gons in, ha ha!'

'Have you come to the right place!' cried Mr G.W.P. merrily. 'Step this way, sir, mind the step; we make a little speciality of musical-instrument cases. There now, I'm sure you'll find the box of your dreams amongst this little lot!' I gave him a suspicious squint, for everyone knows that 'box' has another and naughtier meaning, but he did not seem to be pulling my plonker. There was in truth great store of stoutly-constructed musical-instrument kennels; it was a rare and bizarre sight. I had the measurements of the Mannlicher in my mind's eye (any art-dealer worth his salt can glance at a frame and tell whether it will fit any picture in his stock or whether it can or cannot be cut down to size without altering the sweep of the carving) and I soon selected a perversely-shaped box or case designed, I don't doubt, for a baritone saxophone and haggled over it just long enough to avoid arousing suspicion in G.W.P.'s breast.

I stuffed my execrable gents' natty suiting and co-respondent shoes into the instrument-case and homeward plodded my moody way, as weary as any Stoke Poges ploughman, pausing only at Lillywhite's to buy a checkered golfing-cap of the sort which I had until then believed only to exist in the works of P.G. Wodehouse. I used my Yorkshire accent in Lillywhite's, to throw them off the scent, d'you see. The secret-agent cloak was by now falling across my shoulders so snugly that I felt like an ivy-mantled tower. I aroused, I believe, no suspicion; even without the accent they would have taken me for a North-Country man, no other would buy such a cap.

Jock flicked a baleful eye on the instrument-case when I arrived at the flat. The other, non-baleful eye, the glass one, was pointed at the empyrean or ceiling in a way which suggested that, could it speak, it would have said, 'Oh my Gawd.'

'Pray put this banjo-coffin into the wardrobe in my dressing-room,' I said in dignified, masterly tones, 'and I beg you not to glance inside, for the contents shock even me: the effect of them upon an honest ton of soil like yourself . . .'

'You mean "son of toil", Mr Charlie.'

'Perhaps I do, perhaps I do. Be that as it may, tell me now, without evasion and in your own words, omitting no detail however slight, what is for dinner tonight?'

'Madam is out,' he said smugly. 'Playing bridge.'

'So?' I said haughtily. 'Are you trying to tell me that I must send out or, God forbid, *go* out for dinner? Is there nothing in the pantry? Are you, Jock, supping off bread and cheese? I find this hard to believe, for you were ever one to eat above your station in life.' His eyes glowered, one at the floor, the other at the cornice, above his station in life.

'I was just going to have a bit of a snack,' he mumbled in as civil a voice as he could muster.

'Yes?' I prompted gently.

'Yeah, well, a coupla *blintzes* with caviar inside and some sour cream what I found left over, didn't I, and a few kipper fillets soused with wine I bought out of my own pocket and I can prove it; then nothink but a Minute Steak what was going to waste, wrapped round a liddle concodgion of me own made out of chicken-livers and that.'

'Are you trying to tell me,' I said levelly, 'that there is only enough for you?' He pondered loyally awhile.

'Bit short on the caviar side,' he said at last. I handed him my keys.

'Ten minutes OK, Mr Charlie?'

'You mean ten minutes after you have produced the drinks tray?'

' 'Course.'

'Then; right, Jock.'

'Right, Mr Charlie.'

When Johanna returned I was in bed with an improving book by St Francis de Sales or perhaps Le Marquis de Sade, I forget which, and was not quick enough to snap out the bedside light. She had won at bridge, she always does; this elates her. She was radiant. She sang as she danced about the room, scattering garments both here and there.

We cannot all afford oysters and Guinness's stout but I promise you that there are times when a little £20 jar of Beluga caviar will fill the gap admirably.

The next day, sure that Jock was in his pantry doing useful things and that Johanna was in the shower, I huddled on my new 'clothes' and was about to slink out of the flat unobserved. Johanna caught me in the very act of slinking and staggered about laughing like a little mad thing at the sight of my rainbow garb. She has one of those rippling, silvery laughs which are quite enchanting when they are directed at anyone but oneself.

'Hush!' I commanded. 'If Jock sees me in this suit he will give in his notice. He has his pride, you see.'

'But, Charlie, dearest,' she murmured between one silvery ripple and another, 'why are you dressed as an undertaker? And does the black, important box contain your embalming equipment?'

'I see nothing to laugh at,' I replied stiffly, 'in the sight of a Briton true preparing to assassinate his Sovereign against his better judgment.'

'I am sorry, Charlie,' she said soberly. 'I didn't realize that you were in *disguise*.'

'Well, I jolly well am,' I said.

As I passed the kitchen there was a muffled, flatulent sound, too treble to be one of Jock's.

'Jock,' I said sternly, 'the canary is constipated again. I have no faith in the new vet. Pray telephone the Zoo and ask their advice.'

'Right, Mr Charlie,' he said – and then, *sotto voce*, he said something which sounded like, 'Give him a look at your new suit.'

I walked – nay, slunk – for what seemed miles until I was well away from those parts of London where any friends of mine might live, then I hailed a taxi and directed it to the City, where there was only an outside chance that I might encounter my stockbroker or the chief of my Lloyds' syndicate. In my pocket I had a map of the Royal Route which I had torn out of Jock's newspaper, which is the kind of newspaper which Jock reads. (Fleet Street calls them 'tit-and-bum rags' but Jock is ever faithful to Shirley Temple; what he dearly loves, true-born Briton though he be, is those candid snapshots of junior royals taking an 'arser' from a

47

horse in a *puissance* trial. Perhaps he sometimes also spots the stick of type in the corner which tells of 15,000,000 homeless in West Bengal. Perhaps. His social conscience is a couple of notches higher than the World Council of Churches, but that's about it.) In my pocket, as I was saying before you interrupted me, I had a map of the Royal Route. My *Times* had not specified in the 'Court Circular' – and probably would not say until after the event – which kind of vehicle Her M. would be travelling in but, since this was a State Occasion (a Reception and Luncheon at the Cordwanglers' Hall with foreign royals present), I was hoping that the Royal Party would be in one of the State Landaus – open tops, you see – rather than in one of those great, weighty Daimlers or Rolls-Royces which every amateur assassin knows to be bullet-proof.

My newspaper route-map showed that the Royal Progress was to pass briefly through a grotty little City street on its way to Cordwanglers' Hall and it was to that very street that I directed my cab, and there that I had the cabbie decant me, over-tipping him just enough to give him the impression that I was not a native son of London, but not enough to make him remember me. Those of you who have ever been unlucky enough to be a secret agent or hired assassin will understand how my mind was working.

Up and down the grotty street I toddled, the instrument-case bumping cruelly against my thigh, but not a single BED AND BREAKFAST sign could I descry. What I did descry on my third toddle was a tall, narrow-shouldered, grubby building with the name of a firm of solicitors on the ground-floor windows and an assortment of dirty lace curtains in the windows of the upper floors. A skinny slattern in curlers slouched in the basement area, listlessly pushing dirt about with what had once been a broom.

'Goot mornink!' I said, raising my golfing-cap in a Continental sort of way and smirking amiably. She looked up at me from the 'area'; her eyes were those of a long-retired whore who had never really enjoyed her work.

''E's out,' she said, dismissively.

'I voz wonderink –'

'*Out*,' she repeated. The atmosphere was heavy with the scent of overdue hire-purchase payments.

'I voz wonderink vedder you might haff a small room I could use in ze evenings . . .'

'Yer what?'

'Ya, to play wiz my instrument, you onderstand.'

'Yer *what*?' I realized that, from her position down in the 'area', she could not see my saxophone-case and might have misconstrued me a bit. I raised the case and waggled it.

'My vife,' I explained, 'doz not vish me to play wiz it at home any more. It makes her ongry wiz me.'

' 'Ungry?'

'Ya,' I said, inspired, 'hongry. Then she eat too much, you understand, and become fat an dis spoil our loff-life pecoss I cannot stand fat vomen.' I eyed her with undisguised admiration; she smoothed the ratty house-coat over her skinniness.

Ten minutes later I was the tenant of a second-floor room overlooking the street, having paid a modest rental one month in advance and having agreed that I should only practise my instrument during those hours when the solicitor downstairs was not practising law, that I should not entertain *friends* in the room and that I should not use the bathroom. There was a wash-hand basin in the room, you see, to receive any peremptory calls of nature.

At home that night I passed a hateful couple of hours with my tape-recorder and an album of some overpaid saxophonist of the early 1940s, recording bits and pieces of the fellow's beastly art and repeating phrases again and again as though striving to achieve what a saxophonist would probably call perfection. I shall not name the musician for, who knows, he may well be alive to this day (there is no justice, none) and, to my certain knowledge, the Performing Rights Society is very much alive and poised like a pussy-cat at a mousehole.

For the next few days I played the part. The Great Game. Wore the mask. Worse, I wore the suit and, dear God, the very shoes. Each evening I would creep to that narrow house in that shabby street in the City, clad in the shameful attire, and mount the stairs after fluttering a lecherous eyelash or two at the landlady. Ensconced in the mean room, smelling of undernourished mice (yes, the *room*) I would play over the tape of the nameless saxophonist, occasionally varying the volume, stopping and starting and so forth, while I peered through the window, measuring angles and distances and fields-of-fire until I could stand the bloody saxophone no more, whereupon I would shuffle downstairs, side-step the now clean and lipsticked but still skinny landlady, and pace moodily down the street towards a taxi-point. The moodiness of the pacing, I need hardly say, was because I was pacing out distances in the street and relating them to my field-of-fire. I reckoned that the State Landau would be clocking up a brisk 12 mph on the day. Trigonometry was the only thing I was good at when I was at school. Well, it was the only thing the masters *knew* about that I was good at.

Look, let me make it quite clear that I liked none of this at all, not any of it. I don't speak of wearing clothes which George Melly would scorn, nor of the shoes, the 'banana specials' which still visit me in my dreams. I am speaking, seriously for once, of the basic rottenness of it all. This country had accepted my family, had been good to us, had allowed us to become moderately rich and had never pointed the finger of scorn. Why then was I using all my wits to send its Sovereign to a premature grave? Well, yes, my wife had told me to do it, which is a pretty good reason for most chaps to do most things, especially if, as in this case, there was a strong hint that I might find myself slightly dead if the product did not please. There was also the dread Colonel Blucher, who had made it clear that I was to play along with Johanna until otherwise instructed. None of this made me feel any better about my activities; I was sharply aware that Jock's sense of values was better than mine.

However, in those days I was a man of iron, and was dedicated to the ideal of staying alive – an ideal which seems paltry in retrospect but seemed sensible at the time. Staying alive has a kind of immediacy about it: ask anyone who has been confronted with the choice between life and death.

So I oiled the rifle, visited the horrid house, smirked at the landlady, played the saxophone-tapes, wore the suit, the shoes; nay, even the golfing-cap itself. You have read about the Spartan boy with the fox in his bosom gnawing at his vitals but making no murmur? Very well, I have made myself clear.

'Jock,' I said one morning, to Jock, 'Jock, I need a little help.'
'Mr Charlie,' he said heavily, 'if it's about the matter what we discussed a few days ago, then before you say another word the

answer is "no". I wouldn't shop you, not even if it was ever so, you know that, but I carn 'elp. Not with that.'

'Not even a touch of driving after the event?' I wheedled.

'Sorry, Mr Charlie, I coulden turn a wheel of a jam-jar in such circombstations.'

'Very well, Jock, I daresay I shall manage single-handed. I respect your principles and attach no blame to you. But if I should be, ah, *nicked*, may I depend upon you to visit me in the condemned cell?'

' 'Course.'

'And perhaps bring me in a pot or two of caviar? The real Grosrybriest, I mean, not the stuff we put out at parties.'

' 'Course.'

'And perhaps,' I added wistfully, 'a jar or two of those partridge-breasts in jelly, eh? I mean, I hear frightful tales of what prison governors consider "a hearty breakfast" for the chap about to do his hundred-yards dash to the gallows. Greasy mutton chops with chips and beans and, and . . . *things*.'

'Don't you worry your head about none of that, Mr Charlie, I'll see you right, I got friends in them places. Anyway, they done away with capital punishment, didn't they? You won't draw much more than, ooh, say twenty-five years. A doddle. Do it standing on your head. Only thing to remember is, don't let them big black queers catch you in the showers.' I did not shudder for I wished to retain Jock's respect, but the effort cost me a few hundred calories.

'Look, Jock,' I said gently, 'you are right about the abolition of capital punishment but there is one thing they can still top you for.'

'Reely?'

'Yes.'

'Like what?'

'Like High Treason.'

9 Mortdecai prepares to put himself beyond the pale but wishes that he had a better class of landlady

Her manners had not that repose
Which stamps the caste of Vere de Vere.

Lady Clara Vere de Vere

The dreaded day came. As I left the flat Jock wordlessly handed me my hat and umbrella. I refused the latter; it takes more than a mere umbrella to make an assassin feel like a gentleman. Nevertheless, as I waited for the lift, I found myself humming a stave from the National Anthem, the bit about 'Long may she reign'. Clearly, some Freudian bits in the back of my brain were longing for *rain*, you see, so that the Royal party would be travelling in a nice bullet-proof limousine rather than in the open State Landau. London weather let me down, as it always does: the sun shone as mercilessly as a bank-manager's smile.

I travelled by tube – subway? – to the nearest station to my City lodgings and entered the Public Lavatory. (It was early in the day, you see, the Stock Exchange was busy and Parliament was in session so there was little danger of being accosted.) I changed into the suit, the shoes, the cap.

A few minutes later; well, there I was at the window, sliding the telescopic sight onto the Mannlicher, my fingers twitching with

trepidation about the abominable act I was about to perform –
twitching, too, with fury and revulsion at the way my skinny
landlady had unequivocally brushed herself against me on the stairs
and suggested that I might join her for 'a glass of summink' in her
boudoir.

'Oftervords, oftervords,' I had mumbled, trying to muster a leer
although well knowing – nay, hoping – that there would be no
oftervords.

So there I was, the lovely Spanish mahogany stock of the rifle
becoming more and more slippery with sweat, no matter how often
I wiped my guilty hands on the trouser-legs of the hated suit. My
wristlet-watch, although a creation of Patek Philippe himself, ticked
ever more slowly, as though it had been dipped in the very best
butter.

At last there was to be heard a distant sound of hooraying,
then a sort of galumphing noise which betokened the advent of
horse-drawn carriages full of Royals and their Head of State guests.
I wiped the hands once more, allowed the rifle-muzzle to protrude
a further inch or two (for I could descry no security-idiots on the
rooftops across the street) and cuddled the butt to my shoulder,
telescopic eye-piece to watery eye. Here they came – in the bloody
State Landau, sure enough – all of them doing that wonderful,
inimitable Royal wave of the hand which only Queen Elizabeth
the Queen Mother can do properly. Obviously, I couldn't do it:
the murder, I mean, not the wave. I must have been mad to have
thought that I could. (When St Peter, at the Pearly Gates, gives
me that form to fill in, the only claim I shall be able to make in
mitigation is that I never shot at a sitter in my life.) (Naturally, I
don't count rats, carrion-crows, ex-presidents of Uganda and that
sort of thing.)

Nevertheless, my cowardly, regicide right hand seemed to have a
life of its own; it drew back the bolt of the Mannlicher and shoved it
forward to usher a cartridge into the breech. It jammed. The bolt,
I mean – or rather the cartridge. I wrenched the bolt back fiercely
until the distorted cartridge sprang free and whirred past my ear to
strike a tasteful colour-print of Van Gogh's 'Two Pansies Sharing a
Pot'. I crammed the bolt forward again and it jammed again. The
cavalcade was about to pass the point where my field-of-fire would
be ineffective. I cursed Jock with love and respect (I had checked

those cartridges that very morning – who else could have nobbled them?) but, with thoughts of survival in my mind, wrestled with the bolt-action so that I could loose off just one shot to show that I had tried. It was just as I had cleared the third cartridge and clunked in a fresh clip that I found out why there had been no security-idiots lumbering about on the rooftops across the street. It was because they were kicking in the door of my squalid room. Just behind me.

Now there are two ways of kicking in doors. The first, which I was taught by a gentleman in Philadelphia, is quick, neat and almost soundless. These chaps used the other method. Had I been a dedicated villain I could have shot them into bite-sized helpings before they delivered the third kick, but my heart was not in it. When they at length tumbled in through the wreckage of the door I lifted them to their great feet and dusted them off courteously. The door had not been locked but I did not tell them this, I didn't want to spoil their day. Each of them arrested me again and again, urging me to say things which might be used in evidence against me and sticking evidence-tabs on everything in sight, while the skinny landlady gibbered and squawked behind them, averring that she had suspected all along that I was not a true-born Englishman.

The copper's voices were fierce, grave and *proud*. This was a Tower of London job, you see; your true regicide is not submitted to the squalor of Wormwood Scrubs where he might have to rub shoulders with muggers, wife-bashers, child-rapists and common property-developers. I was special. (My only regret, as they snucked the handcuffs about my wrists, was that I had not made it perfectly clear to Jock that the little jars of partridge-breasts in jelly are quite useless without fresh brown bread and butter.) The coppers scarcely hit me at all but they searched me thoroughly for incriminating documents such as five-pound notes, gold cigarette-cases and so forth but all they found was the receipted bill for the suit I was wearing. I hope they did not give GENTS' WARDROBES PURCHASED a bad time.

The frisking was disgracefully inefficient – I had to remind them about the small of my back, where evil men often tape a 'shiv' or ground-down razor. While I giggled three tall men loomed in the doorway, brushing aside the debris with fastidious feet. No common British coppers, these, the very feet told one that. They were in fact Colonel Blucher and a brace of his myrmidons.

Blucher brandished a plastic triptych bespattered with the marks of important rubber stamps. The coppers stopped arresting me and started calling Blucher 'Sir'. Someone told the landlady to shut up, for which relief much thanks, and there was a sort of tableau. Then Blucher thanked the bobbies civilly but in the flat sort of voice which means 'fuck off'.

I do not know who reimbursed the landlady for her burst door and shattered dreams but it was not I. As we left she made a gesture which she should not have known how to make, for she was clearly not a showjumper.

'In Ongary,' I told her, 've make zat sign like zis' – and I demonstrated, using fewer fingers.

Inexplicably, Blucher seemed pleased with me. Inexplicably, too, he seemed incurious about my regicidal ploy but I told him all about it nevertheless, for attempted assassination always makes one babble; everyone knows that.

'And I suppose it was your lot who jimmied the cartridges,' I ended, gratefully.

'Why, no, Mr Mortdecai; it wasn't us at all.'

'Ah, then Jock is as patriotic as I suspected all along.'

'Well, no, I wouldn't say it was Jock, either.'

'Who then?'

'I really couldn't say.' I knew what that meant. I *thought* I knew what that meant.

They dropped me off at the wrong end of Brook Street, for security reasons I daresay. The walk did me good. Jock opened the door with an expressionless face and, as I passed through the kitchen, thrust a lusty drink into my hand with a similar lack of emotion. The first sip told me that he had understood that this was no time for such niceties as soda-water.

Johanna was in the drawing-room, her lovely eyes gummed to the television set, whereon there was a chap playing something wonderfully tedious on a tin-whistle made of solid platinum.

'Look, Johanna,' I said apologetically . . .

'SSHHHH!' she said. (There are certain instruments which seem to exercise an unaccountable fascination on female human beings. Did you know, for instance, that in ancient Athens there was a law against chaps playing flutes under girls' windows? There was nothing about giving them bunches of flowers, boxes of chocolates

55

or mink coats, but playing the flute was reckoned to be taking an unfair advantage; even *clever* girls succumbed to it. I'm not making that up, I'm really not; ask any Greek Historian. Ask him in that lucid interval between the after-luncheon nap and the cocktail hour.)

When the chap had finished his tootling and was shaking the spit out of his valuable whistle, I moistened my own whistle with what was left of the valuable Scotch and said –

'Look, Johanna, I'm awfully sorry but . . .'

'It's all right, Charlie dear, please don't go on. I couldn't bear to hear you explaining how you failed me. Even the best men can break under stress.' I thought about that one, for I knew that she was not a woman to use words carelessly. Many a bitter rejoinder and witty retort sprang to mind.

'Ah, well, yes,' was what I decided to say. Even she could not think of a riposte to that one. We dined early, later, because this was the night when our lovely Italian cook comes and 'obliges' and she likes to get away early because of what she calls 'Binko'. (You probably won't have heard of 'Bingo', it's a game where the odds are slightly worse against the player than at the 'fruit-machine' but you don't have to wear your palm out pulling the handle. It's jolly good for the economy too, they tell me; you see, if a chap earning £80 a week is giving his wife £20 of that for Bingo and encouraging greyhounds himself with a similar amount, well, he's not going to settle for any lousy, vile-capitalistic differential of bloody 5%, is he?)

We dined early, off a simple *bollito misto* and in a flurry of sparkling conversation like, 'Pass the salt, please, dear,' and 'Oh, dear, I'm sorry about this wine.' My final *jeu d'esprit* was, 'Johanna, darling, I think I'm going to get an early night, d'you mind?' She was ready for that punch; she gave me her sweetest smile and said that she didn't mind a bit; there was a horror movie on TV starting right now.

It must have been two hours later when she crept into my dressing-room and said that the horror-movie had frightened her dreadfully.

'There, there,' I mumbled sleepily, patting her where her night-dress should have been. Then she asked me what had gone wrong in the assassination ploy and I told her that the cartridge just wouldn't slide into the breech. She couldn't seem to comprehend at first, so

56

I sort of demonstrated. A few minutes later she said that she almost understood except the bit about the bolt-action. I went downstairs and made a couple of drinks. Playing for time, you understand.

She fell asleep perhaps half an hour later; ballistics is a very boring subject.

A little before dawn she shook me awake again. I was surly; I always am at that hour.

'Charlie, dear,' she said, 'there's one thing I don't understand.' I made unconvincing sleep-noises but to no avail. 'You see, Charlie, there were supposed to be *three* cartridges in the clip, weren't there?'

'Oh, very well,' I said.

10 Mortdecai is given a perfectly simple, nay, delightful task and makes a dog's breakfast of it

> . . . And the thicket closed
> Behind her and the forest echo'd 'fool'.
>
> *Merlyn and Vivien*

'All the same, Charlie dear,' she said as I pushed a listless rasher around my breakfast-plate, 'all the same, you didn't do awfully well, did you? With the *assassination*, I mean? I bet a CIA man would have checked every cartridge; the CIA brass accepts no excuses, they say.' The only retort I could think of was one such as I could never think of using a gently-nurtured millionairess, so I held my tongue and stabbed spitefully at a fried egg. 'Maybe,' she went on, 'that assignment was a little tough for you – as you often say, you are no longer a young man, are you?' Employing a strength of wrist and hand which I did not know I still possessed, I divided a slice of crisp fried bread with one stroke of the knife, sending half of it skimming across the room like a clay pigeon. 'So,' she said, 'I have thought of a little task for you which you will find simple and delightful.'

I made guarded, mistrustful noises which may or may not have been audible over the munching of fried bread.

'All you have to do is to make friends – make *great* friends – with a beautiful young woman. She is a sort of business-associate of mine in a confidential enterprise and I have a feeling that she is leaking. Oh do stop raising your eyebrows in that silly way, dear; you know I mean that she has been chatting a bit too freely with our uh competitors. I want you to get close to her, spend freely as though you were tired of carrying all that money around; this will make her gaze at you lovingly. Then start to wheedle; see if she is as careless a talker as I suspect. You might hint that you are a researcher journalist for one of the English Sunday papers, hunh?'

My knife and fork crashed down on my plate–a lesser plate would have cracked from side to side – and I stood up, giving an Arctic glare which would have withered a lesser woman.

'There are some things,' I said stiffly, 'which a chap simply cannot be asked to do. Assassination, yes. Impersonating a Sunday journalist, no.'

'Forgive me, dear,' she said hastily, 'I was perhaps lacking in, uh, insight when I suggested that. Just hint, then, that you are a heavy investor and that you have heard that she might be on the inside of some nice little deal such as you love to buy a piece of and that you have a wallet to prove it. But get close to her first, win her confidence; I'm sure she will find you adorable. Well, gosh, *I* do, don't I?'

I sat down again but my breakfast no longer held any charms for me; it looked like a cruel parody of a painting by Kandinsky.

'Very well,' I said at last, 'how and where do I make pals with this lady?'

'Tonight, darling. It's all arranged. Her name is Loretta. You are to be her partner at a reception: it's only at one of those Gulf Arab Embassies so you don't have to hunt for a white tie and tails, a simple tuxedo will do. Sorry, I mean dinner-jacket.'

Loretta proved to have one of those wonderfully flower-like, vulnerable faces; her eyes seemed always to be on the point of brimming with happy tears and her generous lips seemed to have been bruised with a thousand savage kisses. I found myself longing to protect her, which is what it's all about really, isn't it? Bridegroom though I was, I became painfully desirous of finding whether the rest of her bore out the promise of that lovely face.

After the reception and after what passes as a buffet in that class of Embassy she shuddered delicately at my suggestion of a visit to

59

a night-club. (I, too, shuddered a little but mine was a shudder of relief at not having to spend a great deal of money. I mean, I'm not *mean*, I'm really not, but fifty pounds for cheap champagne and a surplus of decibels has never struck me as good value. '*Quantum meruit*,' is what I say.)

'Take me home,' she murmured. Her murmur was of the brand which sends the familiar tingle galloping up from the base of the spine to the dorsal region. I took her. Home, I mean. 'Home' proved to be an apartment in a discreetly splendid block of flats off Curzon Street. The porter discreetly failed to see us but his back was benign. If ever a porter's back registered the words 'Bless you, my children,' that porter's back did so.

At the door of her apartment she handed me the key – I cannot bear bossy women who pretend to be able to open a door unaided – and stood facing me in such a position that I would have to stand very close to her indeed in order to reach the keyhole. Her great, violet-coloured eyes gazed up at me, swimming with the aforesaid unshed tears, her lips trembled tremulously and, in short, she was exuding all those infinitesimal signals which are supposed to tell a chap that a girl expects to be kissed, and that right speedily. I fell to the task with a will. She was very good at it. When her breathing quickened I found the keyhole and, still locked in each other's arms, we fox-trotted into her apartment. It was a lavish sort of pad, full of flowers and dominated by a monstrous sofa drawn up in front of a blazing fire of genuine logs. She vanished for a moment and returned bare-footed with a bottle of Armagnac and two glasses. I forget what the Armagnac was like, I was spellbound by the sight of her perfectly-shaped little toes as she twiddled them in front of the blaze.

As a conversational opener I lamely pointed out that this was well-known to be a sure way of catching chilblains and, inexplicably, she burst into laughter. Then she fell upon me frantically. Our mouths met and clamped together with all the mindless determination of a pair of bar-magnets. For a minute or two, or it may have been three, nothing was to be heard but the succulent sounds of face-chewing, the crackle of the logs and the bee-loud noise of certain zip-fasteners. (If ever I am forced by the soaring price of blackmail to write my memoirs, I have determined to entitle them *The Zip is my Undoing*.)

Suddenly, when it became abundantly clear that Loretta complaisantly expected me to work my wicked will on her, I unstuck myself from her embrace with a guilty start. Was I not a bridegroom? Was I not in love with my bride Johanna? The answers were 'Definitely' and 'Yes, I suppose so,' in that order. I had been told to 'get close' to Loretta – was I, perhaps, exceeding my brief? Loretta was languorously making it clear that I was certainly exceeding my briefs, if you will forgive a little vulgarity just this once.

'Look, ah, darling,' I gabbled, 'I've just had the most awful thought.'

'It's all right,' she murmured, 'I took my pill this morning.'

'No no no, I didn't mean that; I meant that I absolutely promised to telephone my, ah, business manager before –' I stole a glance at my watch '– before midnight. He flies to Frankfurt or one of those places at crack of dawn. Could I possibly . . .?'

'*Hurry,*' she said, handing me the telephone. I dialled. Johanna's cool and lovely voice answered. Summoning up what rusty remains of the German language I could recall, I addressed her throatily.

'*Ah, Herr, er, Johann! Hier ist Charlie Mortdecai!*'

'Darling, are you drunk already?'

'No, no,' I cried, still employing the German tongue, 'canst thou German understand?'

'Well, sure, Charlie dear; your German is a little different from mine but I think I can make out.'

'Good. Understanding is what I need shall. There is here something of a small difficulty. To retain the confidence of our friend it seems necessary that I to bed take her must. What shall I do? Hullo? Hullo? Canst thou me hear?'

'Yes, dear. You mean you want a "Green Card", hunh?'

'What is that? Ah, yes, now I understand.'

'Well, OK, just this once. But Charlie . . .'

'*Ja, Herr Johann?*'

'You are not to *enjoy* it.'

'No, Herr Johann. Goodnight.'

'Oh, and Charlie?'

'*Ja?*'

'Save some, hunh?'

'*Zu befehl, Herr Johann,*' I said. I wiped a furtive bead of sweat from the brow and hung up. Turning back to Loretta I said,

'Sorry about that, darling. Frantically important business. Sure you understand.'

'*Naturlich*,' she said in tones of frosty sweetness. '*Es scheint mir dass du versucht hast von deiner Frau eine Freischute zu bekommen, und ich kann mir auch denken für was.*'

'What what what?' I asked reasonably.

'I mean, does she say it's OK to screw?'

'Oh dear, oh God,' I thought, 'I used my real name on the bloody telephone.'

'Ho ho,' I said aloud, archly, and for want of anything more sensible to do or say I enfolded her in my arms and kissed her passionately. She had re-zipped herself – all the weary work to do again – but as my fingers tugged at the rip-cord she stood up.

'Goodnight, darling,' she said.

'How do you mean, "goodnight"?'

'Well, I suppose I mean sort of "goodnight".'

'But but but . . .'

'Yes, it would have been such fun but I mean to go on living.'

'Eh?'

'I mean I don't want to get killed this week. Or any week. Here is your hat and umbrella. Please do not think hardly of me; I think you are cute, I have always loved stupid men. Oh and darling, do button yourself up in front – the nights are cold, you might catch chilblains.'

The porter was reading behind his desk in the foyer. His face was benignly blank but it seemed to me that his eyebrows rose a fraction as I shambled past him.

'Goodnight,' I mumbled.

'Good*night*, sir,' he answered puzzledly and went back to his copy of *Forum*. He had probably been reading about premature ejaculation.

At home, Johanna, too, raised an eyebrow, far lovelier and more damaging than that of the porter.

'Home so soon, Charlie dear?'

I snarled in a muffled sort of way and poured myself one of the largest whiskies-and-soda of my career. I did not punish the soda-water syphon too hard. Wordlessly, Johanna handed me two

E capsules from a little gold *drageoir*. I swallowed them sulkily.

'I'm blown,' I said at length.

'*Blown*, Charlie? You mean Loretta . . .?'

'No, no; I mean my *cover* is blown – don't you ever read spy-stories? Loretta knows who I am, the bitch speaks German. Better than I do, in fact.' She seemed to smother a smile.

'But of course she does, dearest; she *is* German, you see.'

'You should have told me.'

'You should have asked.' I restrained the words which sprang to my lips for I was not one to use vile language in front of women, never having been married before, you understand.

'Anyway,' I said, when the blessed whisky had got a firm foot-hold on my bloodstream, 'the operation failed. I got nothing out of her.'

'Nor, uh, into . . .?'

'I cannot bear coarseness in women.'

'Don't be so stuffy, Charlie; I didn't for one moment expect her to prattle. She is very highly-trained indeed. As a matter of fact it was you I was checking out, not her. A kind of initiative test, you know?' I digested this, along with another whisky and s., which might have been the big brother of the previous one. My blood boiled with chagrin and frustration while many a bitter reflection on the nature of womankind occurred to me. It seemed to me that the only way to retain my tatters of self-respect was to stalk off to my bed in a marked manner.

'I think I shall go to bed,' I said in the distant tones of a man who has drunk both Armagnac and Scotch whisky and who has, moreover, been thwarted in the very act of a passionate encounter.

'Bed?' she said. 'Great! Can I come?' I studied her with a slight stirring of grudged admiration. She stood up with a little movement, shrugging off her *peignoir* to reveal a shameless little creation in black lace which seemed to be precariously supported only by her out-thrust breasts. The black lace ended just where her long and lovely legs began; had she not been a natural blonde one might have been at a loss to detect the hem-line. My look of admiration changed subtly into one of affection – I was reminded of my earlier rôle of 'heavy investor'.

'Can I?' she repeated meekly.

'I don't know,' I said, 'but I'm pretty certain that I could.'

She trotted towards the bedroom. I am not a lustful man but there is something about the sight of a beautiful woman trotting upstairs before me, clad in that kind of night-attire, which arouses the beast in me, I know not why.

'Charlie?' she said, a few moments later, 'Charlie?'

'Mm-hmm?' I panted, engrossed.

'Charlie, are you pretending that I am Loretta?'

'Certainly not,' I lied. 'I am thinking of my fag at school, if you want to know.'

'You are vile and base,' she murmured happily.

'Charlie,' she said the next morning.

'Oink.'

Firmly extricating my face from between her breasts she repeated the name.

'Yes yes,' I said petulantly, 'this is still I. Whom did you expect it to be? Onassis?'

'Listen, Charlie – no, stop that – just for a moment anyway; I have to talk to you. Your date with Loretta last night was only your second assignment but you must admit you made a bit of a cock-up of it, didn't you?'

'Don't admire your turn of phrase,' I grumbled sleepily.

'You know quite well what I mean. Now, if you are to be really useful to me – no, *stop* it, I didn't mean that – you must be trained.'

'Rubbish. I am trained. By experts. In the War.'

'Yes, I know; I have your War Office dossier in the desk downstairs. It cost me two hundred pounds.' (I awoke at this point.) 'You scored very high in unarmed combat and sabotage and shooting people but that was twenty-five years ago, right? And you never took the subversion course, did you?'

'Forget,' I said, feigning a sleepiness which I no longer felt.

'Well, you didn't. They tried to get you into that scene just after the War and you gave them some flippant reply about flat feet and cowardice.'

'The cowardice bit was true.'

'Well, dear, you are booked in this very evening to start a course at our very own Training College.'

'Oh no I'm not and anyway, what do you mean "our"? Who is this "we"?'

'Yes you are, darling. And "we" is me and some girl-friends of mine; I'll tell you all about it one day soon. You'll love the College, Charlie.'

'Oh no I shan't, because I'm not bloody going.'

'Lovely old house near Leighton Buzzard.'

'I'm going back to sleep.'

'Are you sure, darling? About going back to sleep?' I did not, as it turned out, go back to sleep until some eight minutes later, after she had wrung from me my slow consent, to name but one.

Since I am incapable of telling falsehoods I must confess that, when I married Johanna, I had been keenly relishing the prospect of a great battle for power between her and Jock. Alas, Jock had fallen under Johanna's spell and was by now a mere pawn, anticipating her lightest wish. Had I, in my bachelor days, requested breakfast at half-past noon, which was when it was requested that day, Jock would have summoned a cab and sent me off to the nearest Lyons Corner House. Today, his only comment as he brought on the corn-flakes, the kippers, the kidneys and the kedgeree was a genteel request about when Madam would require luncheon.

'Why are you making those weird, growling noises, Charlie?' asked Johanna. 'You sound like the Big-Cat House in the Zoo!'

'It is the smell of these kippers which makes you think of that zoological enclave,' I said, hoping that Jock would hear me and suffer a little. In a little while, crammed with kedgeree and strong, sweet coffee, I felt emboldened to reopen the subject of the Training College for Young Ladies, making it clear that any assent wrung from me while under the influence of natural blondes was inadmissible under English law. In short, I was not going there.

'Look,' I explained in a reasonable voice, 'all that rubbishy, reach-me-down judo and karate that they teach silly women at night-classes is junk. The women believe they are achieving results because, while they are striking absurd Kung-fu attitudes, waving their podgy hands about in absurder ways and making ultimately absurd noises with their mouths, the well-paid instructor is not about to step forward and deliver a round-house left into her belly while he delivers an old-fashioned right hand into her lipstick, is he? Although I bet he would often like to do so. But he is held back by the gentlemanly instincts which say that you do not strike ladies in vulnerable places, which is most places in ladies. I have never quite understood these prejudices myself because I am not a true-born Englishman, but they exist nonetheless.

'Your common rapist or mugger,' I went on, 'has no such compunction. He does not wait politely while the lady waves her hands at him in minatory ways, nor is he daunted by any Oriental noises she may emit. He simply steps forward and gives the object of his desire a bunch of fives in the moosh – regardless of the valuable crockery implanted there by her dentist – and follows it up by a similar punch just below her cross-my-heart living-bra. This never fails. (Policewomen, of course, know a trick or two; this means that they stay conscious maybe thirty seconds longer and spend maybe thirty days longer in hospital.)

'My advice,' I went on didactically, 'to any woman assailed by rapist or mugger would be as follows. In the case of a rapist: instantly lie on your back, raise your heels in the air and cry, "Take me, take me, I *want* you." This will disconcert almost all rapists, especially if the lady happens to be the kind of lady that only a rapist would look at twice. If he is so intent upon his purpose as not to be cowed by this simple ploy but persists in his purpose, why there is little harm done; lie quite still, try to enjoy it. The choice is a simple one: a brief and possibly not unpleasant invasion of one's physical privacy – or a painful bashing causing the loss of one's good looks and perhaps one's life. Who, after all, misses a slice from a cut cake, eh? In any event, on no account endeavour to have the rapist apprehended, for his lawyer will certainly convince many of the jury that you led him on and the trial will be more painful than the ravishment itself.

'In the case of a mugger, instantly hand him your purse – for you will scarcely be so stupid as to be carrying anything valuable in it – kick off your shoes and *run*. Run like the wind, screaming loudly. Scream like a steam-whistle; such chaps are most averse to noise when about their chosen trade. My life-long study of the art of warfare has taught me that running away is certainly the most cost-effective type of fighting. It doesn't win many battles but it saves you a lot of troops. Ask any Italian general if you catch him out of his hair-net. Or, indeed, if you can catch him at all.'

Having delivered those few, well-chosen words I reached for a kipper in the manner of a lecturer about to take a sip of water.

'Charlie,' she said mildly, 'our College isn't really much like those night-classes in judo. You'll find out when you get there.'

'But my dear, haven't I just made it clear that I am not going to your beastly College? Must I say it again? *I am not going to the College.*'

That evening, on my way to the College, I stopped at St Alban's to drink a little beer and purchase a couple of flat half-bottles of Scotch, in case the College should prove to be teetotal. I also made a telephone call to Blucher – after that assassination fiasco, he had conceded it might be more 'secure' to give me a number and 'procedure' for getting in touch with him in emergencies. I dialled the memorized number, let it ring the prescribed twelve times, hung up, counted out thirty seconds then dialled again. A warm voice answered instantly, saying that it was the Home and Colonial Stores – a likely story, I must say.

'Please may I speak to Daddy,' I asked, gagging over the childish mumbo-jumbo, 'Mummy's very poorly.'

'Oh dear, what a shame. Are you far away?' I gave her the number of the call-box; hung up; lit a cigarette. A fat harridan loomed outside the kiosk, glaring at me and pointing at her wristwatch. I recked not of her. She rapped on the glass, displaying a fistful of coppers and mouthing at me. I leered at the money and commenced to unbutton my top-coat. She went away. The telephone rang.

'Hullo,' said Blucher's voice, 'this is Daddy. Who is this?'

'Willy here,' I said from between clenched teeth.

'Why, hi, Willy. Are you at a secure telephone?'

'Oh, for Christ's sake. Look, I'm on my way to some kind of a Training College, it's called Dingley Dell if you'll believe that. It's near . . .'

'I know where it's near. Say, what's that dingus you Britishers wear when you're playing cricket?'

'I don't understand. We wear lots of things when we play cricket.'

'I mean the thing you wear under your pants, to kind of protect your family jewels, you know?'

'You mean a "box", I suppose. But what the hell . . .?' Had I not known him to be a humourless man I might have supposed him to be amused.

67

'Is there a sports store there in St Alban's?'

'I could not say. But if there is one it will certainly be closed by this time of the evening.'

'Gosh, that's tough. Oh well, good luck, Willy. Keep in touch.' He hung up. I drove off, musing furiously. My breast was seething with many an emotion but jollity was not among those present.

11   Mortdecai takes a bit of stick and drops the phrase 'gentler sex' from his vocabulary

> I read, before my eyelids dropt their shade,
> 'The Legend of Good Women', long ago
> Sung by the morning star of song, who made
> His music heard below.
>
> *A Dream of Fair Women*

Dingley Dell, for all its preposterous name, was indeed a stately pile so far as I could see in the dusk. As I navigated the stately drive an inordinate number of stately floodlights bathed both it and me in the radiance of some half a million Watts. A chunky girl in breeches met me at the foot of the steps.

'Mr Mortdecai? Oh, super. Now I can let the dogs out as soon as you're safely indoors. My name's Fiona, by the way. Just leave your keys in the car, I'll put it away.'

I carried my own bags up the steps to where a plumpish butler was silhouetted against the light.

'Welcome to College, Mr Mortdecai,' said the silhouette in what I took to be effeminate tones.

'Yes,' I said.

'You have just time to bathe, sir. We do not change for dinner. Allow me to take your hat and coat.' He took them, also my umbrella. As I advanced gratefully to the great log-fire blazing in the fireplace of the hall I saw the butler leap at me, whirling my umbrella in the general direction of my lower jawbone. I ducked, of course, for ducking is one of my more polished skills, and took the umbrella away from him by rolling it over his thumb, then I dropped (but stay, let me explain: experts never *whack* at people with sticks, umbrellas and things, for the movement is a clumsy one, easily out-manoeuvred and incapable of doing any damage unless the stick be a right heavy one, which makes the manoeuvre even clumsier. No, the use of such a makeshift weapon is to lunge, stiff-armed, at the midriff: even if the ferrule does not pierce the skin it can be relied upon to smarten up the liver, spleen or diaphragm in an agonizing and often lethal way.) I dropped, as I was about to say, into a stiff-armed lunge at the midriff, calculated to do great harm to the sturdiest butler, but at the very latest split-second I perceived to my dismay that he, the butler, was in fact a she-butler and my point wavered, passing over her hip. She snatched it *en passant* and twitched it further, so that I staggered towards her in time to receive a raised knee. The knee was clumsily timed, I was able to take it harmlessly on my chest and, as I stumbled past, seized the ankle and threw her. Keeping my grip on the ankle I twirled it vigorously so that she rolled over and over and pitched up with a satisfying noise against the wainscot. Face down. I placed a foot in the small of her back.

'Freeze,' I snarled angrily, for I was angry. 'Freeze or I'll stamp on your kidneys until they pop like rotten tomatoes.'

'Oh well *done*, Mortdecai, awf'lly well done!' boomed a voice from the minstrel's gallery. 'Ethel, you may get up now – but extra combat-classes for you all this week, I'm afraid, dear. You made an awful nonsense of that attack, didn't you?'

By now the owner of the voice was descending the great staircase; she was a massive creature, all beef down to the ankles, just like a Mullingar heifer. She advanced towards me, hand outstretched in a jovial way. I made to take the hand but hers slipped upwards and caught my thumb in an iron grip, bending it cruelly backwards. Well, I remembered how to deal with that, of course: you sit down, roll backwards and kick the offending hand away with the flat of both feet.

'Capital, capital!' she boomed. 'Shan't have much to teach *you* in the dirty-fighting class. Now, you see, we run a taut ship here and you must be on the *qui vive* at all times. For your own good, you know. But since this is your first night there'll be no more surprises until after breakfast tomorrow. Honour bright.' I relaxed. She smashed a great fist into the pit of my stomach and I subsided, whooping for breath, onto the carpet.

'Subversion Lesson Number One,' she said amiably, 'don't trust anyone. Ever. No, please, no lower-deck language; some of the girls are *prudes*.' I stood up warily, planning a move. 'No, Mr Mortdecai, you are not allowed to strike me, I am the Commandant. You call me Madam. Have you a gun?'

I pretended, snobbishly, to misunderstand. 'A shot-gun?' I said heavily, 'No, I did not bring one. I was not told that you would be offering me any shooting.'

'I mean, as you well know, a side-arm – a pistol if you prefer.'

'No. I do not commonly come armed when invited to country houses.' I spoke as stiffly as I could.

'Then we must fit you up. What do you fancy? I always use this' – and she plucked out a horrid old cannon – 'but then I'm old-fashioned, you see.' I sneered at the weapon.

'Service Webley .38 on a .45 frame,' I sneered. 'Should be in a museum. Kicks like – like a female butler.'

'Perhaps,' she said placidly. 'But it suits me.' She absently loosed off a round which whirred past my ear and caused a log in the fireplace to leap pyrotechnically. My ears sang with the roar and adrenalin squirted from my every pore. 'What weapon would you prefer, Mr Mortdecai?' I pulled myself together.

'Smith & Wesson,' I said, '.38 Special Airweight.'

She nodded approvingly, strode to the house-telephone.

'Armourer? Ah, Nancy; one Airweight, one box of graphite cartridges, one of solid, four spare clips, cleaning kit and a Thurston pocket holster.'

'*Shoulder*-holster, please,' I said defiantly, for my figure does not lend itself to the trousering of pistols.

'No, Mortdecai, you'll be wearing combat clothes, no time to unzip your blouse, you know.' A chubby little matron bustled up with two cardboard boxes. The pistol was still in its original grease. I handed it back in a lordly way.

'Pray clean it,' I said lordlily, 'and while you're about it, file off that silly foresight.'

'We look after our own pieces here,' she snapped. 'And you can have the foresight off in the morning when you report to the armoury. That's *if* I decide you don't need it.'

'Clean it now, Mortdecai,' said the Commandant, 'and load it with the graphite rounds. They pulverize on contact, you know, quite harmless unless you get one in the eye. You'll just have time before dinner.'

The butler, Ethel, showed me to my room and, as I lowered my suitcase to the ground, planted a succulent kiss on the top of my head, just where the hair is thinning a bit. I stared at her. She stuck out her tongue. 'You didn't hurt me a bit,' she pouted.

'Sorry about that,' I said ambiguously.

The room was Spartan: an iron cot, hard mattress, no sheets, no heating, two rough blankets, a deal table and a kitchen chair. I have been in cosier prison cells. I broke out one of my half-bottles and sucked at it vigorously while I cleaned the pistol. Soon both it and I were 'clean, bright and slightly oiled' as we used to say in the Army. I loaded a clip with the graphite rounds but thoughtfully introduced, first of all, one solid cartridge into the bottom of the clip. Emerging from the shower I heard a rasping boom from some hidden loud-speaker: 'Mortdecai – moving target outside your window – SHOOT!' Shrugging a shoulder, I scooped up the Airweight from under my pillow, flung back the curtains, flung back the casement window, all in jig-time. I could just see a shadowy man-size target trundling jerkily across the lawn. Flipping off the safety-catch I squeezed the trigger. There was a resounding click.

'Lesson Two, Mortdecai,' said the loudspeaker, 'always keep your pistol loaded and within reach.'

'It *was* bloody loaded,' I snarled.

'I know. I took the clip out while you were under the shower. Careless, very.'

'How the hell am I supposed to shower with a pistol about me?' I yelled.

'Sponge-bag,' said the loudspeaker succinctly.

When the dinner-gong roared I strolled warily downstairs, happy in the awareness of my pistol-heavy trousers pocket. There's nothing like a nice new pistol to dispel a feeling of castration. Not a soul struck at me. Taking a line from the grimness of my quarters, I had been dreading dinner but I was agreeably surprised. Hare soup, a casserole of pheasant with apples *à la Normande*, a soufflé and one of those savouries that women make, all washed down with a couple of decilitres of something which tasted quite like Burgundy.

'Excellent,' I said at length, 'quite delicious,' and beamed amiably down the huge refectory-table. There were two or three silent men present but most of the staff and students were women, some six or eight of whom were undeniably nubile. Following my gaze, the Commandant said off-handedly, 'Would you care for a girl to keep you warm tonight?' I gulped, which is not a thing one should do when drinking brandy, it makes it go down the wrong way. Much of mine went down my shirt-front. 'I daresay,' she went on absently, 'that one or two of them will be feeling randy – it's all that violence on television, you know. No? Well, perhaps you're wise. Need all your strength tomorrow.'

I turned my attention frantically upon the middle-aged woman on my right. She proved to be one of those astrology-bores that you meet everywhere nowadays and promptly asked me under which Sign I had been born.

Haven't the least idea,' I said, pishing and tushing freely.

'Oh, but you *must* know! What is your birth-date?' It seemed only civil to tell her, especially since she did not ask the *year*, but I took the opportunity to deliver my set-piece lecture about the stultifying folly of those who believe, in the third quarter of the Twentieth Century, that being born at one particular time and place will govern the whole of one's character and future. 'Why,' I perorated, 'this would mean that every triplet would be run over by a 'bus at the same time as his two siblings! Robert Louis Stevenson once wrote a sentence which has been the guiding-star of my life: "Children dear, never believe anything which insults your intelligence." Reading that at an impressionable age has, I am confident, formed my nature much more positively than the moment, some er, *chrm*, forty years ago when a fashionable *accoucheur* glanced at an unreliable time-piece and, realizing that he had another appointment, decided to spare my mother any further vexation by calling for the high forceps. Surely you can see that?'

She, the astrology-bore, was wearing that rapt, attentive look which women use when wishing to flatter pompous idiots. Being an experienced pompous idiot, I know that this look means that the woman is not listening at all but is merely waiting for you to stop making noises with your mouth so that she can do a spot of uttering herself.

(As it happens, and if you must know, I was born on the last day of September, because my father begat me on the Christmas night of a year which I do not propose to divulge; I know this to be true because my father told me so in front of my mother and several of her friends – he was like that. When he saw my face fall he quite misconstrued my feelings and explained apologetically that he had been drunk at the time. My mother did not speak to him for weeks afterwards but few people noticed this because, by then, she was not speaking to him much at all, anyway. She was a woman of great beauty and dignity, although unpleasing in almost every other way you could imagine and a good few which you could not.)

When I had drawn to a close and had vouchsafed my birth-date the astrology lady seemed thrilled. 'You're a Libra, then, how wonderful! Guess what my sign is. Oh, do!' I ransacked my mind for zodiacal signs. 'Virgo?' I said.

'*Silly*,' she said, lightly slapping my wrist. 'I'm a ram – Aries. We rams are made *for* Libras.' Well, I couldn't correct her Latin, could I, so I just eyed her guardedly. Her face would have passed for an old but once expensive handbag and the crocodile-hide of her neck and bosom would have attracted a snappy bid from Gucci's luggage-factory. 'Not Wanted On Voyage' was the phrase which sprang to mind.

'Oh, come, come,' I said diffidently.

'No, no – I must go, mustn't I, Commandant? Goodnight, dear Libra. My name is Kitty, by the way . . . if you care to know.' With that she left the table, smiling at me. People with teeth like hers should not smile. For a sickening moment I feared that she might be off to my bedroom, to await me there like a sacrificial ram.

'Do please stop grinding your teeth, Mr Mortdecai,' said the Commandant as soon as Kitty was out of earshot. 'She is really a

74

most capable person except for the astrology nonsense.' I could not quite stop grinding the teeth.

'If only,' I grated, 'if *only* such capable people would spare a moment to apply a dab of logic onto what they call their thinking; if only . . .'

'If only,' mocked the Commandant. 'If only! Paah! That is a phrase for kiddies to say to their teddy-bears. If only your uncle had wheels he'd be a tea-trolley. Come to that, if only your aunt had balls she'd be your uncle.' I glowered at her, for this was, after all, not the Australian Embassy.

'*My* aunts,' I said in a rebuking sort of voice, 'all possess balls. Indeed, I can call to mind few aunts who do not sport a cluster of such things. I cannot claim ever to have *rummaged* an aunt but I'm prepared to offer any amount of seven-to-three that . . .'

'Enough!' said the Commandant, raising a commanding hand. 'No wagers are permitted here, pray remember that you are not in a WRNS mess.' I would not have minded offering five-to-two against that proposition also, but took the coward's way out and said that I was awfully sorry. Then I said that I was awfully tired, too, and asked permission to leave the festive board. (The stopper, I noticed, was firmly in the neck of the brandy-decanter.)

I pined to clock up a few sleeping-hours but it seemed that I must first collect my 'lessons' from the Commandant's Office; these proved to be an arm-aching load of Xeroxed brochures about how to Kill/Maim/Cheat/Lie/Deceive/Subvert/Communicate/ Bewilder/Terrorize/Persuade/Forge/Impersonate/Evade/Explode/ Compromise and do all sorts of other horrid things to other people. A second stack was about how to recognize Aircraft/Weapons/Ships/ Missiles/CIA Agents/Narcotics and Counterfeit Currency while at the same time Living in Rough Country/Surviving at Sea/Confuting Interrogative Techniques and Mastering Five Simple Ways of Suicide (three of them almost painless).

Under my breath I muttered a short word concerning the hidden attributes of aunts.

'Cheer up, Mortdecai,' roared the Commandant, 'you're only here for three weeks and – only the first twenty days are painful!' She must have got that one out of the *Beano* comic.

'Ha ha,' I said politely. 'Goodnight, er, Madam.'

'Goodnight . . . oh, wait a sec – *catch!*' and with this she threw a blotting-pad towards me. Well, I wasn't born yesterday, as I have often freely admitted. I let it fall at my feet, making no attempt to catch it, and I had the Airweight out and pointing at her equator before she had even begun to haul out her old Webley.

'Oh, jolly good, Mortdecai,' she crowed, 'oh full marks!'

'Old stuff,' I said, closing the door behind me.

The only nice thing that happened to me that day was two minutes later, that night. No one was in my bedroom: no sacrificial rams, no half-assed Amazons hoping to sublimate their castration-complexes by boffing me on the head or other soft, vulnerable parts. Someone had been there, all right, because my suitcase had been unlocked – I had expected that, for any school-boy, indeed, any airport iuggage-handler can open the ordinary suitcase in a trice, using only a set of those feeler-gauges which you can buy at any garage. I was unconcerned, for the smaller suitcase is made of sterner stuff: it has a combination lock with three cylinders, each bearing ten numbers. I cannot say off-hand how many permutations this affords but I would guess that it would take the average chambermaid something like a million years to hit upon the right one. Even your average chamber maid does not have that kind of time to spare unless she is exceptionally ugly and there are no tired business-men in the hotel.

'BAD, Mortdecai,' quacked the loudspeaker as I drew a pair of pyjamas from the larger suitcase, '*bad*. Lesson Four.'

'*Three*,' I snapped.

'No, four. Never leave incriminating matter in easily-opened luggage.' I allowed myself a smug smirk.

'Anything incrim . . ., that is to say, *private*, is in the other, smaller suitcase.'

'The other, smaller suitcase was the suitcase I meant,' said the loudspeaker. I tried the smaller, unopenable suitcase. It, too, was unlocked. As I gaped the hated voice squawked out again.

'Our research has shown us that people in middle life find it difficult to memorize random numbers; they tend to utilize numbers which they are unlikely to forget. If you must set your lock to the numbers of your birthday – 30th of the 9th, right? –

then never tell the date of your birthday to people like Kitty. *That* was Lesson Three.'

I muttered something obscure.

'What you suggest, Mortdecai, I have tried once or twice. It gave me little or no pleasure.'

'I'm leaving,' I said flatly. 'Now.'

'Ah, yes, well, that's not really awfully easy: all students' bedrooms are automatically time-locked and cannot possibly be re-opened until *reveille*. No, please don't look at the window, don't; the grounds are full of Fiona's Dobermann Pinschers and the Dobermanns are full of blood-lust. You'd have to shoot an awful lot of them before you even got near the electrified fence and Fiona would be *cross* if you hurt even one of them. She lives for those doggies. She's a sweet child but her temper is ungovernable and she will insist on carrying that silly old sawn-off shotgun.'

I began to understand that the loudspeaker was trying to tell me something. I sat on the edge of the bed, for I always fume better in a seated posture. How, I asked myself, had the old she-butch known that I had been casting wistful looks at the window? My eye fell upon the big looking-glass which commanded both my bed and the entrance to the bathroom. I snapped out the light, stole to the mirror, flattened my nose against it. Sure enough, there was a faint glow to be discerned; the unmistakable glow of a cigarette being puffed upon by an ageing Girl Guide. It was the work of a moment to find my First Aid Kit, to tape a First Field Dressing across the mirror and to switch the light on again.

'Oh, *well* done, Mortdecai, there's good stuff in you after all.' said the loudspeaker. 'That was going to be Lesson Five, after the girls had watched you get into your sleeping-suit, ho ho.'

I did not deign to answer but marched into the bathroom to ply an angry toothbrush and conceal one or two trifling matters which had not been in either suitcase. On the bathroom mirror a message was scrawled in lipstick: 'PLEASE DO NOT HIDE THINGS IN THE LAVATORY CISTERN: IT ONLY MAKES WORK FOR THE PLUMBER.'

Huddled in my comfortless bed, I made shift to study the thinnest of my lesson-brochures: the one entitled *Mastering Five*

Simple Ways of Suicide, for this seemed to fall in with my mood at the time. I was shuddering my way through the passage about how to bite through the large blood-vessel at the base of the tongue and breathe in the resultant blood until asphyxia supervened, when the lights went out.

'Soddem,' I said to myself, composing myself to sleep.

12 Mortdecai finally realizes that he is not attending a night-class in self-defence for old ladies

Comrades, leave me here a little, while as yet 'tis early morn:
Leave me here, and when you want me, sound upon your bugle horn.
Locksley Hall

Towards morning, in that half-awakened state when the worst and best dreams come, my repose was marred by hideous visions of female dominators: Catherine the Great, Mrs Bandaranaike, the Erinyes, Mrs Indira Gandhi, Leila Khaled, Ulrike Meinhof, Marion Coyle, Fusako Shigenobu, the Valkyries, Eleanor Roosevelt, Ermyntrude of the Bloody Sword, Mrs Golda Meir, Carrie Nation, the Empress Livia . . . all trooped before my inward eye, gibbering and cursing and waving their blood-boltered hands, red to the elbows. I was bracing myself to receive comfort from the vision of Mrs Margaret Thatcher, for I have ever been a staunch Tory, when to my delighted relief I was aroused into full wakefulness by a whirr and a clunk from the time-lock on my door.

'Wakey wakey, Mortdecai,' cackled the hateful loud-speaker. 'Three minutes for a shower, one for brushing teeth, two for shaving. Draw a tracksuit from the Quartermaster in eight minutes, be at the Gym in ten. Any questions?'

'Tea?' I questioned feebly.

'No, Mortdecai; PT. Do you a power of good. You can skip it if you like but the only entrance to the breakfast-hall is through the Gym.'

PT was hell. People made me prance absurdly, climb up and down wall-bars, hurl myself at hateful vaulting-horses and try to do press-ups. Then they threw monstrous medicine-balls at me. I panted and groaned my way through it until a bell rang and we all trooped into the showers. They were communal, unsegregated showers. Kitty twinkled at me as she soaped her luggage-like carcass and the younger girls played *pranks* on me.

Breakfast, on the other hand, was unrivalled. It was one of those lovely country-house breakfasts where you lift the lids off silver dishes on the sideboard and find eggs and kidneys and chops and bacon and kippers and haddock and kedgeree and fried ham and devilled turkey and scrambled eggs and grilled tomatoes and, when you sit down, there are two sorts of tea as well as coffee and jam and three sorts of marmalade and people keep bringing you more and more hot toast. I ate heartily for, although I do not love such things, I knew that I must keep my strength up, you see.

'This is your last time to sit at the head of the table beside me,' said the Commandant. I made rueful noises, muffled by the piece of toast (laden with that black, chunky marmalade which Oxford makes so well) which I was gnashing. 'Yes,' she went on, 'another guest will arrive before luncheon and it is the privilege of the latest-arrived to sit on my right hand, naturally.' I opened my mouth to make the kind of joke that chaps like me make but closed it again.

'Quite understand,' I gurgled, sluicing a recalcitrant shard of toast down with another cup of capital coffee.

'Ladies!' she suddenly bellowed – ignoring the weedy males at the table – 'Ladies. Captain Mortdecai will be reporting to the Armoury in five minutes to shoot-in his new pistol. According to the custom of the College, when he emerges he will be Fair Game for 24 hours.' People laughed and said 'hooray' and things like that, but the piece of toast jolted to a halt on its way down the Mortdecai gizzard.

'?'I asked courteously.

'It means,' she explained courteously, 'that from 1010 hours you are Fair Game. It is the custom here with new students, whatever their age, sex or weight. Let me put it like this: it will be open season on C. Mortdecai from the hour stated. Your fellow students will take all reasonable care to avoid maiming you seriously, for it is all in fun, you see. Some of your predecessors have survived their Fair Game Day with little more than the loss of a tooth or two.' She gazed at the butter melting into her toast and heaved what might well have been a sigh of regret for happier days, days when no pat of butter durst slink into a piece of toast without written orders signed by herself.

'Good luck, Mortdecai,' she said dismissively.

No retort sprang to my lips.

It was a bad day; a rotten day. (It was like a compressed version of that hateful first term at a fourth-rate Public School when you are hounded and persecuted and you can't lock yourself into the lavatory to cry because the lavatories have no locks and you spend all your private-study time writing frantic, tear-spattered letters to your parents, imploring them to take you away although you know they will only reply in a jocose way, using phrases like 'forming your character' and so forth.) When I say that the pleasantest two hours of this first day at the Terror College of Dingley Dell were spent high up in the fork of a Douglas Fir or some other hateful fourth-rate conifer, being shot at with graphite bullets, I think I have said all.

I lost not a single tooth, but the black eye I sported at dinner excited some tasteless ribaldry. I recked not of it, for dinner was, once again, superb; it seemed to heal all wounds. They tried to spoil the *Navarin d'Agneau* for me by saying that it was my turn to wash up but at this point I dug in my heels. There are some things a white man simply does not do. Yell for mercy from armed lesbians when halfway up a Douglas Fir or other conifer, yes. Wash up after them, no.

The place of honour beside the Commandant was empty throughout dinner; the new guest or victim had clearly not yet reported aboard. I was glad not to be sitting there bandying polite remarks with Madam, nor having to avert my gaze from Kitty's appalling and treacherous bosom. In my new place, halfway down the table, I was flanked on the one hand by an amusing, scholarly American who told me that he guessed I could call him a kind of Sinologist, and on the other by quite the nubilest girl on the premises. She had

81

an engaging giggle and a blouseful of the most ravishing tits you can imagine. She promised that she would take over my washing-up chores for me and then confided that I had hit her with a graphite bullet that afternoon and raised a *drettful* bruise which she couldn't show me just then because she was sitting on it.

So soon as the stopper clunked into the neck of the brandy-decanter I pleaded fatigue – which was no less than the truth – and chugged up to my bedroom. Tomorrow morning was to be devoted to Theory, which meant that I must master an instructional brochure or two before folding the hands to zizz. First I mastered a generous slug out of one of my half-bottles, then selected the *Racial Impersonation* booklet to take to bed with me. The chapter entitled 'Somato-Ethnic Ambience-Values' seemed just the thing to induce a wholesome slumber but I was wrong – for the eleventh time that day. 'Somato-Ethnic Ambience-Values' proved to be about all kinds of fascinating things; I read avidly. It seems that these S-E-A-Values are all about what ethologists call the *Umwelt* – the area of alarm around members of the brute creation, such as human beings. It seems that we are all born with, or acquire, a racial sense of personal territory around our bodies and that outside this inner periphery of 'privacy' there lies an outer sphere of 'friendliness' which may be penetrated by permission or mutual agreement. Thus, if you are interviewing someone whom you wish to humiliate without actually saying so, you seat him just far enough away from yourself to make him feel vaguely ill at ease, to make him speak just a little louder than he cares to – and to enable you to raise your voice in a minatory way. Most tycoons learn this dodge when they are mere suckling managing directors – and it was not the least of Hitler's secret weapons. On the other hand, ask the bloke to come behind your desk and sit a couple of feet from you and he feels admitted to your ring of dentifrice confidence.

Similarly, if you are impersonating an Arab or Levantine, you must chat with other Arabs or Levantines belly to belly: if you step back from the dread gush of garlic and dental caries you will cause raised eyebrows, be your disguise and your mastery of the language never so perfect.

There were lots more fascinating nuggets, some of which I knew already. I knew, for instance, that you don't touch people's turbans but then I have never desired to. I knew that amongst Muslims you don't touch food with your left hand but I didn't know that to touch almost anything with it can be construed as a deadly insult in certain circumstances. (Muslims, you see, only use the left hand for one purpose. Shortage of water in the desert, you understand.) I knew, too, that a closed-lips smile from certain kinds of Chinese means 'I don't understand,' but I had not known that a broader smile means 'You are embarrassing me,' and that a smile revealing the teeth means something quite else again. Chinese restaurants, I felt, after reading the brochure, would never be quite the same for me again. (I was comparatively innocent at the time; had I been given a glimpse into the future I would have been through the window in a flash, prepared to take my chances with the Dobermanns and the electric fence.)

I was still poring over these gobbets of useful lore when the lights went out and, thirty seconds later, the dyke-like voice of the loudspeaker told me that the lights were about to go out.

I composed myself to sleep by trying to visualize just where the bruise on my charming dinner-partner was situated. Had I been younger and less fatigued, such thoughts would have kept me awake.

13 Mortdecai is dismayed to find that this game is not being played for bobby-pins, nor even for money

With prudes for proctors, dowagers for deans
And sweet girl graduates in their golden hair.

The Princess

The Theory Morning went well; when it came to my turn I was able to do a pretty convincing imitation of a Levantine, for I had begged a clove of garlic from the kitchen; the Instructress fell back in disorder when I came bellying up to her, whining and waving my hands and gurking out great poisonous gusts of that prince of vegetables.

My pretty table-mate at luncheon also reeled back aghast but I had saved a snippet of the garlic against this very contingency and she chewed it obediently. 'Why,' she cried a moment later, 'I can't smell you at all any more!' I enquired courteously after her bruise and learnt that it was still quite drettful and that she had meant to wub arnica into it but couldn't quite weach it herself. We looked at each other speculatively.

This did not prevent her, later that afternoon, from doing her best to smarten me up painfully during the 'Seek and Destroy' exercise in the extensive shrubbery and plantation: indeed, she playfully planted, from quite twenty feet away, a graphite bullet squarely

84

into the rolled-up pair of woollen socks which I had prudently placed where a cricketer keeps his box.

'You shall pay for this,' I muttered, gazing at the scarlet stain with which the crotch of my combat-trousers was splashed. (I was on the White side of this particular ploy or *Kriegspiel*, you see, while she was Red and our bullets were appropriately tinted.) I dutifully reported myself dead to the nearest Umpire, who tittered, sprayed an aerosol detergent on my red badge of honour and sent me back into the fray blushing. Craftily, I slithered across the lawn to the ditch or ha-ha, wormed along it until I was past the shrubbery, slithered out again and took up my position in a small, unkempt patch of scrub on the fringe of the plantation. (I was taught, long ago, always to choose the smallest piece of cover which will hold you; if you are behind the most barely adequate of the hummocks or bushes you will be the last to be rushed and may well be able to rake the other chaps with flank-fire while they are rushing the bigger ones. I don't know what they teach soldiers in these days of neutron-bombs. Prayer, perhaps.)

I had chosen my spot well; not a single sinner passed within range for the best part of an hour and I almost think I was beginning to doze off, lulled by the fragrance of myrtle, pine-needles and many another pleasing pong such as botanists relish on a warm afternoon. I was aroused from my musings by the faintest of scraping sounds from, of all places, the direction of ha-ha. 'Har har!' I thought, 'Gotcher!' for I was confident that this scraping sound was from my nubile friend; confident, too, that she would either surrender and offer to show me her bruise or, failing that, give me a sight of her on the skyline so that I could match up the bruise with another.

Nothing of the sort. The student who emerged from the ha-ha was small and skinny and, against all the rules, not wearing the College combat dress. What she was wearing was a sort of hooded track-suit of dull sky-blue – rather like the old French Army field-colour – but striped and slashed diagonally with dark green, as was her face. But I am no milliner; I simply shot her in the chest.

It was a lovely shot. Have you ever swung to a really fast pheasant and known, even as you pulled the trigger, that you could not possibly have missed, that the bird will drop tidily, quite dead, so close to your feet that your dog will have nothing to do but thump his tail approvingly? No? Oh. Well then, have you ever, at the poker-table, drawn a card to a 7, 8, 9, 10 straight with the absolute certainty that the card will be a 6 or a knave? No? *Really* not? Then, clearly, you are a golfer and will know the feeling that golfers never tire of describing: the feeling just as you finish your swing that this is a really meaty one which will send your ball right onto the green and make you wish that you weren't just playing for a lousy fiver.

This was, as I say, a lovely shot at that distance; it hit the girl on the central vertical axis, exactly half-way between the navel and the clavicle. Had it been a real bullet it would have collected a goodly chunk of her sternum and shredded it through the aorta, not killing her quite instantly but giving her perhaps a second and a half in which to regret that she had not chosen some other career.

Her reactions were slow, or perhaps she was simply a dullard; she checked in her stride and looked down stupidly at the 'wound', touched the splash of white powder in a puzzled sort of way, raised her fingers to her lips and tasted them. I raised my head from behind the hummock and cheerily told her that she was dead. She shot at me, which was against the rules. I wasted no time in protesting, for her bullet struck a stone in the hummock and screamed away *en ricochet* – no graphite bullet that. 'Bitch!' I thought angrily and squeezed off a couple of rounds at her camouflaged face – this, too, was against the rules. One of them must have connected for she screamed and clutched at her eyes. The odd thing was that she was screaming in no European language that I had ever heard and the screams were delivered in a round tenor voice. A *man's* voice.

As I stood up a shot came from another direction and I felt a strong snatch at the waist of my combat-blouse: another camouflaged Oriental was emerging from the ha-ha. I knew I was down to the last round in the clip – the solid, cupro-nickel coated round – but I have always set my personal safety before that of people who are trying to kill me. I shot him in the head. He died uncomplainingly, passing no remarks.

A third man clambered out of the ditch, similarly camouflaged. This was a bad thing, because my pistol was empty and the spare clip was filled with graphite only. As I scrabbled in my pocket a genteel sort of sound, like a bank manager's fingers drumming on his desk-top, was to be heard from the plantation behind me. The man rose to his full height, stared down at his chest as puzzledly as the first chap had stared, then dropped dead. I swung around, still trying to drag the clip from my pocket.

Johanna emerged from the trees, holding a curious kind of machine-pistol of a brand I had never seen before.

'What's new, pussy-cat?' I quavered valiantly. She planted a wifely but perfunctory kiss on my cheek before trotting over to the ha-ha to seek out any further fiends in human shape. She found none. We took the chap with the sore eye back to the College with us.

Over a cup of tea in the Commandant's office, or 'den' as she chose to call it, we chatted of this and that. Johanna's cup of tea was what she calls a 'General Montgomery', which is a fearful kind of dry Martini and so called because the proportion of gin to vermouth is twelve to one. Mine was a richly-deserved Red Hackle De Luxe – a fluid expressly designed to twitch people back from the very edge of the grave – while the Commandant was demurely sipping neat Navy rum. The actual teapot seethed unloved upon its tray.

'Look,' I said. They looked, politely.

'Look, why were those awful people trying to kill me, eh? Eh?'

'They weren't,' said the Commandant crisply.

'Well, you would certainly have had me fooled.'

'Charlie dear, they were not trying to kill you *in particular* is what Sibyl means. Yes, dear, this is Sibyl but you must continue to call her Madam while you're here. (Oh Charlie, dear, please don't let your mouth hang open like that.) They were infiltrating the Command Post, you see.' I didn't see.

'Where's that?' I asked.

'Why, here, dear.'

'No no no, quite wrong, this is Dingley Dell College, ask anyone.'

'Well, yes, dear, but it's a few other things as well. All sorts of things, in fact.'

I had a nasty feeling that someone would soon say that I should not trouble my pretty head with such things, so I shut up.

'In fact,' Johanna said with becoming modesty, 'it was probably me they were hoping to kill. I was kind of expecting it, you know? That's why I wasn't at dinner last night, sitting on – OK, *at* – Sibyl's right hand. I arrived here just after dawn, when Fiona would have locked her doggies up, and spent the day in the plantation or whatever you call it in Britain and there I was, just in time to save your life, wasn't I, darling?'

'Indeed you were,' I said bitterly. 'Indeed you were. Forgive me for not having thanked you at the time. Let's see, how many times does that make?'

She gave me a long, level look which should have stuck out between my shoulder-blades but I was not abashed for I have received many such looks in my career. It takes a very long and level look indeed to abash a dealer in Old Master paintings.

'Who, then,' I asked curtly, 'were these avenging angels? Mere fortune-hunters? Cast-off lovers? I feel I have a right to know, you know.'

This time she raised an eyebrow. Long, level looks I can cope with, but when Johanna raises an eyebrow strong men have been known to rend their garments. I quailed. My question had been in bad taste.

'Sorry,' I said.

'They were from 14K.'

'That's 14, Quai d'Orsay?' I asked brightly. 'Assassination rules; *Au Quai*?' They looked at me. I fancy I did a spot more quailing.

'No, Charlie dear, it means Number 14, Po Wah Road, Canton, China. That used to be the headquarters of a sort of Tong – they call them Triads now in the newspapers – formed by the old Nationalist Government or, to be exact, by Madam Chiang, Sun Yat Sen's grand-daughter, which amounts to the same thing – in 1945 as a "bulwark against Communism". They're still anti-Communist but they have kind of diversified their operations in the last twenty years or so. They're into the Golden Triangle in a big way now.'

I both boggled and blushed, as any chap would who has shared many a loving jest with his bride about her being a natural blonde. She gave me another of the looks; there was little kindness in it.

'Charlie, even you must have heard of the Golden Triangle; it is the opium-growing area bounded by the hill-country of Burma, Laos and Thailand. You must have realized what all those nasty little wars are about. Well, 14K desperately needs acetic anhydride and they can only get it from us. *Now* do you see?'

'No,' I said frankly.

'Oh, golly. Acetic anhydride is for refining morphine. It's essential. Refining opium into morphine reduces its bulk and increases its value; refining morphine into heroin does the same – in spades. You can buy a kilo of Number Three in Bangkok for a couple of hundred pounds; as heroin in Hong Kong it's worth maybe £6000 wholesale, which means, say £30,000 on the streets. If you can get it to Amsterdam you can triple that, even after paying off the narcotics-gendarmes who have starving mistresses and a mortgage to support. In New York . . .'

'Yes, yes,' I said, 'I know all that, although the prices seem to rise every week. And I know about the Police Sergeant in Hong Kong who has fifty-six bank accounts, too. But when I said "No" I meant "No, I don't know who this *us* is – I mean this 'us' who has a half-Nelson on the acetic what-d'ye-call-it." Who, in fact, is this "us?" ' I asked with a fine disregard for the niceties of the English tongue. She exchanged a quick glance with the Commandant.

'Oh, I see,' she said. 'Yes, well, I guess you might as well know. "Us" are – oh, hell, you've got me doing it now – *we* are – or rather we're friends with – the Woh Singh Wo, probably the most ancient Tong in China.'

'Oh, ah,' I said feebly.

'Yes. We're in a sort of league with them. It's a little complicated to explain just now . . .'

'White slaves?' I asked curtly. She stared at me, then giggled in that annoying silvery-tinkle way.

'No, Charlie, you have it upside down, dear.'

'Sometimes, yes,' I said stiffly, for I do not care to have my bedroom fads spoken of in public, 'but what do you mean? Are you – we – *against* white slaving?'

'Well, yes, you might say that. Yes, that's very good, Charlie.' She went off into the silvery laugh again.

'Now look here,' I said, trying to control the Mortdecai temper, 'I'm not an inquisitive man but would you mind telling me, just between the three of us . . .'

'Four,' she said. I counted us. We were three.

'Eh?' I said.

'No, Ho,' said a voice behind me. I laid an egg as I whirled round. There, behind me, bulked a massive Chinese gentleman in a silk suit. I still don't know how he got there.

'Charlie, this is my friend Mr Ho. Mr Ho, this is my husband.' The Chinese chap made noises both respectful and disbelieving.

Leabharlanna Poibli Chathair Bhaile Átha Cliath

Dublin City Public Libraries

I pulled myself together and ransacked my mind for a telling remark.

'How do you do,' is what came out.

'I manage,' he said. I smiled, not showing the teeth.

There fell a sort of silence. Mr Ho did not sit down. Johanna and the Commandant – I would never learn to call her Sibyl – looked at their laps as though they had embroidery there. It fell to me to biff the ball of conversation about.

'Mr ah, Ho,' I began, in the jovial, over-civil way in which one addresses chaps whose skins aren't quite the same colour as one's own.

'No, *Ho*,' he said.

'Eh?'

'No, not eh, not ah ho: *Ho*,' he insisted. I began to feel like the straight man on a Linguaphone record; decided to assert myself.

'What's your line of business then, Mr Ho?' I asked jovially.

'Hut,' he said. There was little in that remark for me so I let it fall to the floor, hoping that the maid would brush it under the chair next morning.

'Charlie dear, Mr Ho is saying that he *hurts* people. He does it for a living, you see.'

'Oh, ah,' I said.

'Charlie dear, the phrase "oh ah" is very rude in Cantonese.'

I said a very rude word in English, then subsided into a sulky silence.

'Mr Ho, would you like to bring the prisoner in, please?' said the Commandant. He did not reply. I glanced at him: he was not there. I reckon that I can shift the Mortdecai carcass around fairly noiselessly but this man was quite uncanny; he was even better than old Wooster's manservant who, as is well known, used to shimmer for England.

'Mr Ho is the Red Stick for the Woh Singh Wo in England,' said Johanna hurriedly. 'That's sort of, uh, *enforcer*.' He was back in a twinkling, carrying the prisoner over his shoulder as casually as you or I might carry a beach-bag, if we were the kind of person who carries beach-bags.

'Interrogate him,' said the Commandant, 'but please don't make a mess. The carpet is a costly one.' Mr Ho dumped the man on the floor, took a plastic Pak-a-Mak out of his pocket and threw it at him. The man unrolled it, lay down tidily on it. He was quite naked except for a bandage on his face where my bullet had hit him but his other eye was open and alert. He showed no signs of fear except that his penis had sort of shrivelled up as though he had just come out of a cold bath.

'If you're going to torture him,' I said, 'I'm leaving.'

'Probabry not necessary,' said Mr Ho. 'If he is professional, will know I can make him talk, will not waste our time. Most torture is crap; it amuses torturer onry; makes innocent man confess to anything, makes guilty man rie, makes stupid man dead too soon. Gestapo rubbish.

'Professional torture simple.

'First, hut very much at beginning. Most peopre do not rearise how much pain huts.

'Second, remove male members. Most peopre talk before this.

'Third, remove eyesight.

'Fourth, promise quick death. That is all. Watch.'

He produced a black doctor's bag. I trembled at the thought of the dreadful instruments he would take out of it but the contents were positively homely. One ordinary electric iron, which he placed tidily at the soles of the prisoner's feet. He did not plug it in. The prisoner raised himself on one elbow and watched dispassionately. Then Ho laid a coil of thin wire with wooden handles at each and – such as grocers use for cutting cheese – on the man's genitals. The man's face did not display any emotion but his penis seemed to shrivel a little more. Then Ho produced a teaspoon and laid it on the carpet at the level of the man's remaining eyeball and a long, tenpenny nail which he laid on the man's left breast.

The man seemed to appraise these ordinary, workaday objects – how sensible of Mr Ho to carry nothing incriminating – and came to a decision. He uttered a series of polite, deprecating quacks in what was probably Cantonese.

'There!' said Mr Ho kindly. 'He is professional. Says he knows one thing. Only one. Will say it, if kill quick; now. OK?'

Mr Ho cleared away everything except the long, tenpenny nail, which he left over the man's heart. The man rattled off a string of syllables in the same polite and unemotional tones he had used before. Mr Ho wrote things on a piece of paper and handed it to the Commandant.

'And what the hell is that supposed to mean?' she bellowed. Johanna took the slip of paper and shook her head, passed it to me.

'It's a map-reference,' I said in my cold, war-experienced, adjutant's voice. 'LSE64 is the sheet number, Ordnance Survey. H6 is the kilometre square. 625975 is the ground reference.' The Commandant snatched it and pressed a tit on her buzzer-console, asked for 'Library' and told someone called Annie to find sheet LSE6$_4$ and that right speedily. We waited, in silence and various degrees of fraughtness. Apart from Mr Ho, the least agitated member of our tea-party was the Chinese prisoner, who was gazing absorbedly up the Commandant's skirt. I was glad to note that his penis had unshrivelled itself a goodish bit. Ah well, whatever turns you on. For my part, I'd hate to go to eternal bliss with the memory of an old bull-dyke's directoire knickers imprinted on my retina for all eternity but that's what makes horse-races, isn't it?

Annie the Librarian brought in the map. Johanna and the Commandant looked at it. Rather in the way they had looked at me.

'Oh, dear,' said Johanna.

'Oh, shit,' said the Commandant in her coarse way. 'They know where, er, our man er *you-know-who* is.' She tried to work out the six-figure reference and snarled. I explained that the first figures go laterally, the others vertically. 'You must put it across a woman before you can get it up her,' I explained, quoting an old Army mnemonic. They glared at me but let me find the spot. It was an **ANCIENT FORT** overlooking a main road in a featureless waste of Yorkshire moorland.

'Mortdecai must go,' said the Commandant briskly. 'He's expendable.'

'Hoy!' I protested.

'Sibyl didn't mean it like that, Charlie dear,' said Johanna worriedly.

'Also he's crafty; a survivor; can shoot a bit,' added the Commandant, hoping to mollify me. She addressed herself to her buzzer-console again: 'Sandwiches for two days please, kitchen: high-protein ones, none of your fancy egg-and-salad; one litre flask of strong black coffee, no sugar; one litre bottle of Scotch

92

whisky. To be in Mr Mortdecai's car, which will be at the door in five minutes exactly.'

'How do you know I don't take sugar?' I asked rebelliously.

'*No* gentleman takes sugar in black coffee. Besides, it's bad for you. No, I'm not talking about your disgraceful waistline. Sugar and alcohol together trigger off your insulin and give you hypoglycaemia – symptoms are faulty judgment, undue fatigue, anxiety, inner trembling.'

'I get the last two when ordered to go and find people called *you-know-who* on lonely Yorkshire moors at five minutes notice,' I retorted. 'Anyhow, how do I recognize this chap, how will he recognize me and what do I do if I find him?'

'He will be on foot, if we're lucky,' she said cryptically. 'He answers to the name of Freddie. Just tell him what has happened and he'll know you're genuine.'

'Thank God I don't have to approach a complete stranger and whisper to him that the moon is shining brightly and wait for him to say that the price of fish and chips is going up,' I quipped.

'Try not to babble, Charlie dear.'

'If possible, get him out of there fast, and back here in one piece. If he can't come, take a message. If he's, ah, unable to speak, search him.'

'For what?'

'I don't know,' she said simply.

'I see.'

'Now, pop upstairs, get warm clothes, stout shoes and a couple of clips of cartridges. The real ones.'

'What about him?' I asked, indicating the patient prisoner. 'He's heard all this; probably understands English. And shouldn't someone see to his poor eye?'

'Irrelevant,' she said absently, 'he's been promised a quick death – a kindness really, because if we were to let him go his friends would give him a slow and exceedingly nasty one. Mr Ho?'

She gave Ho a half-tumbler of raw vodka which he handed to the naked chap. The chap tossed it off in one gulp, nodded appreciatively. Mr Ho gave him a lighted cigarette. He took two deep and happy drags then ground it out on the carpet (in his place I'd have said I was trying to give them up, of course; I couldn't have wasted such an opportunity). Then he lay down again on the Pak-a-Mak and made not a tremor as Ho knelt beside him, measured off one hand's-breadth below the left nipple and, finding the space between the appropriate ribs, positioned the point of the six-inch nail, holding it in place with an index finger on its head. Then Ho turned to me and politely said, 'Prease, he try to kill you – you wanna kill him?'

'Goodness, no,' I gabbled, 'I mean thanks awfully, kind of you, very, but I've already killed one chap today and I'm trying to . . .'

'Mr Ho,' said the Commandant, 'I think it might be better if you did it outside. You'll find a girl called Fiona at the kennels, she'll show you where the graves are.'

Mr Ho left the room in a marked manner – a little hurt, I fancy – the prisoner folded the Pak-a-Mak neatly, bobbed politely to the company and trotted off behind him.

I hope that, when my own three oranges turn up on the Celestial fruit-machine, I shall accept the jackpot of mortality with as much dignity.

'Goodbye, Charlie dear,' said Johanna. 'Drive carefully.'

'Good luck, Mortdecai,' said the Commandant gruffly.

'Yes,' is what I said.

14 Mortdecai's interest in bird-watching falters

What does little birdie say
In her nest at peep of day?

Sea Dreams

I must say I do approve of seagulls. Most petty criminals nowadays are so bad at their jobs – don't you agree? – while gulls are as dedicated as traffic-wardens and a great deal cheerier about their chosen vocation. They (the seagulls) gather in the grey light of dawn, shouting dirty jokes at each other and screaming with ribald laughter, waking up slug-a-beds like you and me, then when they have decided what to do that day, off they fly – and how good they are at flying, not an erg of energy wasted – scrounging, stealing, murdering and generally fulfilling their slots in the ecology. At lunchtime, when we are munching our first brandy-and-soda of the day, they congregate again in some spacious field, their bellies full for the nonce, and stand there in silence, sensibly digesting and *loafing* until it is time for another worm or two (in the case of the little Black-headed sort) or a tasty dead dog (in the case of the Greater Black-backed buggers). How wonderfully uplifting it is to watch them wheeling and swooping in the wake of a car-ferry, waiting for idiots to purchase British Rail sandwiches and throw them overboard after one disgustful bite! The very poetry of motion!

When all the world and I were young and people still knew their proper stations in life, seagulls were something that happened at sea, only occasionally calling in at the shore to defecate on your nice new sun-hat so that Nursey could give you a bad time. Nowadays you see them everywhere, raiding dustbins and queueing up outside fish-and-chip shops instead of swimming in their nice oil-slicks and eating up their nice, freshly polluted herring-guts.

The assorted seagulls who were grouped at the foot of the **ANCIENT FORT** were not exhibiting the poetry of motion, nor where they loafing, nor yelling like spoiled brats as seagulls should. *Waiting* is what they were doing. Waiting around a bundle of old rags. As I drew nearer they all rose into the air in a sulky fashion, except for a Greater Black-backed (*Larus Marinus*), big as a Michaelmas goose, who remained perched on the bundle of rags. Foraging for something. I broke into a run. The gull's beak emerged from the raggedy man's face, gulping something white and glistening from which scarlet ribbons hung. The bird gave me a murderous, yellow-rimmed glance from one of its eyeballs then flapped insolently away. I had nothing to throw at it.

When I had finished vomiting, I turned the raggedy man over onto his face and ran down the fell-side to the road. I should of course have searched him as ordered but, to tell the truth, I was filled with horror at the thought that he might still be alive. That may sound strange to you but you weren't there, were you? I had, of course, left my car some miles away and had walked across the moors to the map-reference and the **ANCIENT FORT** and the raggedy man. I waved down a passing car and had great trouble persuading the television-sodden driver that he was not on 'Candid Camera' and that no, I really wasn't Robert Morley, before he became grudgingly convinced that a man was actually dying or dead and that he must take me to the nearest telephone. From there I telephoned Blucher's secretary and gave her all the *nu*'s that were fit to print.

'Wait there,' she ordered. Since I still had one and one-half sandwiches and an almost-full pocket flask I fell in with her wishes. Night, too, fell. One hundred years and one almost-full pocket-flask later a Cocteau-like motor-bicycle policeman came roaring out of the gloaming, followed in a few moments by a 'bad-news wagon' (that means a police-car, *hypocrite lecteur*) and an ambulance. I led them all up to the **ANCIENT FORT** breaking each of my legs several times en route. There were several brief altercations: when the Sergeant berated me for having turned the raggedy chap over onto his face 'thus possibly destroying evidence'. I explained that certain feathered friends had been destroying evidence even more effectively. He did not believe me until they turned the chap over onto his back again, whereupon the dashing, fearless motor-bike copper was ill all over the Sergeant's brand-new shoes, starting another altercation which, conjoined with the ambulance-men's bitter discussion about overtime, fairly made the welkin ring. I found it all a bit sordid.

'Trotskyist pig!'

'They cost me nineteen pounds ninety-five only last week!'

'Get no bloody home-life in this job, do we?'

'Filthy Maoist revisionary!'

'I should afford such shoes on my pay.'

'Got the shop-steward in your pockets, haven't you, eh?'

'They're supposed to have the rubbed-off wet-look and look at the buggers now!'

'Well, at least I'm not in the bosses' pockets, I can say that . . .'

'Drop of turps will have 'em good as new in no time . . .'

'No, it's not the bosses' *pockets* you're in, comrade . . .'

'You calling me a brown-nose, brother?'

I stole away, murmuring 'Oh dear, oh dear' and musing on dialectical materialism and the Majesty of the Law. I was quite right: I had indeed left almost half a sandwich in the telephone-box. It occurred to me to telephone Blucher again, hoping to get him in person this time. He was not in the least amused. Had I searched the man? Why not? Was the chap dead? What did I mean I wasn't sure? Why wasn't I there beside him, watching every move of every copper? I began to feel like Macbeth in Act II, Scene 2, where his wife says 'Infirm of purpose; give me the daggers,' when the door of the booth or kiosk was flung open and the Sergeant demanded to be told who it was that I was telephoning.

'Sweet, cuddlesome dreams, my own dearest little fluffy-puss,' I said into the receiver as I replaced it in a dignified fashion, before turning upon the fellow and raising a brace of icy eyebrows. (I yield to none when it comes to eyebrow-raising; I was taught by my father himself, who could have eyebrow-raised for Great Britain had he

Brainse Ráth Maonais
Rathmines Branch
Fón / Tel: 4973559

not been so haughty.) The Sergeant cringed a little, as I had been cringing under the lash of Blucher's ice-maiden voice. This cringing of his gave me time to wonder what kind of pressure Blucher could have applied – and to whom – and what I was supposed to do – or be.

The necessary, hasty trip to the mortuary over, we all pitched up at the cop-shop of the county town – I cannot remember its name but I shall always think of it as Heckmondwyke – where I was given great mugs of tea and met an Inspector of Detectives who positively bulged with intelligence and well-feigned friendliness. He asked me only the most natural and obvious questions then told me courteously that a room was booked for me at the cleaner of the two local hostelries and that the Detective Sergeant would take me there. Oh yes, and would pick me up in the morning, so that we could foregather at the morgue.

'Didn't seem awfully interested, did he?' I said nonchalantly as the Sergeant decanted me in front of what I suppose I must call the hotel.

'Well, only an old tramp,' said the Sergeant.

'Ah,' I said.

Dinner was 'off', of course, for it was by now quite eight o'clock, but an embittered crone, after I had bribed her richly, made me a bowl of soup and something called am-an-eggs. The soup was not good but she had at least taken the packet off before adding the warm water. I prefer not to discuss the am-an-eggs.

It would be idle to pretend that I slept well.

Well, there we were next morning, all well-washed, shaven, after-shave fragrant; costly our habits as our purse could buy. (Indeed, rather costlier in the case of the Detective Constable: policemen in expensive suits *worry* me.) It was shaming to look at the dirty old corpse on the mortuary slab. Refrigeration had only a little abated the richness of his bodily odours. His mouth gaped open in a derisive way; the teeth in his mouth were few – and few of them could have met. The Inspector took his time looking at the teeth.

'Even a tramp,' I said crossly, from my guilty heart and from between well-dentifriced ivory-castles, 'even a tramp could have got himself a set of gnashers from the National Health. I mean, dammit.'

'That's right,' said the Inspector as he rose from peering into the carrion old mouth.

We trooped into the room where the tramp's pitiful clothes and other gear were laid out on a trestle-table, together with the prescribed three copies of the list of these possessions. Our nostrils were assailed with the cloying horror of a lavender-flavoured aerosol 'air-freshener' and the Inspector snarled at the uniformed bloke in charge.

'I might have wanted to *smell* these things,' is what he snarled.

'Sorry, sir.'

'Anything that turns you on . . .' murmured the Detective Constable by the door. The Inspector pretended not to have heard – help is hard to come by these days and, in any case, he had noticed the Detective Sergeant's deadly glance at the DC: the glance which says that certain DC's are going to find themselves lumbered with a nasty little bit of extra duty tomorrow.

The objects laid out on the trestle-table were not a suitable sight for the squeamish. In the matter of underclothes the deceased's policy seemed to have been 'live and let live', not to mention 'increase and multiply'. There were several layers of these intimate garments and its was apparent that the local police had not found a volunteer to separate them. The Inspector braced himself and went about the task himself: he was a man of iron. Then he checked, against the list, the pitiful, trumpery possessions from the corpse's pockets and haversack. He checked them as minutely as a prosecuting attorney might scan President Nixon's Christmas-present list.

There were ancient, nameless scraps of what might once have been food. There was a retired baked-beans tin with two holes in the edges to take a loop of wire; the inside was caked with tea, the outside with soot. There was a twist of plug-tobacco engraved with tooth-marks: whether by man or beast it would be hard to say. There was a cheap, blunt, celluloid-handled penknife of the sort which is made to sell. To schoolboys. Something stirred in my mind. There was a piece of soap, gnarled and grime-fissured. A tin box containing a dozen red-top matches and half an inch of candle. A coloured photograph from a 'girlie' magazine – a 'beaver-shot' as they call it, much creased and be-thumbed. An onion, the sweating heel of a piece of cheese and some cold fried potatoes, neatly packed in one of those foil-lined cartons they use in Chinese take-away restaurants. Grubby twists of paper containing sugar, tea, salt . . . ah, well, you know the sort of thing. Or perhaps you don't; lucky you.

Oh yes, and there was a nice, clean £10 note.

The Inspector at last rose from his absurdly detailed inspection of the chattels, blew his nose and shook himself like a dog.

'Not a tramp,' he said. His voice was flat; he was not accusing anyone.

'Not?' I asked after a pause.

'But . . .' said the Sergeant after a longer pause.

'Sir!' huffed the DC.

'Use your eyes, lad,' said the Inspector. 'The facts are as plain as the nose on your face.' The DC, being well-gifted in the nose-department, fell silent. This was the point at which I began to take the Inspector seriously.

After he had signed receipts and things and had shrugged off his subordinates he carried me off to the cop-shop canteen, where he regaled me with delectable tea and the finest and crispest ham-rolls I have ever sunk tooth into.

'Well,' I said, when the crust-munching noises had died down, 'are you going to tell me or not?'

'Teeth and toenails,' he answered cryptically.

'Eh?'

'Aye. No blame to you for not noticing, but those twits out there are supposed to have been taught to use their eyes.'

I kept my mouth shut. I, too, had been taught things of that kind long ago, but there was no profit in telling him the story of my life and I hoped, in any case, to hear him spell out his thoughts as to an innocent bystander, for there is no more rewarding experience than to listen to a man who is really good at his job. This man was very good.

'First,' he said, licking a trace of mustard from a capable thumb, 'when did you last see a genuine old-fashioned foot-tramp in England?'

'Why, now I come to think of it, not for a hell of a long time. Used to be part of the landscape, didn't they, but I can't say that I –'

'Right. I said *foot*-tramp to rule out Romanies and didicoys and such. I don't reckon there's six real tramps walking the roads of

England today and there haven't been since, oh, about 1960. The casual-wards are all closed down, so are the pay-flops; and the Rowton Houses are all turning into Commercial Hotels. They say there's a few old stagers still trudging Wild Wales, but that's it.

'Moreover, your real old tramp used to have a regular beat of about two hundred miles, so he'd pass through any given "manor" maybe once in a good summer and three times in winter. Even those morons out there who call themselves detectives would certainly know any walking-gent who went through the manor regular.'

'Meths-drinker?' I asked.

'No. None of the signs. And meths-drinkers haven't the strength to walk any distance. And they usually have a flat half-bottle of the rubbish taped to the small of their back in case they get nicked. And they don't eat. Our man liked his food – if you can call it food.'

'So?'

'So, second,' he said, examining his forefinger for any lingering mustard, 'you were dead right when you worried that he'd not got himself a set of dining-snappers off the National Health. In fact, as a glance at his gums and canines would have told any *real* policeman, he had once owned a costly set of bridgework – not your National Health sort – and had only parted with them a few months ago. Say, about the time he took his last bath.'

'And third?' I prompted.

'Third,' he said, holding up his middle finger in a gesture which would be considered vulgar in Italy, 'third, no scissors.'

'No scissors,' I repeated in an intelligent sort of voice.

'No scissors. In me early days I've looked over the belongings of many a tramp found dead in a ditch. Some of them had pictures of the lass that drove them onto the road, some of them had rosaries, some had a little bag of golden sovereigns and I remember one that had a New Testament in Greek. But the one thing that they all had was a good, strong pair of scissors. You wouldn't last long walking the road if you couldn't cut your toenails. A tramp's toenails are his bread and butter, you might say. Our man here didn't even have a strong sharp knife, did he? No; not a tramp, definitely.'

I made the sort of admiring noises you used to make when your geometry-master triumphantly said 'QED'.

'I don't mind telling you,' he went on, 'that I regret saying that bit about him not being a tramp in front of the Sergeant and the DC. But I know that you can be relied on to keep your mouth shut, sir' – I jumped a little at the 'sir' – 'because obviously neither of us wants idiots like them wondering why someone would be wanting to pass himself off as a tramp in *this particular* part of the country.' He looked narrowly at me as he said that last bit: I did my best to look inscrutable, hoping to give the impression that I well knew the special fact about 'this particular part of the country' and that I might well have, tucked into my left boot, a very special kind of identity-credential too grand to be shown to common coppers.

'Funny about that nice new tenner he had on him,' mused the Inspector. 'Looked to be fresh from the mint, didn't it?'

'Yes.'

Not even folded, was it?'

'No.'

'What was the number on it again, did you happen to notice?'

'Yes,' I said absently – *stupidly* – 'JZ9833672, wasn't it?'

'Ah, yes, that was it. Funny, that.'

'How d'you mean, "funny"?' I asked. 'Funny that I should remember it? I have an eidetic memory for numbers, can't help it. Born with it.' He did not take the trouble to check my statement – he was good at his job, he knew I was lying.

'No,' he said, 'I meant funny that it's from the same series as a large number of perfectly genuine tenners that the London lads reckon have come into the country not a month ago. From Singapore or one of those places. You must admit that's funny.'

'Hilarious,' I said.

'Yes, well, goodbye now, sir, we really can't detain you any longer.'

'Oh, but if I can be of any further help . . .'

'No, sir; what I meant to say was that I'm sorry we can't *detain* you. In custody, as they say. Like, for instance, dropping you in the Quiet Room for a couple of days and then having two or three of the lads beat the shit out of you until you told us what this caper is all about. Would have been nice,' he added thoughtfully. 'You know, interesting. We jacks are an inquisitive lot, see?' I may have gulped a little at this point.

'But you seem to have some very heavy friends, sir, so I will just bid you a friendly farewell. For now.' He shook me warmly by the hand.

Outside, waiting for me, there was one of those lovely black cars which only police-forces can afford. The uniformed driver opened the door for me. 'Where to, sir?' he asked in a uniformed sort of voice.

'Well,' I said, 'as a matter of fact I have a car of my own which I sort of left just off the road about, let's see, about twenty miles away; it's a . . .'

'We know where your car is, sir,' he said.

15 Mortdecai loses faith in matrimony, takes holy orders *pro tem* and sees a dentist more frightened than a dentist's client

But the jingling of the guinea helps the hurt that Honour feels

Locksley Hall

When your kitchen sink is blocked and you have to summon a plumber because both it and the maid are making threatening noises, he – the plumber – unscrews the thingummy at the bottom of the wonderfully aptly-named U-trap and shows you triumphantly the mass of detritus that he has liberated from it, with all the pride of a young mother exhibiting the malevolent squashed-tomato which she assures you is a baby. This great, greasy gobbet of nastiness (I refer, of course, to the sink-occlusion, not to the family-planning error) proves to be a closely-matted cupful of vegetable-peelings, pubic hair and nameless, grey, fatty matter.

What I am trying to describe is the condition of the enfeebled Mortdecai brain on its – my – return to the Training College or Command Post or whatever.

'Ah, Mortdecai,' growled the Commandant gruffly.

'Charlie, dear!' cried Johanna.

'Drink?' I muttered, subsiding into an armchair.

'Drink!' snapped Johanna absently. The Commandant leapt to the booze-cupboard and made me a drink with surprising alacrity and rather too much soda-water. I filed the surprising-alacrity bit away into that part of my mind where I file things which I must think about when I feel stronger. Then I filed the whisky and s. into the most confidential part of the Mortdecai system and called for another.

'So you found him, Charlie dear?'

'Yes.' A thought squirmed in my brain. 'How did you know?' (I had, you see, telephoned no one but Colonel Blucher.)

'Just guessed, darling. And you wouldn't be back so soon if you were still looking for him, would you?'

'Glib,' I thought bitterly. 'Glib, *glib*.' I often bitterly think words like 'glib, *glib*' after listening to things which women have said; I'm sure I'm not alone in this.

'And how are you, Charlie? I hope it wasn't a horrid experience?'

'Not at all,' I replied bitterly. 'Wonderful shake-up. As good as a week at the seaside. Stimulating. Refreshing.' I gargled a little more.

'Do tell us all about it,' she murmured when the noises had died down. I told her almost all about it. From A to, let us say, W – omitting X, you see.

'And of course you wrote down the number of the nice, new, fresh ten-pound note, Charlie?'

'Naturally,' I said. Two panic-stricken glares focused upon me.

'But only,' I added smugly, 'upon the tablets of my memory.' Two batches of panic-stricken female breath were exhaled. I raised an eyebrow of the kind my mother used to raise when parsons preached unsound doctrine at Mattins. They gazed at me expectantly while I pretended to ransack my memory; then the Commandant took the hint and refilled my glass. I delivered the serial-number of the note in a gift-wrapped sort of way. They wrote it down, then the Commandant went to her desk and fiddled with absurd secret drawers (look, there are only just so many places in a bureau where a secret drawer can lurk – ask any antique-dealer) and produced a slim little book. They compared the number I had given them with the nonsense in the slim little book, looking cross, grave and worried in that order until I lost patience and rose to my feet. Secret Service games are boring even when played by men.

'Off to bed,' I said. 'Tired, you see. Must go to bed.'

'No, Charlie dear.'

'Eh?'

'I mean, you must be off to China; not bed.' I did not even try to absorb such nonsense. 'Rubbish!' I cried manfully, snaring the whisky-decanter as I swept out of the room. I did not sweep far, for Johanna called me back in masterful tones quite unbecoming in a bride.

'You will like it in China, Charlie.'

'Oh no I bloody won't, they'll take one look at me and send me off to be politically re-educated on some co-operative farm in Hunan. *I* know.'

'Well, no dear, I didn't mean Red China – not this time anyway – more Macao, really. It's independent or Portuguese or something – I guess it amounts to the same thing. A great gambling centre, you'll love it.'

'No,' I said firmly.

'Flying First Class in a Jumbo. With a bar.'

'No,' I said, but she could see that I was weakening.

'A suite in the best hotel and a bankroll to gamble with. Say a thousand.'

'Dollars or pounds?'

'Pounds.'

'Oh, very well. But I must go to bed first.'

'OK. In fact, goody.'

'I'm sorry I cannot invite you to share a nuptial couch,' I added stiffly, 'my bed is some two feet six inches wide and there are enough electronic bugs in the room to start an epidemic.'

'Yes,' she said obscurely.

When I emerged from the shower, briskly towelling the Mort-decai tum, Johanna was in the said 2′ 6″ bed.

'I've had the bugs turned off, Charlie.'

'Oh yeah?' I said in American.

'Yeah. I kinda own this joint, you know?' I winced.

'I didn't know,' I said stuffily, 'and there still isn't enough room in that bed for two.'

'You wanna bet, buster?'

There was enough room. And I mean that most sincerely.

106

'I think that, on the whole, I'd better take Jock with me,' I said later, during the interval for refreshments. 'After all, three eyes are better than two, eh?'

'No, Charlie. He is too conspicuous, people would remember him, whereas you're kind of unremarkable, you sort of melt into the background, you know?'

'No, I didn't know that,' I said stiffly, for that is the kind of remark which stings.

'Anyway, dear, he's a xenophobe, isn't he – he'd probably hit all sorts of people and attract attention.'

'Oh, very well,' I said. 'Back to the grind,' I added, but not out loud of course.

Johanna drove me to London the next morning. She is a wonderful driver but I used the passenger's brake a goodish number of times; the journey was, in fact, one long cringe for me. We finally pitched up unscathed at Upper Brook Street, W1, having stopped briefly at one of those places where they make passport photographs of you while you wait.

'But I already *have* a passport,' I said.

'Well, dear, I thought you'd like a nice new one.'

From the flat she made a number of guarded telephone calls to all sorts of people; the upshot was that by late afternoon I was the proud possessor of First Class tickets on a Boeing 747 and a Vatican City passport, complete with all necessary visas and made out in the name of Fr Thomas Rosenthal, SJ; occupation: Curial Secretary. I didn't think that was very funny and said so, huffedly.

'Darling,' she said, 'I do realize that at your age you wouldn't be just a Fr still, but if we'd made you a Monsignore or Bp or something the airline people would make a *fuss* of you and that wouldn't be secure, right? Tell you what, I'll send the passport back and have them promote you Canon. Hunh? Would you settle for Canon?'

'Oh, leave it alone, Johanna; I'm truly not sulking. The Church wouldn't be the first career I've muffed. Anyway, I'm not at all sure they have Canons in Rome and Monsignores have to wear puce breeches, I think.'

'Oh, good. I knew you wouldn't mind being a simple Fr. You have a kind of wonderful modesty . . .' I raised a deprecatory hand.

'I shall of course need a few strings of rosary-beads and a Breviary or two – I'm sure you've thought of that.'

'Charlie, darling, you're supposed to be a *Jesuit*, remember? They're not into all that stuff.'

'Of course not; silly of me.'

I don't mind admitting that I enjoyed the flight; I was the only First Class passenger and the stewardess was most attentive. Most attentive. I began to understand why Johanna had taken such pains over me the previous night, if you see what I mean. (If you don't see what I mean, congratulations on a clean mind.)

My hotel was of a *luxe* which surprised me: *tout confort moderne* would be understating by a bushel and a peck. It was not quite like that one in Bangkok where you have to shake the sheets each night to rid your bed-clothes of little golden girls, though the management of this one was certainly doing its best. But you don't want to hear about that sort of thing, do you?

In the morning I sprang out of bed with a glad cry and promptly sprang into it again with a whimper. I was never strong, even as a boy, and on that morning I felt so enfeebled both in body and mind that I doubt whether I could have hit the ground with my hat. Certainly, I was in no state to play at Secret Agents with Sinister Orientals. Jet-lag and other factors had me by the throat, to name only one organ; I built up my strength by having first one delicious breakfast and then, after a two-hour digestive nap, just such another, washing them down with nutritive glasses of brandy and soda which, in that sort of hotel, you can summon up without the aid of floor-waiters: you simply press the appropriate tit on a 'Refreshments Console' which looks for all the world like a miniature cinema-organ.

By lunch-time I felt able to totter down to the restaurant and recruit my strength properly; I had something green and crisp and tasty which was evidently the pubic hair of mermaidens but which the waiter assured me was fried seaweed. Then there were slivers of duck cooked in a sort of jam; a delicious goo made of the swim-bladders of some improbable fish; deep-fried dumpling-like things each containing a huge and succulent prawn, and so on and so forth: there was no limit to their inventiveness.

There was also something to drink which they said was distilled from rice. It had the deceptively innocent taste which made Pimm's No. 1 such a handy drink for seducing girls when I was at University. I went gratefully back towards my room, smiling at one and all. I was in that delightful stage of not-quite-drunkenness when one overtips happily and there was no lack of minions to overtip. I even pressed a sheaf of currency into the hand of someone who proved to be an American guest; he said, 'OK, Father, whaddya fancy?' Realizing my mistake, and remembering my clerical kit or garb, I waved an airy hand and told him to play it for me on anything he fancied: it would all go to the poor. Then I found my room, crashed the Mortdecai turnip onto the pillow and completed the cure with a couple of hours of the dreamless.

By late afternoon the cure was completed and I felt strong enough to open the sealed envelope of instructions which Johanna had given me at Heathrow Airport.

'Lo Fang Hi,' it read, 'Doctor of Dentistry and Orthodontics.' Clearly a poor joke but nevertheless I looked him up in the telephone-book (even if you do know that the Chinese keep their surnames where we keep our Christian ones, a Chinese telephone directory is a skull-popper) and found him. I telephoned him. A shrill and agitated voice admitted to being Dr Lo. I resisted the temptation to say 'Hi' and said, instead, that I was a toothpaste-salesman – for that was what I had been told to say. What he said was that I might come around as soon as I liked, indeed, he suggested I came very soon. Yes, very soon *indeed*, prease. I hung up, musingly. The Roman collar had been tormenting my neck and I recalled that I had rarely seen a toothpaste-salesman in a cassock, so I changed into an inconspicuous little burnt-orange lightweight which that chap in the Rue de Rivoli ran up for me in the day when £300 would still buy a casual suit.

The address, to my surprise, was not 'In the Street of the Thousand Baseballs, 'Neath the sign of the Swinging Tit' as the old ballad has it, but in Nathan Street, Kowloon, which proved to be a dull, respectable sort of boulevard, reminiscent of Wigmore St, London W1. (I do not know who Mr Nathan was nor why he should have such a street named after him; indeed I know nothing of Mr Wimpole, no, nor even Wigmore, although I could tell you a thing or two about Harley.)

The cab-driver spoke American with a pronounced Chinese accent. He was also the proud owner of a sense of humour: he had evidently taken Buster Keaton's correspondence-course. When I told him to take to No. 18, Lancaster Buildings, Nathan Road, Kowloon, he leaned over his seat and eyed me in a tiresome, inscrutable way.

'Cannot take you there, buddy.'

'Oh? And why not, pray?'

'Can take you to Rancaster Birradings, Nathan Rod, but not Number 18.'

'Why not?' I asked, a tremor in my voice this time.

'Number 18 on third floor; taxi does not fit into erevator.'

'Ha ha,' I said stiffly, 'but I notice that your meter is running; laugh on your own time, or while driving me capably to Lancaster Buildings, Nathan Road.'

'You a poreeseman?'

'Certainly not. I happen to be a toothpaste-salesman, if you must know.'

He wagged his head respectfully, as though I had said something impressive, or perhaps funny. He took me to Lancaster Buildings in an expert and blessedly silent fashion. On arrival I under-tipped him by precisely $2\frac{1}{2}$% – not enough to cause a scene but just enough to make it clear that taxi-drivers should not jest with sahibs.

Number 18 was indeed on the third floor of Lancaster Buildings and the door to Dr Lo's consulting-room was clearly inscribed RING AND ENTER. I rang, but could not enter, for the door was locked. Hearing sounds within I rapped irritably on the frosted glass, then louder and still louder, crying words such as 'Hoy!' All of a sudden, the door opened, a large, tan-coloured hand reached out, grabbed the front of my lightweight Paris suit and whisked me inside, depositing me upon an uncomfortable armchair. The owner of the tan-coloured hand was grasping a large, crude Stechkin automatic pistol in his other tan-coloured hand and waving it in an admonitory sort of way. I understood his desires instantly, for the Stechkin is by no means a lady's handbag-gun, and sat in my nice chair as quiet as any little mouse.

There was a patient in the dentist's operating-chair, being attended to by a brace of dentists. At first it seemed odd to me that the dentists were wearing dark-blue mackintoshes, just like the chap with the Stechkin, while the patient was wearing a white dentist's smock. (Sorry, a dentist's white smock.) I began to believe that the patient was, in fact, Dr Lo and that the dentists were quite unqualified in dentistry, especially when I noticed that they were using the drill on him although he refused to open his mouth. When Dr Lo – for it must have been he – passed out for the third or fourth time, his assailants were unable to bring him round. He had not uttered a word through his clenched teeth, although he had squealed through his nose a little, from time to time. I remember thinking that Mr Ho would have done much better, making much less mess.

The chaps in blue mackintoshes conversed in quacking tones together for a while, then turned on me.

'Who you?' asked one of them. I clapped my hand against my jaw in a piteous way and mimed the miseries of a tooth-ache sufferer. The man took my hand away from my jaw and slammed it with the side of his heavy pistol. Then he picked me up from the floor, sat me back in the chair.

'Tooth-ache better now?' I nodded vigorously. 'You recognize our faces again maybe?' There was no longer any need to mime suffering.

'Goodness, no; you chaps all look the same to . . . I mean, *no*, I have a terrible head for figures, that's to say faces or . . .'

He shifted the big pistol to his right hand and slammed me with it again. Now I really did need a dentist. He had not, in fact, rendered me unconscious but I decided to be so for all practical purposes. I let my head loll. He did not hit me again.

Through half-closed eyes I watched the three mackintoshed persons take off the clothes of the unconscious Dr Lo. He was a well-nourished dentist, as dentists go. One of the nasties took something out of his coat-pocket and threw the cardboard outer wrapping over his shoulder. It landed at my feet: the brand-name was 'Bull-Stik' – one of those terrifying new cyanoacrylic adhesives for which there is no known solvent. If you get it on your fingers, don't touch them, it will mean surgery. One of the three men spread it all over the seat of the dentist's chair and sat the naked Dr Lo down upon it, legs well apart. Then they played other pranks with the stuff which you will not wish to read about and which I would gladly forget. To tell the truth, I passed out in good earnest. Delayed shock, that sort of thing.

111

When I came to my senses I found my mouth full of little hard, pebbly scraps which I spat out onto my hand. Well, yes, assorted fillings, of course.

The three mackintosh-men had left so I tottered over to where Dr Lo was sitting. His eyes were more or less open.

'Police?' I asked. He made no sign. 'Look,' I said, 'you've got to have an ambulance and they'll call the police anyway; it will look odd if we don't call them straightaway.'

He nodded his head slowly and carefully, as though he had just come to realize that he was a very old man. He was, in fact, in his forties – or had been that morning. I, too, felt that I had aged.

'First,' I said (I couldn't talk very well because of the damage to my teeth; he couldn't talk at all for reasons which will occur to you), 'first, what have you got for me that I must take away?' His head rotated slowly and his gaze fastened on the wall beside the door. I went over to the wall. 'This?' I asked, pointing to a rather bad scroll painting. He shook his head. I pointed in turn to several framed diplomas designed to reassure the customer that Lo Fang Hi was licensed to yank teeth within reason. He went on shaking his head and staring mutely at the wall. There was nothing else on the wall except some fly-dirt and a vulgar toothpaste-advertisement featuring a foot-high Mr Toothpaste Tube with arms and legs, surrounded by a score or so of actual tubes of the said dentifrice. That is to say, it had once been surrounded by such tubes but these were now scattered on the floor, each one burst open and squeezed-out by the nasties. I prised Mr T. Tube himself off the wall. He was filled with a fine white powder.

I have no idea what heroin and cocaine are supposed to taste like, so I didn't do the fingertip-tasting thing that they do on television if you're still awake at that time of the night, but I had little doubt about its not being baby-powder.

I was never a star pupil at mental arithmetic but a quick and terrified calculation taught me that I had become the proud but shy possessor of something more than half a kilogramme of highly illegal white powder. Say, eighty thousand pounds in Amsterdam. More to the point, say fifty years in nick. I cannot say that I was much gratified; I am as fond of eighty thousand pounds as the next man – for I am not haughty like my brother – but I do prefer to

112

have it quietly dumped for me in the Union des Banques Suisses, rather than carrying it around in an improbable toothpaste-tube full of prison-sentences.

Dr Lo started to make alarming noises. I have always been a charitable man but this was the first time that I had ever blown a Chinese dentist's nose for him. He could not, of course, breathe through his mouth. Then I telephoned for an ambulance and policemen and scrammed, for I am a survivor.

Back at the hotel I telephone Johanna – did you know that you can *dial* London from China? – and told her, guardedly that all was not well with her toothsome friend and that her husband, too, had known better days. She told me to get some change, walk down the street to a telephone kiosk and ring again. This I did, for I am ever anxious to please. Soon we were in touch again, on a wonderfully clear line.

'It's really easy, Charlie dear,' she said when I had unrolled the tapestry of my dismay. 'Do you have a pencil or pen?'

'Of course I have,' I snapped 'but what the hell –'

'Then write this down. Secrete the uh dentifrice about your person. Take an early flight tomorrow from Hong Kong to Delhi. Then Delhi to Paris. Then take Air France Flight ZZ 690 to J.F. Kennedy Airport, New York. Can you spell that? OK. Now, in flight, go to the toilet – sorry, dear, I'll never get used to saying "lavatory" – and unscrew the inspection plate behind the pan. Hide the stuff in there. At Kennedy, walk through customs and book on Flight ZZ 887 to Chicago: this is the same aircraft but it's now a domestic flight – no customs, get it? In flight, retrieve the dentifrice. Call me from Chicago and I'll tell you what to do next. OK?'

'No,' I said.

'How do you mean, "no", dear?'

'I mean, sort of "no". It means, no, I won't do it. I have seen a film about San Quentin penitentiary and I hate every stone of it. I shall not do it. I shall flush that stuff down what you call the toilet as soon as I get back to the hotel. Please do not try to persuade me for my mind is made up.'

'Charlie.'

'Yes?'

'Remember when I coaxed you to have that vasectomy done just after we were married?'

'Yes.'

'In that cute little clinic?'

'Yes.'

They did not perform a vasectomy.'

'Good God!' I cried, appalled. 'Why, I might have had a baby!'

'I don't think so, dear. What they did do was implant in your, uh, groin a tiny explosive capsule with a quartz-decay time-system. It explodes in, let's see, ten days time. Only the guy who put it in can take it out without activating a kind of fail-safe mechanism, so please don't let anyone meddle with it: I kind of like you as you are, you know? Hey, Charlie, are you still there?'

'Yes,' I said heavily. 'Very well. Just give me those flight numbers again. And Johanna?'

'Yes dear?'

'Tell the chap who knows how to take the gadget out of me to be very, very careful crossing the road, eh?'

16 Mortdecai takes a little more drink than is good for him and is frightened by a competent frightener

Being of noble fostering, I glance
Lightly into old Laggan's ingle-nook . . .
Rabbits or snipe-fowl – even nicer things:
Has any longer title – God-remitted?

The Old Poacher

I stayed not upon the order of my going, nor even to lose my £1000 at the tables in far-famed Macao, but crammed everything – well, almost everything – into my suitcase and went down to the desk to pay my bill and book a ticket on the night-flight. The desk-clerk – how is it that they all contrive to look the same? – said that he had something in the safe for me. Had there been anywhere to run to I daresay I would have run. As it was, I made a nonchalant 'Oh, ah?' The desk-chap twiddled the safe and fished out a stout envelope; it was addressed in a scrawly hand to 'The Friend of the Poor' and the clerk had omitted to remove the clipped-on piece of paper which read 'For the overweight, Jewish-looking guy who wears his collar back to front and drinks too much.' I am not proud, I opened the envelope: it contained a note saying 'Dear Father, I played your dough at the craps table and made five straight passes and then faded a couple other shooters taking the odds and got lucky and I

115

taken 5% for my time and trouble and I hope the poor will offer up a prayer for yours truly . . .' The other contents of the envelope were a quite improbable wodge of currency notes of all nations. Hotels like the one I had been staying at have, of course, all-night banking facilities: I bought a cashier's cheque for my winnings (and most of my £1000 walking-about money) and sent it to the poor, as my conscience dictated. The only poor I could think of at the time was C. Mortdecai in Upper Brook Street, London, W1. I shall always remember that nice American as the only honest man I have ever met.

Painlessly gaining the price of another Rembrandt etching for the rainy-day scrap-book usually has a soothing effect on the nerve-endings but, long before my taxi-cab dumped me at the airport, I was quaking again. This was not necessarily a bad thing; had I been able to put a bold front on I would certainly have been apprehended as an obvious malefactor but, twitching with terror as I was, the customs chaps and security thugs wafted me through as a clear case of St Vitus' Dance or Parkinson's Disease – well-known occupational hazards among Curial Secretaries.

All went as merrily as a wedding-bell until the penultimate leg of the journey: Paris to New York, via Air France. A little too merrily, indeed, for by then I was a bit biffed – you know, a little the worse for my dinner, which had been several courses of Scotch whisky – and on my journey to the lavatory or toilet I sat, quite inadvertently, on the laps of several of my fellow-passengers. Their reactions varied from 'Ooh, aren't you *bold!*' via '*Ach, du lieber Augustin*' to '*Pas gentil, ça!*', while one impassive Chinese gentleman ignored me completely, pretending that his lap was quite free of any Mortdecai. Having at last locked myself in the loo or bog, I found that I had failed to arm myself with the necessary screwdriver with which to unscrewdrive the inspection-plate.

Back to my seat I teetered, watched narrowly now by the stewardess. When she came to enquire after my well-being I had decided upon a *ruse*: I would tell her that the zip of my trousers was jammed and that she must find me a screwdriver so that I could free the Mortdecai plumbing system. Alas, my usual fluent French deserted me – look, can *you* remember the French for 'screwdriver' when you're biffed? – and I had to resort to a certain amount of sign-language, pointing vigorously at my fly while vociferating the word 'screwdriver' again and again. Her English was little better than my French.

' "Screw" I onderstand,' she said demurely 'but what is zis "draivaire", hein?'

' "Draivaire",' I said wildly, ' "drivaire" is like, yes, *conducteur*!' and again I frantically pointed at that area of my trousers where my personal lightning-conductor is housed. She clapped her hands gleefully as understanding came to her.

'Ah! Now I onderstand! You weesh me to tell the *conducteur* – the pilot – that you weesh to do to him what Général de Gaulle has done to the whole French nation, not so?'

'Oh, sweet Christ and chips and tomato sauce,' I sighed, subsiding into my seat. This baffled the stewardess; she went away and brought another stewardess, a polyglot of dusky hue and tenor-baritone voice.

'I doth spake English a few better what she,' growled this new one, 'exprime what be this thou askings?' But she knew what a screwdriver was (it's *tournevis* in French, as any sober man can tell you). Five minutes later the perilous powder was safely screwed up behind the lavatory pan and I was pulling myself together on the lavatory floor.

'Pull yourself together,' I told myself sternly. 'You must excite no suspicion. You cannot afford to be lodged in some foreign nick with a quartz-decay timing-system nestling beside your *vas deferens*. A low profile is what you must keep.' So I strolled down the aisle to my seat, twirling the screwdriver and whistling a nonchalant bar or two from *Cosi Fan Tutte*, having craftily left my trouser-fly agape to encourage onlookers to understand the object of my mission. I don't suppose anyone gave me a second glance.

Everything continued to go wonderfully smoothly and soon, soon I was in wondrous Chicago and little the worse for my journey. (I suspect that the much-vaunted 'jet-lag syndrome' is nothing more than the common hangover of commerce. Certainly, I felt no worse than I would normally expect to feel at that time of day.)

The windiness of Chicago is grossly over-described: I was much windier myself. On the journey to my hotel I strained my eyes out of the taxi's windows, hoping to catch a glimpse of some mobsters cutting-down dirty, double-crossing rats with 'type-writers' or blasting their molls with 'pineapples' but none was to be seen. When I complained of this to the cabbie he chuckled fatly.

'Nixon we got,' he said over his shoulder, 'who needs Capone?' I pretended to understand. Well, I'd heard of Capone of course: he'll have a place in history, won't he?

My hotel was really just the same hotel that I've stayed in all over the world except that it was a bit taller than most. They'll never take the place of Claridge's or the Connaught; still less the duplex penthouse suite in the Bristol (that's in Paris, France) but at least you know where you are in these new ones. You know exactly the size and springiness of your bed, exactly what the room-service will be like if you can get them to answer the phone – and you know better than to put your shoes outside the door.

I visited the loo or toilet – who would not? – and found the porcelain pan protected by the usual strip of 'sanitized' paper. (This reassures Americans that they may sit safely, for Americans are terrified of germs, everyone knows that. Hotel-managers love it for its 'cost-effectiveness': whipping a piece of paper around the receiver and giving a blast of aerosol takes far less time than actually cleaning it. Only Arabs are not fooled: they stand on the seat.) Then I had a brisk shower (the shower was programmed to scald you or freeze you; you didn't stay under it long – 'cost-effectiveness' again, you see) and, having put on a fresh clothe or two, I had a brisk debate with myself. The upshot was that I telephoned Blucher before Johanna, for reasons which will occur to you. Blucher seemed full of merriment.

'How full of merriment you seem, to be sure,' I said sourly.

'Well, Mr Mortdecai, to tell the truth I just took a call from a Chinese gentleman – he doesn't exactly work for me but he sometimes throws me a bit of news just for laughs, you know? – and he tells me that you sat on his lap when you were about forty minutes out from Paris, France.'

'An unexpected air-pocket. I rebuked the *conducteur* – sorry, the pilot – for his clumsy driving.'

'An air-pocket at 30,000 feet? Yeah, of course. And the screw-driver bit – don't tell me you tried the old toilet-inspection-panel routine? You did? You really did?' Had I not known him for a humourless man I might almost have thought that he was stifling a laugh.

'Hey,' he went on, 'did you taste the stuff since you retrieved it? I mean, it may really *be* tooth-powder now, huh?'

'It may very well have been that in the first place, for all I know.'

'Hunh? Oh. Yes, that's good thinking. Well, I'd say you should just call your lady now and do exactly what she tells you. Some of our fellows will be sort of close at hand with fresh diapers for you but you won't see them. And don't call me again until you get back to the UK unless something comes up that you really can't handle. OK?'

'You mean, like death?'

'Oh, golly, *no*,' he said seriously. 'If you get dead do not on any account call us; we'd have to disown you, that's the ground-rules, right?'

'Right,' I said with equal seriousness. Then I said, 'I suppose you wouldn't care to tell me what this is all about?'

'Right,' he said. I hung up. Then I called Johanna.

'Darling!' she cried when I told her the news. 'Wonderful! Now, just you sit there by the telephone with a drink and I'll have someone come and see you.'

'Do you know what time it is here?' I squeaked, outraged.

'I know what time it is here, Charlie; what time do you have there in Chicago?'

'*Dinner*-time,' I snarled, for the Spartan boy's fox was indeed gnawing at my very vitals.

'Well, just sit there with *two* drinks, dear; the person who's coming to see you will give you a lovely dinner, I promise.'

'Oh, very well,' I said, as I have so often said before. Another revolt quelled, another outpost surrendered. Why do nations pay great salaries to Generals when women can do the job just as well without even using an army? I decided on a spot of toothbrushing – as well as the drink, of course, not instead of.

'Why, why, why Mortdecai?' I asked myself as I burnished the teeth still extant (my initials are, in fact, C.S.v.C. Mortdecai, but let it pass, let it pass), 'why are you suffering these slings and arrows?'

The answer was simple, for the question was merely rhetorical: suffer these slings and arrows or lose my end of the life-death trade-in I had agreed to with Blucher. I have no particular objection to death as such; it pays all bills and lays on others the chore of hiding the pornograms, the illegal firearms, the incriminating letters: all these things become of little importance when you have six feet of sod o'er you. On the other hand – I distinctly remember saying 'on the other hand' gravely to my toothbrush as I rinsed it – on the other hand, d'you see, death was not something I was actually craving just then. For one thing, I was not in a state of grace and, more to the point, I was burning with desire for revenge upon the perfidious Johanna who had played that horrid prank with the quartz-decay capsule implant. (On the 'plane I had thought of asking the stewardess to listen to my *vesiculae seminales* and tell me if she could hear anything ticking, but once again my command of French had failed me. In any case, it is possible that she might have thought it an odd request.)

'Heigh-ho!' I thought, then trotted briefly down to the hotel's drug-store where I made a purchase or two. I don't think they had ever before been asked for half a kilo of baby-powder. I also bought some stout envelopes and stamps. Lots of stamps. A brief trip back to my room, another to the post office and soon I was relaxing in an arm-chair, my jet-lag symptoms reacting well to the treatment I was pouring into them but my hunger unabated. Only such a man of iron as I could have resisted the temptation to ring for a sandwich or two but I placed my trust in Johanna: if she says there is a good dinner in the offing, then the offing is what the said dinner is in.

Not that I didn't feel a twinge of trepidation as I awaited my host. By the time the door-bell rang I had arranged the odds in my mind: seven to three said a Mafioso with padded shoulders who would *frisk* me before treating me to *spaghetti coi vongole* plus deep-fried baby *zucchini* with the flowers still attached and lots of fried *piperoni* on the side, while ten would get you seven that it would be a slinky she-sadist who would frisk me only with contemptuous eyes before making me take her to Sardi's or somewhere like that and buy her pheasant under glass – the most boring grocery in the world.

I was wrong, not for the first time. Who oozed into my suite when I answered the bell was none other than the portly Chinese gentleman upon whose lap I had roosted for a while in the Boeing 747.

'Harrow,' he said civilly. I glanced at his tie.

'Surely you mean Clifton? Oh, yes, sorry, I see; harro to you, too. Have a drink?'

'Thankyou, no. I bereave you are hungry? Come.'

I came. Went, rather.

You will hardly be surprised to learn that it was a Chinese meal with which I was regaled, but in a Chinese restaurant of no common sort, nor of the nastiness I would have expected from my first impressions of Chicago – a city which seemed intent upon finding how low a lowest common denominator can be. (I hasten to say that some of my best friends may well be Chicagoans – without actually advertising the fact – but have you ever snuffed the scent of the Chicago River as it slides greasily under the nine bridges in the centre of the Windy City? Alligators have been known to flee, holding perfumed handkerchiefs to their noses. As for the carrion gusts from Lake Michigan itself, 'Faugh!' is too mild a word by half.)

This restaurant, as I was saying before I caught ecology, was not one of those where oafs stir three or four dishes together and eat the resultant mess with chips and soy sauce, while the waiters watch inscrutably, thinking their own thoughts. No, it was one of those rare ones which has no menu – people just bring you a succession of tiny dishes of nameless things to be eaten one at a time and without soy sauce. I tried not to disappoint these dedicated waiters and gifted cooks; tried, too, to earn a reputation for being the fastest chopstick in the Northern Mid-West.

My host's name proved to be either Ree or Lee: my uncertainty about this is perfectly genuine. At Oxford we had a Korean professor who trilled his name unmistakably as 'Ree' but insisted on writing 'Lee'. He saw no anomaly in this.

As we dabbled in the finger-bowls, my courteous host murmured courteously that he bereaved I had a package for him. I dabbled thoughtfully.

'That may well be,' I said guardedly, 'or, perhaps, not. What?'

He gazed at me civilly. I replied with equal civility.

'You see, I have no instructions about lashing out samples of toothpowder or dentifrice to one and all, however delectable the dinner they give.'

'Mr Mortdecai,' he said heavily, or as heavily as chaps like that can, 'you are surely experienced enough to know that in this particurar rine of business it is not considered porite, or even safe, to pray, ah, sirry buggers. We have, you understand, certain resources, ah?'

'Oh, goodness, yes,' I hastened to say, 'goodness yes. Indeed, I've had the pleasure and privilege of meeting your Mr Ho. Ah? That's really why I've sort of taken out insurance. I mean, I've a simple-minded sort of mind, you understand, no trace of a death-wish or any of that rubbish: self-preservation is so much more fun than self-destructiveness, don't you agree? Eh? Or rather, "Ah", eh?'

'What sort of precautions have you taken, Mr Mortdecai?'

'Oh, well, I've sort of entrusted the toothpowder to the US Mails: an incorruptible lot, I'm told. Neither frost nor sleet nor trade unions prevents these messengers from etc. And it's gone to a safe address. Old-fashioned, I know, but the best I could think of at the time. I'm sure you understand.'

'Mr Mortdecai,' he murmured suavely, pouring me another cup of delicious tea, 'if you have met my subordinate, Mr Ho, you must surely rearize that this safe address can be ericited from you in ress time than it takes to say what I am saying.'

'Oh, my word, yes; I quite understand that, but the address is no secret at all, you may have it for the asking. It's the Commercial Attaché at the British Embassy in Washington – he doubles in security co-ordination or whatever they call it now, as I'm sure you know. Old school-friend of mine; knows my face, you see. I sort of worked for him in the 1940s if you know what I mean. He's quite potty about security, wouldn't dream of handing the package to anyone but me. And I mean, me *unaccompanied*, of course. And if I didn't say the right sort of words he'd give me a cosy bedroom in the Embassy for as long as I needed it. You see?'

He thought a while but without ostentation.

'I see,' he said. (An English chap would have said 'Yes, I see, I *see*,' but your actual Oriental is economical with words.)

'How much do you want?' he asked.

'Money?' I asked disdainfully. 'Nothing at all. Still less, God forbid, any part of that costly tooth-powder, for I fancy I know what happens to people who own such things when other people wish to own them. No, all I wish is a little information. I have become tired and vexed, you see, at being used as a cat's-paw in matters about which I know nothing. This prodding from random directions insults my intelligence. I am prepared to fight under almost any flag if the money is good, but I do need to have a squint at the flag first. I am too overweight to play, ah, silly buggers.'

I could tell by the way he mused over this that he was a clever man. How much cleverer than me he was, of course, remained an open question.

'That is quite understandable, Mr Mortdecai,' he said at last, 'and it seems to me that your case-officer has been running you without a proper regard for your interrigence and, ah, other quarities. I agree that you should be given a view of the frag under which you are fighting – but you rearise that I must first get a little crearance. Ah?'

'Ah,' I agreed. He invited me to his office. We entered. That sounds easy, but entering the office of a clandestine Chinese gentleman seems to involve being goggled at through peepholes, scanned by metal-detectors and listening to the office-owner mur-mur into voice-sensitive locks – all that stuff which so destroys the quality of life nowadays. Death, too, now I come to think of it. He gave me a glass of the actual John Smith's Glenlivet to sip while he dialled a number so prodigal in digits that it had to be somewhere far, far away. His polite stare at me while he waited for his connection bore no trace of hostility but it had the effect of making me feel far, far away from home and loved ones; one would have thought that he was costing me out in terms of coffin-wood – or perhaps concrete and baling-wire. I let my tummy sag out fully, hoping to make myself look less cost-effective. The telephone crackled at last.

'Harro!' he said. '. . . may make more noise,' I murmured, for I can never resist finishing a quotation. His stare at me sharpened and he switched into a language which sounded like a malicious send-up of a Welsh newsreader but was, I suppose, one of the many brands of Chinese. He clacked and grunted and fluted awhile then listened intently while similar noises from his interlocutor made the instrument positively vibrate in his hand. This went on for a time then, in beautifully-modulated but outdated French, he said, *'D'accord. Au'voir, re copain.'* Showing off, I suppose. Having replaced the receiver he said to me, 'Would you rike to wash your hands, Mr Mortdecai?' I inspected said members: they were indeed sweating profusely. How had he *known*?

Returning from his richly but curiously appointed lavatory, I moved into the attack.

'Well, Mr Ree?' were the stormtrooper words which spear-headed my attack.

'Thankyou, yes,' he replied. My attack was wiped out. I felt just like an infantry subaltern who has thrown away a platoon against a machine-gun emplacement he forgot to mark on his map. (Listening to the Colonel's remarks afterwards is not nearly so unpleasant as sitting down to write twenty letters to next-of-kin while the people in the Orderly Room pretend you're not there. The worst bit is when your batman brings you your dinner to the foxhole or bivvy-tent, saying 'Thought you might be too tired to dine in Mess tonight. Sir.' But I reminisce.)

Having delivered the devastating 'thankyou, yes,' Mr Lee or Ree fell silent, studying me again. I did not break this silence; I felt that it was his move.

'Mr Mortdecai,' he said after a demoralizing interval, 'are you a discreet man? No, prease do not repry, that was not a question but a warning. A rittre more Grenrivet? Good. I keep it for speciah occasions.' Those words 'speciah occasions' hung delicately in the air between us.

'Now,' he went on, 'my friend has agreed that I should tell you enough to exprain a rittle of our work – just enough to encourage you not to pray any more games with goods worth a great sum of money. The conditions are that you do not mention this conversation to your derightful rady wife; that you do not speak of it to any American Coroners you may happen to know (yes, we know about that but we bereave your rady wife does not) and, of course, you make no expranations to your Embassy friend in Washington, who is, forgive me, prease, a fool. In any case, his office is bugged.'

'Tut!' I said, frowningly. He raised a hand.

'We did not bug it' he said reprovingly. 'The Americans did. They are even sirrier than the Engrish. We bug their bugs after they have instorred them. Much cheaper.

'Now, prease pay attention more crosery. If you were to tell any of these people what I shall now tell you, three very powerful organizations would be offended with you. *Offended*.'

I sighed. How life repeats itself, to be sure. *

'Do go on,' I murmured nonchalantly. My hands were sticky with sweat again.

'First, your rady wife is very fond of you but in such circumstances she would have to rate you "insecure" and pass you over to her people for disposah. Fiona, the dog-girl at the Correge, would bury you. Probabry your wife has enough infruence to ensure that you would be dead before buriah; I do not know.'

I did not shudder, I never let foreigners see me shudder, but he must have seen that the beads of sweat were popping out of my forehead like ping-pong balls.

'Next, once you had given this information to a certain American Coroner, you would now be expendabah and he could prease many of his superiors – who have never approved of his keeping you arive – by "terminating you with extreme prejudice" as he would say. Naturarry, you would be interrogated first and this would hurt.'

'Quite,' I quavered. I don't mind telling you that I detest being hurt.

'Last, you would now be an enemy, in the third crass, of my own organization.'

'Only *third* class?' I asked in the indignant tones which Queen Victoria surely used when she received the Abyssinian Order of Chastity, Second Class; 'What is that supposed to mean?'

'It means we would not kill you.'

'Oh, good.'

A muscle in his face twitched, almost as though he were a British cavalry officer who is trying to puzzle out whether someone has made a joke and, if so, whether or not it would be good form to smile.

'No,' he went on, having clearly dismissed any intention of smiling, 'We would not kill you. We do not kill enemies of the third crass. But after a rittle time you would be asking us most poritery for death. We would not feel able to obrige. After another two or three days – this would depend on your stamina and vitarity – let us say two days – we would rerease you conveniently crose to a rairway-bridge. With a white walking-stick – you would of course by then have lost your sight – which would be taped to

*See *Don't Point That Thing at Me*, last chapters.

what would remain of your hand, and a tendorrar note between your teeth. Sorry, yes, gums – you would no ronger have any teeth, naturarry.'

'Naturarry,' I said bravely.

'The ten dorrars would be for you to give to some indigent passer-by who would help you to a convenient part of the rairway-bridge: you would be anxious for such help by then, you understand.'

I pulled myself together, remembering that I was, after all, partly British. We British do not cringe in the presence of the heathen, nor are we daunted by foreign threats. (Well, all right, Suez was a special case, wasn't it?)

'Mr Ree,' I said, as crisply as the words allowed, 'pray tell me something. Is it true that Chinese, ah, persons, consider themselves to be constipated if they do not achieve at least two motions of the bowels each weekday? I have read this somewhere and I long to know whether it be true.' He considered this for quite half a minute, looking as nonplussed as his inscrutability would permit.

'Yes,' he said after the stated half-minute, 'yes, this is true. But I cannot see why you should ask such a thing. Are there not matters of almost equal importance . . .?'

'I ask,' I said, maintaining the British crispness, 'because I fear for your health. It seems to me that a good deal of surplus, ah, effluent has been escaping from your mouth during the past few minutes. Your digestive tract seems to have lost all sense of direction. In short, if you will forgive me, I begin to find your talk tedious.'

'Ah,' he said.

'On the other hand,' I continued, 'your points are well taken; indeed I have been in accord with you for some ten minutes. If you will now tell me, in your own words, as much of the truth as your masters have empowered you to tell, then you may depend upon it that I shall impart it to no one. First, I am a man of my word. Second, I am not brave.'

'Ah,' he said again. 'But, Mr Mortdecai, our dossier on you must be at fault, for it states that you can lie like a prostitute and are capable of quite absurd bravery on occasion. But it also says that you are sensible, a virtue often mistaken for cowardice.'

I looked at my watch and stifled a well-bred yawn.

'Mr Ree,' I said, 'you have frightened me, as you intended. This was unnecessary for I was already frightened. Your dossier is right in one respect: I am sensible. Tell me some of the truth. We both know that you can and will kill me later if you decide to do so – and unless I contrive to kill you first, which has no part in my plans at present. Meanwhile, perhaps I might have just a touch more of that delicious malt whisky? And enough plausible facts to persuade me to part with the toothpowder, eh?'

How brave I was, to be sure. Mr Ree passed me a Kleenex. I mopped the sweat off my forehead. He began to utter.

'Your wife is Johanna Mortdecai,' he told me. Well, I knew that, of course, but I wasn't about to walk into any straight-line situations; I didn't even nod.

'She is the chief financier – forgive me, financière? – of the Women's Domination Society; arso, Deputy Head of it.'

'You mean Women's *Liberation*, don't you?' I said in the embarrassed tones one uses to foreigners who get words wrong.

'No, Mr Mortdecai. Women's Riberation is a piece of sirriness which was froated to, ah, test the temperature of the water and to mask the rear movement. It was instructive to see how many sirry women were prepared to, shall we say, cut off their bras to spite their breasts.' He had made a joke. I smiled, not showing the teeth. 'Quite agree,' I said. 'I mean, if God hadn't meant us to wear trusses, he wouldn't have given us ruptures, would he?' He didn't smile.

'The Women's Domination Society is very serious. It is probabry the richest private organization in the world; even richer than the Parestinian Popurar Front – with whom they happen to be friends.' I was about to say something valiant about how little I cared for the riches and murderous capacity of the PFLP when I recalled that, some forty years ago, I had promised an aged aunt never to tell a lie. (This was in exchange for a tin of Mackintosh's Quality Street Toffee Selection. Those toffees are long gone – nor would I find them toothsome in this my middle age – but a Mortdecai's promise, even to an aunt, is not to be paltered with.) So I held my tongue.

'They intend,' continued Mr Lee, 'to assume controh of the world.' I gave him that look – often practised before the mirror – which I give to players at stud poker who back into the betting on the fourth card. He was unimpressed.

'How can they *not* win?' he asked. 'First, the terrifying American middre-aged woman controhs quite three-fifths of the wealth of the richest country in the world. Second, the women "behind the curtain" – in the harems of the Musrim world – controh wealth which even Zurich could not count. Third, the female interrectuals of Israel and India have their poriticah worlds by the, ah, borrocks. Fourth, women have the insensate drive of the castration comprex; the same knowledge of inferiority which makes rittre men into tyrants. Arexander the Great was incapable with women; Attira the Hun died trying to achieve an erection; Naporeon had an absurdry small penis (36mm – it was sold at Sotheby's a few years ago) and Adorf Hitrer, as all the world knows, had onry one testicre.'

I shifted uneasily in my chair; he was talking the kind of lunacy which often makes better sense than sense does. Also, I was frantically trying to convert mirrimetres into inches – feet? – in my head.

'Fifth,' he said, spreading his beautifully-tapered fingers on the desk, 'who is to oppose them? Is there one state – other than China – which is not rotten from top to bottom? Can you name one poritician in office who is a strong man – a statesman?'

This was not a rhetorical question; he paused to give me time to answer. I took that time.

'No,' is what I finally said. He nodded a few mirrimetres.

'Sixth and last, they have friends, as I have said. Most of all, they have us.'

'Who are "us"?'

'Issyvoo.'

I boggled as I had never boggled in my life before. 'Issyvoo,' surely, was what the Berliners used to call Christopher Isherwood, the man who will go down to fame as the chap who made the joke about 'the last of the small Spenders'. I allowed myself to raise an eyebrow. He spelled it out for me.

'ICWU. The International Chinese Waiters Union. No, prease do not raugh. Our union – we do not call it that but you would not be interested in its reah name – is the only trury internationah organization in the world. Arso, it is the only Union with no absurd poritical affiriations. Arso, it is the onry Union where the emproyers are equah members with the emproyees. They have to be. Most important of all, it is the only union which has no trouble with brackregs. Such people are given one hour in which to understand that the union is their mother and father. The crever ones understand this in much ress than one hour. The stupid ones; we send a present of money to their families – and a souvenir.'

'Like, say, an ear?' I ventured.

'Something of that sort, yes. But annoyances of that kind do not often happen nowadays. We Chinese, as the world knows, are inveterate gambrers; when you go to your favourite Chinese restaurant and find that it has changed hands it arways means that the owner has lost it at the gaining table.'

'I knew that,' I said.

'The new owner is onry a manager, you understand. He now owes the union a great deah of money, as do all the waiters, according to their station in rife. You understand that all this calls for heavy financing, far more than the union dues can suppry. Your charming rady wife supprices this through her organization. Partry by supporting our cash-flow, partry through making avairable her capable young radies as couriers so that we can, ah, adjust the supply of *medicines* internationarry. I think that is all you need to know, ah?'

'Beauty is truth, truth beauty – that is all . . . ye need to know,,' I said, dipping deep into the Grecian Urn.

'Sorry?'

'Keats.'

'Kits?'

'Yes – it means little pussies.'

'Ah. I can arrange . . .'

'Please do not go to any such trouble; I was simply accepting that I had been given what information you were permitted to give me.'

'I have been frank with you, Mr Mortdecai. You bereave that, I hope.'

'Of course. Santa Claus lives. You shall have your icing sugar. Meet me in Washington tomorrow?'

17 Charlie passes on some perilous groceries and receives a zonk with less than his habitual meekness

Man with the head and woman with the heart:
Man to command and woman to obey;
All else confusion.

The Princess

'What-ho, Charlie!' cried Humphrey as I was ushered in to his tastefully-decorated sanctum or office in the Embassy next day.

'What-ho, what-ho, Humpers!' I retorted courteously. We swapped a few more civilities, freely using the useful phrase 'what-ho'. It saves one thinking, you see, and saves one the chore of trying to remember whether the other chap is married, divorced, queer or whatever. Best of all, it saves one from the peril of asking after the chap's parents. Humphrey, you see, is the scion of a pretty antique Irish family, which means that at least one of his nearest and dearest is chained up in a cellar, living on dry bread and biting the heads off rats for pastime.

Moreover, this what-hoing gave Humphrey the opportunity to draw from his pocket a calling-card upon which, neatly typed, were the words THIS PLACE IS BUGGED. I nodded vigorously in what he probably thought was comprehension but which I intended as agreement; guilty knowledge if you like.

'Too early for a drink, I suppose?' he asked, glancing at his watch.

'On the contrary, damn' nearly too late,' I said, glancing needlessly at mine. 'Wheel on the life-giving fluids without delay.' He went to a cupboard, unlocked it and drew out the two fat envelopes I had sent him, raising his eyebrows and saying, 'Scotch or Bourbon?'

'Both,' I quipped merrily.

'Greedy sod,' he laughed, handing me both packages, followed by a huge brandy and soda which was, in fact, what he knew I would be needing at that time of day. (These chaps don't get into Intelligence merely on charm; never mind what the after-shave manufacturers say.)

We Woostered away for a while, giggling silently at the thought of grim-jawed FBI men and beetle-browed CIA men frantically sending out 'Code Orange-Five Trace Orders' on such ornaments of the Drones Club as Oofy Prosser and Barmy Fotheringay-Phipps. (Indeed, one hopes that they took 'Drones Club' to be the code name for 'The Firm's' new London 'safe-house' – and, who knows, it may well be for all I know.)

While we idly bandied these Woosterisms – and he and I are confirmed bandiers of such things – he slid a scribbling-pad across the desk and I scribbled on it enough news to pay him richly for his kindness. To be exact, I wrote down everything I knew that I knew Colonel Blucher knew, if I make myself clear, together with a couple of other snippets which would put him ahead of the game and give him something to trade with Blucher. I selected with care a few bits to omit: he wouldn't have believed them and, in any case, they concerned my personal safety. ('Idle, intelligent, devious; a survivor,' read the summary of my character on my last school report and I have not changed; I am no butterfly.)

After another invigorating suck at the brandy-tit we parted with many a friendly message to Freddie Widgeon and Honoria Glossop. As he courteously ushered me to the door he paused beside what he no doubt knew to be a well-bugged standard lamp and whispered hoarsely, 'Charlie, *don't believe a word old Mulliner says.*' I gasped but mumbled assent, grinning inaudibly.

Mr Ree was waiting at the rendezvous as advertised, staring politely into space like a man doing long-division sums in his head.

Or working out a fool-proof way of murdering his wife. He offered me a drink but his heart was evidently not in the offer and I, too, was more anxious to do business than to quaff. Frankly, I would rather carry an Irish-made time-bomb around the streets than a package of heroin. If that's what it was.

We walked around the block to a spot chosen by Mr Ree where he was sure that we could not be overseen by stupid, bumbling, British Intelligence blokes. (It will be a sad day for the world when the Oriental gent realizes that Western bumbling is only Eastern guile in a different idiom. Well, a lot of it, anyway.) We sidled into an entry. He opened a capacious briefcase. I slipped a fat envelope into it. He gave me a fraction of a bow and a long, steady look before popping into a large, vulgar, black limousine which had been idling beside a fire-plug under the indulgent eye of a well-paid policeman. I did not much relish the long, steady look from Mr Ree; it was the sort of look which seems to say, 'Mortdecai, this stuff had better be what it's supposed to be: we have ways of making you scream.' I waved a nonchalant hand, confident that the churning acid in my stomach could not be seen by the naked eye. Then I studied the scrap of paper he had pressed into my hand. It was not, as I hoped, a munificent piece of walking-about money: it was better, much better. It read 'MESSAGE FROM WIFE BEGINS QUARTZ-DECAY IMPLANT JUST A JOKE COMMA FEAR NOT COMMA PLEASE DONT BE CROSS LOVE HANNA STOP ENDS.'

'Stop ends indeed,' I snarled.

Before the limousine was out of eyeshot another, even more vulgar black limousine swept up to the kerb – just like they do in the story-books. I gave it no more than a brief and haughty glance whilst I made taxi-attracting gestures to passing taxis. The taxi-drivers did not seem to understand my British gestures. Just as my fears were changing into honest British annoyance, I became aware that respectable-looking chaps were issuing from the limousine – the second, longer, more vulgar limousine, you understand. I recked not of them but continued to beckon imperiously at passing taxi-cabs. It was at that point that I was zonked on the back of the head.

Now you who – forgive me – have nothing better to do than read such tales of daring and true love as this which I now relate, must have read many a description of what it feels like to be zonked on the occiput. Stars burst wondrously, blue-birds twitter, fireworks effulge, bells chime and so forth. None of this is true; none has been written by chaps who have actually experienced such a zonk.

Speaking as one who has in his time received not one or two but several such cowardly buffets, I am in a position to record the resultant phenomena in scientific form, such as any serious medical journal would gladly accept for publication.

(A) The subject feels a distinct zonking sensation at the rear of he bonce or cranium. A momentary agony is experienced.

(B) This causes the novice to say '*Aaargh!*' or words to that effect, according to his ethnic group. The seasoned chap, who is no stranger to zonks, subsides quietly, lest he receive just such another.

(C) The subject then sinks into an untroubled sleep, more dreamless than he has known since puberty.

(D) He awakes, reluctantly, to find himself infested with a shattering headache and a great thirst. Moreover, he is surrounded by large, ugly men who view his awakening coldly, for they are engrossed in a game called three-handed pinochle. He goes back to sleep. It is now but a fitful sleep.

(E) He is awakened again, this time by one of the coarse, ugly men and in a fashion so coarse that I cannot describe it in a narrative intended for family reading.

(F) Full, now, of indignation, piss-and-vinegar, etc, he launches a death-dealing karate-chop at his tormentor, not realizing how enervating have been the effects of the professional zonk. The d.-dealing k.-chop misses by several feeble inches. The ugly chap does not even smile: he *smacks* the patient across the chops with a spade-like hand, back and forth and to and fro. In Brooklyn I understand this is rendered as 'whackity-whap, biff, zap'.

(G) Weeping bitterly with shame and rage, the subject collapses onto the carpet. The ugly chap raises him compassionately to his feet by grabbing a handful of hair.

All these things happened to me in the order named and I have a couple of neuroses to prove it. I was taken to a lavatory or toilet – no wait, it's called a bathroom in the USA – and was allowed to be sick, wash my face and, as my grandmother would say, 'straighten my veil'. (In my will I have bequeathed my collection of euphemisms to the National Trust.)

I felt a little better but my indignation was lessened by no whit. I am assured that there is many a chap who accepts a slosh on the brain-pan with equanimity. Some, I daresay, positively welcome such wallops as aids to meditation; others reproach themselves for not having loved their fellow-men enough. I was never such a one. Being coshed or sapped never fails to fill me with a quite irrational annoyance. We overweight cowards in early middle age have few inexpensive recreations left to us: indignant rage – so long as one's blood-pressure is no worse than 120/80 – is both cheap and satisfying.

It was, then, a furious and unforgiving Mortdecai whose face was wiped and whose trousers were adjusted by large, ugly men and who was half-carried into a darkened room and dumped into a wonderfully comfortable chair. He – I – raged vaguely and luxuriously for a minute or two until sleep slunk up like a black panther and sank its kindly fangs into what remained of the Mortdecai brain. Curiously delicious dreams involving over-ripe schoolgirls ensued – quite unsuitable for these chaste pages. (It has often been remarked that men about to face death on the field of battle or, indeed, the very gallows itself, frantically seek solace in the sexual act. The same is true of the common hangover: a raw egg beaten up in Worcester Sauce or Tabasco is a useful placebo for the hung-over novice; a pint of flat and tepid ale is a kill-or-cure specific/emetic for those with leathern stomachs, while a brace of large brandies marks out your seasoned boozer who knows that he needs an empiric to get him back into the human race as quickly as may be. You may depend upon it, however, that the only sovereign cure for us men of iron is a brisk five minutes of what Jock coarsely calls 'rumpy-pumpy'. It is positively warranted to scour the cobwebs from the most infested skull; no home should be without it. Try some tomorrow. I shan't pretend that you can buy it at all reputable chemists but you will find a registry office in most large towns. I digress, I know, but usefully: these words of mine alone are worth the price of admission.)

The curiously delicious dreams of which I speak were snapped off short by a flood of blinding light and a gentle shake or two at my shoulder. I opened reluctant eyes, sat up, turned my gaze first upon the shoulder-shaker, who proved to be the smallest and fattest of the ugly persecutors. He looked unhappy. I eyed him dangerously, then stared to my front across about an acre of black-glass desk towards a set of apologetic features flickering in the mid-distance.

When my eyes could focus I recognized the apologetic features as those of Col. Blucher.

'Hey, Mr Mortdecai, are you OK?' he asked with what seemed to be anxiety.

'Grrr,' I growled, for neither 'yes' nor 'no' seemed to fill the bill.

'Look, Mr Mortdecai, I'm really very very sorry you were kind of uh roughed up a little . . .'

'*Grrr*,' I reiterated, putting a little more venom into the word this time.

'. . . but you see I had to get you off the street fast and I had to make it look like it wasn't *friends* picking you up and I didn't have any skilled help this side of town and I guess these fellers uh kind of got their orders at second-hand and they're well kind of hostility-situation-orientated . . .'

'Again?'

'. . . hostility-situation-orientated and, well, when guys like these snatch a guy they snatch him real good, hunh?'

'Are you trying to say, Colonel, that these men exceeded their orders?'

'Well, I'd say so.'

'And you will, of course, be rebuking them?'

'Why yes, I guess I shall. Hey, Elmer' – this was to the ugly chap beside my chair – 'Elmer, why don't you go get yourself some chow?' As Elmer turned towards the door I rose to my feet and, in the nasty, rasping voice I developed years ago when I was an adjutant in the Guards, I rasped the word '*Elmer?*'

He span around in a clockwise direction, thus meeting my left hook to the liver and, indeed, aiding it. How it sank in, to be sure. We have all heard of those miraculous punches which 'travelled no more than four inches', have we not? Well, this one must have travelled quite twenty inches and had some 180 pounds of Mortdecai muscle, fat and spite behind it. The ugly chap went '*Urrrgghhh*', or something which sounded uncommonly like it, and folded up like an ill-made Venetian blind. (Jock, you see, had long ago told me that 'when you give a geezer a bunch of fives in the gut, don't think about the gut, nor the abominal wall; just make out that you're hitting his bleeding back-bone – from the front; see?' Jock *knows* about these things, you understand.)

Blucher pressed a buzzer, I suppose, for the other two ugly men entered and, at a gesture from Blucher's pinkie, hauled out their stricken comrade before he could damage the carpet beyond repair.

I sank back into my chair, feeling a trifle more in tune with the infinite. Blucher registered neither approval nor mild reproof although I fancy a corner of his mouth twitched in what might have been amusement in another man.

'Well, now, where were we?' I asked comfortably.

18   Mortdecai does not get the right vibrations

That a lie which all a lie may be met and fought with outright.
But a lie which is part a truth is a harder matter to fight.

The Grandmother

Blucher made a courteous gesture, indicating that he was all ears
and was prepared to lend me them unreservedly. I glanced around
the office; it was clearly not his own but on loan from some Midas-
like business-man, for the walls were bespattered with exceedingly
costly graphics by Münch, Braque, Picasso, Léger and all those
chaps – beyond the dreams of avarice if that's the kind of thing one
likes; certainly beyond the reach of Blucher's salary and outside his
Agency's Scale of Office Furnishings. Nevertheless, in Washington
most places are bugged, everyone knows that, don't they? I skated
the other heavy package of powder across the frozen black lake of
the desk; it landed on his lap with a satisfying thump followed by
a manly grunt of discomfort from Col. Blucher.

'I am prepared to tell all,' I murmured to him, 'but not between
these walls. I am a survivor, you see, and I have a certificate from
my old headmaster to prove it. Let us go for a stroll: a little fresh
air will be jolly good for us both.'

He looked at me incuriously, which meant, of course, that he was
thinking furiously; I could almost hear his synapses crackling and
popping like breakfast cereal. 'Would the lies he could have his lads

137

beat out of me be more valuable than the half-truths I was prepared to volunteer?' was evidently the question which he had fed into his crew-cut nut. He came to the right decision: after all, coming to decisions is what such chaps are paid for – like 'one who gathers samphire, dreadful trade'.

'Hey, that's a great idea, Charlie!' he said. 'Let's go.'

In the outer office the two larger ugly chaps were still playing pinochle, but two-handed now because from the open door of the lavatory or bathroom came a rhythmical '*Urrgh, urrgh*' from Elmer. I paused by their table and cleared my throat. Neither of them looked up. 'Tell Elmer,' I said in the voice of an overpaid physician, 'that he should take more exercise and drink less. The only hard thing about him is his liver.' One ugly chap kept his eyes on his cards (and who shall blame him, because a quick kibitz had shown me that he only needed the last queen to perfect what pinochle-players call a 'round-house') but the other slowly raised his eyes to mine and gave me his best and coldest Edward G. Robinson stare – the one that is supposed to make you think of *gats*, concrete overcoats and paving-slabs dropped into the Potomac River with your ankles wired to them. I have seen such looks done better.

'Well, so long, youse guys,' I said, courteously using their dialect. Neither of the pinochle-players responded but Elmer said '*Urrrghh*' from the lavatory or bathroom.

The way to take a stroll for fresh air in Washington, DC, is to hail an air-conditioned taxi-cab. This I did. I entered the first which offered itself, drawing a vexed look from Blucher. Well, obviously, he must have thought me too half-smart to take the first cab; it would have been the second which would have been in his pay, which is why I took the first, you see. Goodness, how clever I was in those days – barely a year ago!

The driver squinted at us from his little air-conditioned womb of armoured glass and steel-mesh (being zonked is an occupational hazard which even cab-drivers dislike) and asked us courteously how he could earn the pleasure of being of service to us. Well, what he actually said was 'Yeah?' but one could tell that it was a civil 'yeah'.

'Just drive around the sights, OK?' said Blucher. 'You know, Grant's tomb, places like that?'

'And the National Gallery, please,' I chirped up, 'in fact, the National Gallery first. Oh, and could you stop at a shop where I could buy a torch?'

'He means, like a flashlight, from a drug-store,' explained Blucher. The driver did not even shrug his shoulders; he had been driving idiots around all day, we would not even figure in the bleary reminiscences with which he would regale his wife that night as she bathed his bunions.

'Do you care to start telling now?' Blucher asked me. I shot him a glance fraught with caution and cowardice, flicking an eye at the driver. 'Well, hell, why the National Gallery, hunh?' I began to feel a little in command of the situation: I can cower with the best but, given a fraction of an edge, I am happier in the dominant rôle.

'First,' I said, 'I wish to go there. Second, I earnestly wish to rinse my eyes out with some good art after seeing those frightful graphics in your office. Third, the NG, that stately pleasure-dome, is probably the only unbugged place in this fair city. Fourth, I have a long-standing appointment with a chap called Giorgio del Castelfranco, who has a picture in the Gallery which I both covet and suspect. OK?'

'Sure,' he said with policeman-like innocence, 'you mean the guy who was Bellini's pupil in Venice – around about when Columbus was discovering America? Hunh? The guy we jerks call Giorgione?'

'That would be he,' I said bitterly. 'And you can cut out the dialect.'

'Gosh, I really enjoyed your piece about him in the *Giornale delle Belle Arte* last year; you really made that Berenson guy look a right Charlie – gosh, sorry, Charlie . . .'

'That's all right,' I said. 'I have been called worse.' But I sulked all the way to the National Gallery and insisted on paying off the cabbie myself. He examined my tip carefully, interestedly, then handed it back with a charitable sort of look.

Inside the Gallery, I stalked unswervingly past all the lovely art that Lord Duveen had sold to Kress and Widener and fellows like that in the palmy, piping days when Lord Mortdecai (yes, my papa) was peddling piddling pastiches to minor European royalty whose cheques were as good as their word. I halted in an important way in front of the Giorgione and played my torch or flashlight upon it. In a trice a wardress had pounced on me and wrested it out of my hand, making noises like a she-vulture laying its first egg. I handed her my wallet, open at the place which displays my art-historian credentials, and bade her show it to a curator. She was back in another trice or two, spraying apologies and calling me 'Dr Mortdecai' and telling me that I might shine my flashlight at anything. Anything I liked.

'Thank you,' I said, ignoring the explicitness. I shone the torch on this part and that of the painting, making art-historical noises such as 'ah' and 'hum' and 'oh dear', while Blucher fretted, shifting from foot to foot.

'Look, Mr Mortdecai,' he said at last, 'would you care to tell me what it is you're looking for? I mean, we do have to . . .' I shot him a patronizing glance over my shoulder.

'I am looking,' I said pompously, 'for the brushwork of the young Titian in or about the year 1510. I do not see it. It occurs to me that I just may have been wrong about this picture.'

'But gosh,' he said, 'it says right here on the tablet that this art-work is by Giorgione . . .'

'And it may now continue to say so for the time being,' I said with more than usual pomposity, tossing the torch or flashlight petulantly into the nearest litter-bin. (In the US of A they call waste-paper baskets 'newspaper-baskets', which shows a fine sense of values. I like American realists. American *idealists*, of course, are like all idealists: they are people who kill people.)

'But here,' I said, 'is what we have been waiting for.' Blucher stared. A titter of thirteen-year-old schoolgirls was swarming into the shrine of art, frantically shepherded by one of those women who are born to be schoolmarms – you know the species well, I'm sure; some of them have quite nice legs but the thick ankles, the slack bust and the calm panic peering from behind the contact-lenses give them away every time. I know a chap who nearly married one of them: he gave me all the field-identification tips. I cannot remember just what it was that Blucher said but, had he been an Englishman he would have said 'Eh?'

I took his arm and steered him into the formicating mass. The girls tittered, and even *groped* us while their teacher prated, but I, at last, felt safe: there is no directional microphone which can sort out the words of devious Mortdecais from the prattle of pubescence. Blucher twigged, although it was clear that he thought

140

my precaution a bit far-fetched. (He is – I must be careful not to say 'was' – one of those who would be glad to die for the Pentagon's idea of democracy whereas I am a simple man who believes in the survival of the fittest. Since I have no sons it is clear that the fittest Mordecai to survive is me: I'm sure you see that.)

'Well,' he growled into my ear, just loudly enough to overcome the roosting-starlings noise of next year's gang-bang material, 'Well, give me the dirt, Mr Mortdecai.'

'You're going to think I'm an idiot,' I began.

He looked at me strangely. 'I wouldn't touch a straight line like that to save my soul,' he said.

I pretended not to have heard. 'You see, that package of powder, the one I collected from the aircraft; well, I sort of took out a little life insurance. I made up a duplicate package full of baby-powder – how they stared in the drug-store! – and put them both into envelopes and posted them by special delivery to a safe place. When I was satisfied that the chap who contacted me was the right chap I got them out of the safe place and gave one to the chap in question as arranged.' I wasn't watching Blucher's face but I swear I could hear his eyes narrowing. 'Which package?' he asked in a narrow-eyed sort of voice.

'That's the *trouble*,' I wailed convincingly, 'I don't *know*. You see, I marked them "A" and "B" – respectively – but when it came to the crunch I simply couldn't remember which was "A". Nor, if it comes to that, which was "B".' We fell silent. The schoolmarm was droning on usefully about Palma Vecchio although the picture she was discussing was clearly labelled Palma Giovane. It didn't matter: no one was listening. The nymphets were ganging up on us quite terrifyingly, I began to realize what hell it must be to be a pop-singer. Blucher had one hand pressed to his jacket, where the shoulder-holster lives, another on the zip of his trousers or pants.

'The awful thing is,' I went on, 'that the original package, as I think you pointed out, may well only have been tooth-powder in the first place, so there is a fair chance that my er contact . . .'

'Mr Lee,' he interjected helpfully.

'Or Ree,' I agreed, 'is going to be very very cross with me and that you too are going to suspect that I have not played a straight bat.'

'Yes,' he said. That was all he said.

The teacher moved on to another work of some choice and master spirit, shooting hateful glances at us and a few despairing ones at her pupils. We followed. I murmured into Blucher's ear almost all of what Mr Ree had told me. He turned and stared.

'And you *believe* that?' he asked in an incredulous voice.

'Well, it fits all the facts so far,' I said, swatting behind me at a gently-nurtured teenager who was being *impertinent* to me with an electrical vibrator, 'but if you have a more plausible scenario I shall be delighted to hear it.' He thought, then started – nay leapt into the air as though a great insight had come to him.

'An insight?' I asked in my polite voice.

'No, a schoolgirl. Let's please get to hell out of this place, please, *please*? I never knew that schoolgirls could be like this, did you?'

'Well, yes, I did; but then I read dirty books, you see, Colonel.'

There's nothing in a remark like that for chaps like Blucher. He boggled a moment then reiterated his request that we should get out. I fell in with his wishes. We got. We also took a taxi-cab – I let him choose it this time – to an eating-place where they solds us things to eat which tasted like dead policemen on toast. Blucher, clearly, was musing as he ingested his share of the garbage (the coffee in such places is often good; drink lots of it with your food; it's hell on the ulcers but it takes away the taste). I, too, was musing as frantically as a man can muse, for it was evident to my trained mind that the Blind Fury with the Abhorrèd Shears was sharpening them up for a snip at the Mortdecai life-span. I say again that I am not especially afraid of death, for the best authorities tell us that it is no more painful and undignified than birth, but I do feel that I'd like to have a say in the when and where and how. Particularly the 'how'.

'Blucher,' I said, pushing away my tepid and scarcely-touched platter, 'Blucher, it seems to me that there are few, if any, chaps with an interest in keeping me alive. I *wish* to stay alive, for reasons which I shall not trouble you with at present. Your suggestions would be welcome.' He turned his face to me, gave one last chew at whatever was in his mouth and looked at me gravely. There was a trickle of greasy gravy on his chin.

'There is a trickle of greasy gravy on your chin,' I murmured. He wiped it off. 'What was that again?' he asked.

'I said,' I said, 'that it would be nice to stay alive and could you perhaps give me a few ideas.' This time he looked blank, then almost friendly. He turned to the short-order cook or assistant-poisoner and called for more coffee and a toothpick. Then he turned back to me. His face was now benign – I'd never have dreamed that he could command so many expressions in so short a time. 'You know, Mr Mortdecai, I like you, I really do. We could use a few hundred guys like you in this country.' With that, he reached out and kneaded my shoulder in a brotherly sort of a way. His hand was large and hard but I did not wince nor cry aloud.

'About the staying-alive thing . . .?' I asked. His face went grave again and he shook his head slowly and compassionately.

'No way,' he said.

19 Mortdecai finds himself in possession of some art-work which he could well do without and learns about policemen's widows and fishcakes

Gigantic daughter of the West,
We drink to thee across the flood . . .

Hands All Round

I am not one to whimper, for I have found that it does one no good.
I did not even wet myself, although the provocation was intense. I lit a nonchalant cigarette, using only four matches and only slightly burning my valuable Sulka necktie. Blucher, clearly impressed by my British *sang-froid*, offered a sturdy word or two of comfort.

'Until I contact the Controller of my Agency,' he said, 'I have no orders to, uh, effect termination on.you. Like I said, I kind of like you. I'd say you had maybe eighty or ninety minutes before any such orders reach me. Until then, you can reckon that anyone shooting at you is on the side of the bamboo-shoot and water-chestnut princes.'

'Goodbye,' I said, rising.

'Good luck,' he said.

Outside on the pavement I felt curiously naked; I had never before felt so keen a desire for a pair of blue spectacles, a false nose and a large ginger beard, but it was now too late to regret such elementary precautions. A courteous cab sped me to the airport in something less than a hundred years. By the time I had retrieved my suitcase and booked into a London flight my hair had, I was sure, whitened noticeably around the roots.

So far as I could see there was not a single Chinese person on the aircraft. It was not until just before take-off that Mr Lee and a young compatriot boarded. Neither of them looked at me. If it comes to that, I didn't look at them after the first time, I glared straight ahead like a driver who has been stopped for speeding and doesn't much want the policeman to get a sniff of his breath.

I offered myself all sorts of explanations. They can't have known that I'd be on that particular flight, could they? Could they? Or perhaps Johanna had asked them to be my bodyguard, how about that? Perhaps Mr Lee took that flight every day or perhaps he was hastening back to Soho for the Chinese New Year, his bag stuffed with goodies for his grandchildren. He was clearly the kind of chap who would have any number of grandchildren, all of whom he would dote on. Perhaps it wasn't Mr Lee at all: it is well known that all these chaps look alike. My fevered imagination fantasized away until we were thoroughly airborne and the Captain's voice came crackling out of the public address system with the usual wonderfully sincere wishes for an enjoyable flight. 'Ha ha,' I said bitterly, drawing a nasty look from the obviously teetotal lady sitting next to me. The loudspeaker went on to tell us that we would be cruising at large numbers of thousands of feet (aircraft drivers are the last bastion against metrication) and that our air-speed would be an immense number of mph. I felt like complaining at this excessive speed for I was in no great hurry to reach the end of the journey – it is better to travel hopelessly than to arrive.

When the stewardess arrived to take our orders for drinks my neighbour asked for a glass of iced water; I confirmed her worst suspicions by ordering two large brandies, one bottle of dry ginger ale and no ice. I was proud to note that there was scarcely a quaver in my voice. When the wench brought the life-giving potions I heard myself asking her whether she happened to know the date of Chinese New Year's Day.

'Why, no sir, I guess I don't, I'm sorry. But hey, there's two Chinese gentlemen sitting right there in front; just let me finish with the drinks and I'll go ask them.'

'No no no no,' I squeaked, 'I wouldn't dream of –'

'It's no trouble, sir. You're very welcome.'

Soon I saw her leaning over the seats of the two Chinese gentlemen, brightly pointing back to where I sat quaking. They did not look around. She tripped back and said, 'You're out of luck, sir, they say it was three weeks ago. Oh, and they said they were real sorry you missed out.'

'Thank you. How kind.'

'You're welcome.' Officious bitch. I unfolded my *Times* with studied nonchalance, laid it on my briefcase and applied myself to the crossword. I am not one who completes this crossword while his breakfast egg boils to medium-soft but on a good day a medium-hard puzzle lies stricken at my feet in half an hour or so. This was one of the other days. I readily solved 'One who uses public transport – a target, exterminated (9,6)' and wrote in 'passenger pigeon' with a hollow laugh, but after that I seemed unable to concentrate. I blamed this on my briefcase, which did not seem to be affording the usual flat surface. Indeed, it did not seem to be flat at all. I gave it a petulant palpation: sure enough, there seemed to be a fat, cylindrical bulge lying diagonally inside it. Distraught as I was, I was nevertheless certain that I owned no object of that shape and dimensions, or, if I did, it certainly could not be in my briefcase. I undid the catch of the flap and had a cautious grope inside; sure enough, my questing fingers found a stiff cardboard cylinder, measuring some eighteen inches in length and four inches in diameter. I closed the flap and – quaking now as I had never quaked before – reached for the unexpended portion of the brandy. It dashed past my uvula, tonsils, larynx and pharynx without touching the sides. Then I lay back in my reclining seat, regulated my breathing and applied myself to frenzied thought. A bomb or similar anti-Mortdecai device? Surely not: Mr Lee was on that very aircraft. Moreover, the metal-detectors of the security men at the airport would have detected anything of the kind. A monstrous tube of Smarties' chocolate beans from a well-wisher? But I could think of no well-wisher.

Consumed now with vulgar curiosity and death-wish, I opened the bag again and drew out the cylinder. It was light. It was made of cardboard and looked exactly like the cylinders in which people store and dispatch prints and drawings, things like that. I raised one end to my eye and, pointing it at the window or porthole, peered through it. I found myself gazing at the left-hand unit of the bust of my teetotal neighbour. She cuffed it aside and made a noise like an expiring soda-water syphon. I think I said 'Whoops!' but I cannot be sure.

Nothing seemed to be in the cylinder except a roll of heavy paper so I inserted a couple of fingers, gave a skilful twirl and extracted it like a well-buttered *escargot*. Unrolled, it seemed to be a good colour-reproduction of a Rouault gouache painting; closer inspection proved it be a clever *copy* in gouache, all done by hand. I say 'copy' because the original happens to be a rather famous Rouault called *Après-midi d'un Clown* and it is in the Peggy Guggenheim collection or one of those places. It really was beautifully executed, more like a forgery than a copy, for the copyist had laid it down on a jaconet backing and had even added a *cachet de vente*, a couple of collectors' marks and a museum reference number. I tut-tutted or tsk-tsked a bit, because it had been rolled the wrong way, with the paint side inside, a practice which any art-dealer knows better than. My portly she-neighbour was making her soda-syphon noises again and I realized that the painting was perhaps a little *explicit*: in Rouault's day, you see, clowns seemed to spend their *après-midis* in the most bizarre fashion. (For my part, I have never taken much interest in modern art; I feel that it is a subject which calls for a good deal less research.) As I rolled up the gouache and twiddled it back into the cylinder a scrap of paper fell out of the opposite end. It was typewritten and said YOU MAY WELL FIND THIS USEFUL AT HEATHROW. I tore the scrap of paper into as many pieces as it had room for, musing anguishedly the while. I mean, it is not often that copies of famous Rouault gouaches creep unobserved into your briefcase and it is still rarer to be told that they will prove useful at airports. I would have liked to go to the lavatory but that would have meant passing Mr Lee and his friend and, on the way back, they might have *looked* at me. I was in no shape to cope with that sort of thing. I took the coward's way out, I stabbed the appropriate bell-push and asked the stewardess for 'some more of that ginger ale and, yes, perhaps a spot more of that brandy'. My neighbour – I shall always think of her as Carrie Nation – whispered to the stewardess urgently. The stewardess looked at me puzzledly. I looked at the stewardess smilingly but I fancy the smile came out as more of a lopsided leer, really. In a few moments Carrie Nation had been moved to another seat and, more to the point, my brandy had been delivered at the pit-head.

I supped, mused, supped again. Nothing made sense. I made another attack on the virtue of the crossword; it was by the compiler who always tries to work in the word 'tedding' – I suspect Adrian Bell – so I had no difficulty with 'Currying favour with Tory band-leader; making hay while the sun never sets', but the rest defeated me. I gave myself up to thoughts about survival, staying alive, things like that. One good result of this thought or thinking was engendered by the fact that the airport security people with their metal-detectors had not detected the Rouault copy in my briefcase but had pin-pointed my silver pocket-flask in a trice. This had to mean that the two Chinese gentlemen could scarcely be carrying anything more lethal than a cardboard dagger. Their gats, shivs and other bits of mayhem equipment must be in their suitcases, in the hold of the aircraft. Clearly, then, when I arrived at Heathrow, London, all I had to do was *not* to wait for my own suitcase to creak out of the constipated luggage-delivery system but to abandon it, flee through Customs with nothing but my briefcase and take a speedy taxi to Walthamstow or some other improbable place where I might have a friend. Meanwhile, the Chinese gentlemen would be fretting and fuming at the luggage-carousel, impatient for their murder-tackle to appear.

How lucidly one thinks, to be sure, when one has taken just a suspicion of brandy more than one should. I folded my hands smugly across that part of the torso which lies a little south of the liver and had a little zizz. When I awoke, the smugness was still there; I seized the *Times* crossword, gave it a masterful glare and had it whining for mercy in twenty minutes.

I have always sneered in a well-bred way at those idiots who, as soon as the aircraft's engines have been switched off, stand up, clutching their brats and other hand-luggage for quite ten minutes until the surly cabin-crew deign to open the doors, but on this occasion I was well to the fore and sped down the ramp far ahead of the field. Had this been Newmarket, a casual observer equipped with field-glasses and a stop-watch would have hastened to the nearest telephone and had a chat with his bookie.

Ignoring all signs telling people where they might wait for their luggage I galloped straight to the Customs Area and towards the blessed sign which said TAXIS, waving my innocent briefcase at the customs chap. He crooked an authoritative finger at me; I skidded to a halt. 'Nothing to declare, officer,' I cried merrily, 'just the old briefcase full of the old paper-work, eh? Mustn't detain you, sure you're a busy man yourself –'

'Open it,' he said. 'Sir.'

'Certainly, certainly, certainly,' I quipped, 'but do be quick, there's a good chap, or all the taxis will be taken. Nothing in there, I assure you.'

Every once in a while I encounter people who don't like me. This customs chap was one of those. He dwelt upon every least object in the briefcase as though he were an aged *courreur* pawing over his collection of pubic hairs. He left the cardboard cylinder to the last. 'What's this then, sir?' he asked.

'A picture or painting,' I said impatiently, glancing ever and again at the baggage-hall where my fellow-travellers (if I may coin a phrase) awaited their luggage. 'A mere copy. No Commercial Value and Not For Re-sale.'

'Reelly,' he said. 'Let's just have a look, please.' Fretfully, I extracted and unrolled the said art-work. 'There,' I said, 'it's the *Après-midi d'un Clown* by Rouault. It's in the Guggenheim or one of those places.'

'The Weltschmerzer Foundation?' he prompted.

'That's it, that's it; jolly good. It's in the Weltschmerzer, of course. Chicago.'

'Oh no it's not, sir.'

'?'

'It *was* there until last Wensdee; then some villains bust into the place, got away with a million quidsworth of this old rubbish.'

My mouth opened and shut, opened and shut, miming those soundless 'oh's that goldfish make when they want their water changed. I was spared the effort of saying something useful by a civil cough which seemed to come from behind my left shoulder.

A glance in that direction showed me a large, civil chap wearing a mackintosh or raincoat. A rapid swivel of some 270 degrees showed a similar chap, wearing a benign look, behind my right shoulder.

Permit me to digress for a moment. Every sound, professional team of thieves has a 'brain' who plans the villainy; a 'manager' who puts up the working capital; a 'fence' who will buy and sell the loot before it is even separated from its owners; a 'toolman' who knows how to neutralize burglar-alarm systems and to open locks, be they ever so sophisticated; a 'peterman' who can use a thermic lance on a safe or perhaps inject a fluid ounce of liquid explosive and detonate it with no more noise than a sparrow farting in its sleep; a 'hooligan' – regrettably – who will, at need, hit inquisitive passers-by with an iron bar; a 'bent' night-watchman or security-firm employee who is prepared to be concussed for £500 and a small percentage of the take; and – this is the chap you *didn't* know about – a 'lighthouse'. Your 'lighthouse' takes no active part in the actual breaking-and-entering; he simply strolls about with his hands in his pockets. He has but one simple, God-given skill: he can recognize 'fuzz', 'filth', 'Old Bill' or any other form of copper, however plainly-clothed, at two hundred metres on a dark night. No one – least of all the 'lighthouse' himself – knows how he does it, but there it is. There are only three reliable ones in the whole of London and they are paid the same as the hooligan.

What I am trying to say is that, had I been born into a different social stratum, I would have made a handsome living as a 'lighthouse'. The two chaps looming behind my shoulders were unmistakably 'fuzz'.

'Hello,' I said.

'I am Detective Inspector Jaggard,' said the chap on my left, 'and this is Detective Sergeant Blackwell. We are from the Fine Art Squad.' I shot another glance into the baggage hall; the carousel was beginning to rotate and my fellow-passengers were thronging around it. Suddenly I realized why my anonymous benefactor had assured me cryptically that the Rouault might well be of use to me at Heathrow.

'Flash the tin,' I said in my Bogart voice.

'I beg your pardon?' said the DI.

'Let's see the potsy.' They looked at each other, smiling thin smiles.

'Detectives here do not carry gilt shield-badges,' explained the DI, 'but here is my warrant-card, which is almost as impressive and, unlike the "potsy" you speak of, cannot be bought in toy-shops.' It seemed to be a very valid sort of warrant-card. 'It's a fair cop,' I said happily. 'Lead me to the nearest dungeon. Oh yes, and perhaps Sergeant Blackwell might be kind enough to collect my suitcase while you and I go to the Black Maria. It's a sort of pigskin job by Gucci, has my initials on it, can't mistake it.'

'That'll be "C.M." for Charlie Mortdecai, right, sir?' said the sergeant.

'Right,' I said, giving him a nod of approval.

'Then why,' asked the DI, 'does your passport say that you are Fr T. Rosenthal, SJ?'

Like any jesting Pilate, he did not stay for an answer but steered me courteously to one of those large black motor-cars which the better class of policeman has the use of. In a minute or two we were joined by the DS, who had found my suitcase. He did not give it to me. Nor did he drive to what you call Scotland Yard and what coppers call 'Headquarters' – he drove us over Battersea Bridge to that new place on the South Bank which they set up for the Serious Crimes Squad after that train-robbery (remember?) and which now houses all sorts of esoteric arms of the law. Such as, for instance, CII, which thinks up crimes before the villains do and has people sitting on the steps waiting for them. Such as, too, CI, which polices naughty policemen and is known affectionately as Rubber Heels; the late Martland's Special Power Group or SOGPU, and, of course, the Fine Art Squad which is so highly trained that its members can tell which way up a Picasso should hang. (Picasso, of course, is no longer in a position to contradict them.) The whole place is most secure and secret, except that any taxi-driver in London will take you there unerringly.

In a cosy room on the ground floor they formally charged me with illegal entry or something vague like that so that they could get me remanded in the morning, then we ascended three floors in a large lift, passed through a heavy iron door watched over by closed-circuit television, crowded into a much smaller lift and went down eight floors. I am no great lover of the bowels of the earth but the said bowels were just what I craved at the time. They were peopled by large, *English* male policemen: not an American, a Chinese waiter

151

nor a militant woman was to be seen. They ushered me into a simply-furnished, well-lit room, stuck a telephone into a jack-plug, attached a tape-recorder to it and invited me to make my 'privilege phone-call'. I was in no two minds about whom I should call: I dialled Mrs Spon, the best interior decorator in London and the only thoroughly capable person I know. I sketched in the outlines of my plight, asked her to get in touch with my 'brief' (as we rats of the underworld call our lawyers) and with Johanna, and to tell Jock to stand by the telephone around the clock. 'Tell him,' I urged, 'that he is not to go out except on spoken instructions by you or me. If he must play dominoes he may have his friends in and they may drink my beer within reason. Oh, and Mrs Spon, you might make it clear to the brief that I am in no pressing hurry to be sprung – no writs of *habeas corpus* – I wish to clear my name of this foul imputation before breathing free air again.'

'I twig,' she said. I replaced the receiver with a certain smugness: when Mrs Spon says that she has twigged then twig is what she has done. I'd back her to take the Grand Fleet into action after ten minutes of instruction from a Petty Officer, she's like that. She wears wonderfully expensive clothes and has a face like a disused quarry.

'Well now,' I said to my two captors, 'I daresay you'll be wanting to, ah, grill me a bit, eh?' They looked at each other, then back at me, then shook their heads in unison.

'I think you'd better wait for your lawyer, sir,' said Inspector Jaggard.

'For your own sake, sir,' said Sergeant Blackwell. They didn't frighten me. On the floor stood my suitcase, briefcase and the plastic bag containing my duty-free allowance of brandy and cigarettes. I reached for the plastic bag. They didn't hit me. I toddled into the adjoining lavatory and found two plastic tooth-glasses. I gave myself a jolt of the brandy, then poured two drinks for them.

'I think we're on duty, aren't we, Sergeant?' Blackwell consulted his watch. 'Hard to say, sir.' I put three packets of duty-free cigarettes beside Jaggard's glass and two beside Blackwell's, then tactfully visited the lavatory again. When I returned the glasses were empty, the cigarettes pocketed, but I was under no illusions. Policemen like them are not hungry for a free swig of brandy and a packet of king-size gaspers; they had only taken them to lull me into the belief that they were easy-going chaps. But I had observed their eyes, you see; they were the eyes of career-policemen, quite different from the fierce eye of a copper who can be bought. I offered them the key to my suitcase, saying that if they cared to rummage it now I could enjoy the creature comforts it contained, such as soap, clean underwear and so forth. Blackwell gave it a perfunctory rummage; Jaggard didn't even bother to watch, we all knew that there would be nothing illegal in it. Then I indicated that I would quite like a little lie-down and they said that they were, in fact, going off duty themselves and that their guvnor, the Detective Chief Inspector, might be down for a chat when my lawyer arrived. Then they locked me in. I didn't mind a bit – there are times when being locked in is comforting. After a quick scrub at the depleted ivory castles with Mr Eucryl's justly-celebrated Smoker's Dentifrice, I threw myself on the cot and sank into the arms of Morpheus. My last waking thought was one of pleasure that they had not ripped open the lining of my suitcase; it is a very expensive suitcase. Moreover, I tend to keep a few large, vulgar currency notes under the lining in case I ever need to buy a steam-yacht in a hurry.

I cannot have slept for more than an hour or so when the door made unlocking noises and I sprang to my feet – trouserless as I was – prepared to sell my life dearly. It was only a uniformed, fatherly 'Old Bill' who wanted to know what I would like for supper.

'There's a very good Chinese take-away just down the road – hoy, are you all right, sir?'

'Fine, thank you, fine, fine. It's just that I have an allergy to Chinese food. I'll just have whatever's going in the canteen.'

'It's rissoles tonight,' he warned me.

'Capital, capital. Nothing nicer. Wheel them on, do. And, ah, I daresay there'll be a touch of HP sauce or something of that sort, eh?'

'That *and* tomato sauce, sir.'

'Oh, Sergeant,' I said as he began to exit. 'Yessir?' replied the constable.

'Do you have *many* Chinese chaps working in the canteen?'

'Lord love you, no, sir. All the staff is widows of officers of the Force. Their attitude is a bit Bolshie sometimes but when they set their minds to it they make the finest fishcakes South of the Thames. It's fishcakes tomorrow night, sir, will you be here?'

'I hope so,' I said sincerely. 'Wild horses have often tried to drag me away from a well-made fishcake, with little or no success.'

The rissoles were all that a rissole-lover could wish for; they were accompanied by frozen french beans and faultless mashed potatoes, not to mention a full bottle each of HP sauce and tomato ditto, also bread and butter in abundance and a huge tin mug of strong orange-coloured tea such as I had thought only Jock could make. Tears sprang to my eyes as I slipped a packet of duty-free king-sized into 'Old Bill's' kindly pocket.

Stomach assuaged for the nonce, I was about to fling myself once more onto the cot when my eye fell upon the telephone, which Jaggard and Blackwell had carelessly left in my room or cell. I lifted the receiver and applied it to my ear. It was giving off a dialling-tone which meant that they had left it through to an open line.

'Oh, *really*,' I thought. I mean, people don't achieve the rank of DI, or even DS, if they inadvertently leave live telephones about in the cells of International Art Thieves. I applied myself to the problem of how best to squeeze a little gravy out of the situation. At last I decided to muddy the wells of investigatory technique by telephoning Pete the Welshman – a person who often works for me. I should explain that all those people who work for art-dealers – re-liners, restorers, mount-cutters, frame-makers, etc. – are congenital liars and thieves: they observe that their masters sometimes depart from the truth and soon come to believe that mendacity and peculation are all that is required to make a fortune in the fine art trade. How wrong they are, to be sure. Pete is also a Welshman and a fervent chapel-goer, which puts him well ahead of the game. I dialled his number.

'Hello, Pete,' I said. 'You know who this is, don't you?'

'Do you know what fucking time of night it is?' he snarled.

'Look, Pete, let's save the social amenities; this is business. You know that big job . . .?'

'Ah,' he lied unhesitatingly.

'Dump it,' I said. 'Forget it. You never saw it. Right?'

'Right,' he said. A casual listener – and I knew that there would be several – would believe that Pete knew what I was talking about. They would have been wrong. I hung up.

I reckoned that that little chat should guarantee me at least another twenty-four hours in the security of that stoutly-constructed nick. I decided on a digestive nap; fell asleep to dream of fishcakes on the morrow.

20 Mortdecai, crazed by the thought of fishcakes and terrified by the thought of liberty, is held in contempt of court, to name but one.

This madness has come on us for our sins

The Holy Grail

My lawyer woke me up to tell me that no one, after all, wanted to interrogate me that night and was there anything else I wanted. Half-awake, I imprudently told him that what I wanted more than anything was to spend a lengthy sojourn in this very room or cell, for fate's fickle finger was feeling for my fundament and I had to find out, somehow, before I was released, who was on whose side, the only certainty being that no one was on mine. When I say that I said this imprudently, I mean that, had I been fully in my senses, I'd have realized that the place probably boasted more bugs than a Sailors' Mission Refuge. He semaphored meaningfully with his eyebrows – only lawyers nowadays seem to be able to grow eyebrows, even bank managers seem to have lost the art – and I shut up. He said that he would be in court in the morning and warned me sadly, but with a huge wink, that I must prepare myself to be remanded in custody for weeks and weeks. Then he goodnighted me, I changed into pyjamas and in a trice was sleeping the sleep of

156

the unjust, which is quite as dreamless as the sleep of the just if the unjust sleeper has a litre of Red Hackle on his bedside table.

I was awakened by the arrival of another great mug of orange-hued tea and a dish of eggs and bacon. Dawn's left hand was in the sky. The e's and b would not have brought a smile to the face of Egon Ronay but I plied a lusty knife and fork, knowing that I must keep my strength up. The journey to the magistrate's court was on my mind, of course: the route thereto was doubtless thick with Chinese snipers *faisant la haie*.

As it turned out, those fears were groundless, for this de-luxe cop-shop had its own magistrate and mini-court on the premises. It was a cosy little gathering: one ill-shaven Mortdecai escorted by one kindly turnkey, one magistrate who exhibited all the signs of a magistrate who has not had enough sleep, one lawyer giving me the blank sort of look which means 'keep your mouth shut and leave this to me', one haggard Detective Inspector Jaggard glaring at his notebook as though it had said something rude to him; one world-weary clerk and – to my dismay – one Johanna looking quite ravishing in an oxlip-yellow suit and hat.

The clerk droned legally for a while; Jaggard put on a joke-policeman voice while he read bits from his notebook about how he had proceeded from here to there on information received . . . but I must not trouble you with such minutiae: I am sure that you have been in magistrates' courts yourselves. Just as I was expecting the blessed words which would remand the prisoner, C. Mortdecai, in custody for weeks and weeks, revelling in fishcakes far from the madding Triads, the blow fell. My treacherous lawyer rose and submitted that the prisoner's wife, Mrs C. Mortdecai, had received a visit, late the previous night, from a Fr T. Rosenthal, SJ, who had explained how – after some muddle at Immigration – he had found himself in possession of a passport in the name of Mortdecai. And could he have his own passport back, please. And, no, he couldn't be produced in court because he had gone into Retreat at Heythrop and the Preliminary Confession alone would take some twelve hours, not to mention the penance after. 'Just an absurd muddle,' said my brief, avoiding my glance, 'great credit to the vigilance of the police etc. etc.'

I opened my mouth to claim that I was clearly an International Art Thief and deserved more courtesy than this but then I remembered

157

that I had only been charged with Illegal Entry into Her Majesty's Domains. No word of Rouault or his gouaches had passed anyone's lips.

The magistrate apologized to me, hoped that I had not been too much inconvenienced, dismissed me without a stain on my character. I was free to go.

I looked around me frantically: the turnkey was giving a friendly nod, Jaggard was sneering, Johanna was irradiating the most wifely smile you can imagine. I knew that the instant I stepped into the freedom of the street I was a dead man – curiously, too, the thought of those incomparable fishcakes surged into my mind. My best friends would not claim that I am a fast thinker; I like to mull these things over for a day or two, but it was clear that there was no time for mulling. I did a Fred Astaire double-shuffle around the turnkey or gaoler, strode up the steps to the magistrate, right hand outstretched. The beak's expression made it clear that he didn't have a lot of time for these Continental expressions of emotion but, after an inward struggle, held out his hand. I seized it, whisked his frail body from the bench and gave him the heel of my hand in the hooter. Sleepy before, he now became a sleeper in earnest. Hordes of capable people sprang out of the woodwork and restrained me (restrained means 'hit') but I recked little of their blows for, in the twinkling of an eye, I was once again in my comfy cell, secure in the knowledge that bail is rarely allowed to chaps who wantonly alter the appearance of Stipendiary Magistrates. I allowed myself a snort of whisky and poured the rest into the plastic duty-free bag, lest any vengeful copper should try to take it away from me.

I am not one of those who, in times of stress, sits on the edge of a bed gnashing his nails and cursing whichever fool or blackguard made this world: I am more one of those who lies down on the bed in question and snatches a nap. When the door opened at lunch-time I kept the eyes firmly closed. A voice which could only have emanated from one of those fierce young policemen said 'Lunch.' I remained tacit and mute. I heard him lift the empty whisky-bottle, shake it and replace it onto the table with a disgusted slam. He went out, locking the door. After counting from one to ten I opened an eye. The luncheon he had brought was in three of those little white cartons with tin-foil tops such as Chinese take-away places sell. I coaxed a little Scotch out of the plastic shopping bag, mingled it with water and went back to sleep. A dead rat might have coaxed a reaction from my salivary glands sooner than anything with bean-shoots and soy-sauce.

Sergeant Blackwell came to see me soon afterwards; he looked at my untouched lunch and said '*Waste!*'

'Thirty-nine inches,' I quipped, 'bust, forty-two.'

'Neither funny nor plausible,' he said. Both true, of course. Then he took me upstairs to the charge-room and charged me with common assault, actual bodily harm, contempt of court and many another thing including, I fancy, unimaginative potty-training in early childhood, while I hung my head in a suitable fashion.

Back in my cell I asked for something to read; he was back in ten minutes with a tattered Bible.

'I think I've read this,' I said.

'It's all we've got,' he retorted, 'Enid Blyton is only for trusties.'

The Good Book was printed upon fine India paper and the first few pages had been used by sacreligious chaps for rolling fags with (that's *cigarettes*), so that *Genesis* began at the bit where Cain says 'My punishment is more than I can bear. Behold, thou hast driven me out this day from the face of the earth; . . . and I shall be a fugitive and a vagabond in the earth; and it shall come to pass that every one that findeth me shall slay me.' I never did find out what happened to Cain except that he went to the land of Nod which is to the East of Eden; I joined him there.

It was one of those days when a chap simply cannot get a good day's sleep; it seemed I had scarcely closed my eyes before last night's 'Old Bill' was warning me to get shaved for Six o'Clock Court. He watched me with something of admiration in his eye as I plied the disposable razor; many a villain, he told me, had sworn to give that particular magistrate a knuckle-sandwich but none had hitherto made good the threat. I could see that he found it hard to believe that my only motive was a determination to graze upon the fabled fishcakes.

Back in the intimate court-room, the cast was almost the same as it had been that morning, except that my custodian was now the 'Old Bill', the magistrate was one of those soppy, earnest chaps who long to hear of broken homes and deprived childhoods and Johanna was looking esculent in a cinnamon sheath such as you could not buy with a lifetime's trading-stamps. Yes, and there was a flaccid man with a big face whom I had never seen before but who was clearly one of those Harley Street chaps who charge you fifty guineas for telling you to take a long sea voyage and more exercise.

Detective Inspector Jaggard flatly recited the facts about my disgraceful behaviour that morning. It seemed to me that the magistrate permitted a thin smile to cross his face as Jaggard related how his brother of the bench would never again be quite the same around the nose. My brief called Johanna to the witness-box. She dabbed a tearful eye with a couple of square inches of cambric as she told how valiantly I had fought against my, uh, terrible, uh, disability and how she was ready to stand by me until I had conquered it. For my part I gaped. Probably I was meant to gape. Then the flaccid chap was called: I had been wrong about him, his address was not Harley Street but Wigmore Street.

He had, it seemed, been treating me for more than a year and was getting some pretty good results; all sorts of mental diseases with names I cannot remember had succumbed to his therapy and the slight, residual hostility-issue-orientation towards legal authority was fast vanishing and he would stake his reputation that this morning's little outburst was just a preter-ultimate orgasmic sublimation which was, not to put too fine a point on it, a jolly good thing and meant that I was now cured. He also had my wife's assurance that I was very sorry and that I would pay for the nose.

I wagged my head with admiration; so fine a liar was wasted in Wigmore Street. There had been times in his declaration when I had been on the point of believing him myself.

You must have noticed that most magistrates, when looking wise, peer over the tops of their spectacles. This one was trendy: he prodded the gig-lamps up to his forehead and peered under them. He asked the mendacious medico if he could advance any other extenuating circs., had the prisoner been the product of a broken home, a deprived childhood, that sort of thing?

'Oh dear, yes, *very*,' said the liar, speaking more truthfully than he realized, 'but, er*chrmmm*, you understand, at this stage, sure you follow me . . .' and he jerked his head a couple of millimetres in my direction.

'Just so, just so,' said the kindly stipendiary. Beaming at me, he hit me with a hundred quid for his fellow-magistrate's conk

– well, that was the least he could do, I realized that – added a few more bobs for contempt of court, bound me over in my own recognizances to keep the peace and begged me, like any father, to listen to my doctor and loved ones who knew what was best for me. He didn't tell me to give up smoking cigarettes.

Going down the stairs, free as a bird and terrified as a clay pigeon, I accosted Jaggard. 'Charge me with pinching the Rouault,' I whined; 'I'll plead guilty, it's a fair cop.' He stared at me bleakly as only Detective-Inspectors can.

'Unfortunately, sir,' he said (the 'sir' stuck in his throat a bit), 'it seems that just before the robbery your lady wife had agreed to buy that Rouault from Miss Gertrude Weltschmerzer for you. As a wedding-present. I have spoken to Miss Weltschmerzer on the international telephone. She confirms this.' He spoke in the bitter tones of a policeman who has to live and work in a world where 'law and order' has become a dirty phrase. I truly felt sorry for him.

'Well, well,' I babbled, 'that was nice of her, wasn't it. Matter of fact, I'm thinking of buying her an antique pendant.'

'You mean, like a spare?' he said.

I stopped feeling sorry for him.

Downstairs, I collected my possessions, gave the plastic bag of whisky to the kindly Old Bill, along with the remainder of the duty-free cigarettes – who knows when you may need a friend in the Force? – and joined Johanna in her cute little Jensen Interceptor. Not a shot was fired as she drove us to Upper Brook Street. She looked beautiful behind the wheel, as all lovely women do behind the wheels of sports cars. All she said was 'Oh, Charlie, Charlie, Charlie.'

All I said was, 'Yes.'

Jock was at home, looking useful. I had forgotten to bring him any American comic-books but he didn't sulk. I took him aside and murmured an instruction or two about dinner. My conversation with Johanna was desultory.

'Charlie dear, don't tire yourself telling me all about your adventures. I know most of it and can guess the rest.'

'Darling Charlie, why are you keeping away from the windows in that kind of furtive way?'

'Charlie, what on earth are those *strange* brown things you are eating?'

'Fishcakes,' I mumbled from a full mouth and a fuller heart. 'Made by policemen's widows.'

'I see . . .'

'Charlie, I expect you're very tired?'

'Very.'

'*Too* tired?'

'I didn't say that, did I?'

21　Mortdecai takes an educational tour around a food-processing plant and improves his mind no end.

The dirty nurse, Experience, in her kind
Hath fouled me.

The Last Tournament

I awoke the next morning at an earlier hour than usual.

'Johanna,' I said, 'could you please stop doing that for a moment?'

'Shchroombleshly,' she said, indistinctly.

'How much did that Wigmore Street wank-shrink cost you?'

'A thousand,' she said, clearing her throat.

'And the Rouault?'

'Nothing. No, really, nothing – I just happened to have heard that Gertie Weltschmerzer was having to find a really serious sum of money to pay her last-husband-but-one not to publish his memoirs, so I called her and congratulated her on the *convenient* burglary and sort of dropped the name of the president of her insurance firm who happens to be an old buddy of mine and she made the sort of noises that rich women make – you know, like this . . .'

'Later,' I said. 'First the narrative.'

'Where was I? Oh yes, when she stopped making noises like a gobbler – that's what we call a turkey in the States – I sort of reminded her that the Rouault couldn't have been burgled because she'd sold it to me just a couple of days before. She had to think about that for a while because she's a little dumb, you know? and then she said why, *sure* she remembered and she hoped my husband would enjoy it. That's all, except that I feel I ought to check that my husband does enjoy it.'

I managed to enjoy it although it was, as I have said, quite indecently early in the morning.

Jock, announcing his imminent appearance by a polite cough which almost took the door off its hinges (I have taught him that good servants never knock), brought in a tray for Johanna laden with the sort of coffee which you and I drink after dinner but which Daughters of the Revolution pour into their stomachs at crack of dawn. Small wonder that the American Colonies were the first to win their independence – if that's what they still call it. Before I could doze off again my own tray arrived, just a few eggs, a half-dozen slices of toast and a steaming pot of well-judged tea. Jock, you see, although not bred to service, has a heaven-sent knowledge of what the young master will require in the way of tea. I would pit him against any Wigmore Street physician when it comes to prescribing tea: there are times, as I'm sure you know, when these things *matter*. I mean, an art-dealer who has nothing to face that day but a brisk flurry of bidding at Sotheby's needs naught but the soothing Oolong. A morning at Christie's indicates the Lapsang Souchong. A battle-royal at Bonham's over, say, a Pater which only one other dealer has spotted, calls for the Broken Orange Pekoe Tips – nay, even the Earl Grey itself. For an art-dealer in terror of his life, however, and one who has valiantly embarked on Part Two of his honeymoon in early middle age, only two specifics are in the field: Twining's Queen Mary's Blend or Fortnum's Royal. What I'd call a two-horse race. I forget which it was; I only remember that I slunk out of bed before its fortifying effect made me forget that I am no longer a youngster. (That's all right about the 'size of the dog in the fight and the size of the fight in the dog' but art-dealers in their late forties have *livers* to consider; other organs have to take their place in the queue.)

Jock really is a compassionate man when he sets his mind to it: it was not until I was under the shower that he slipped me the bad news.

'Mr Charlie,' was how he phrased it, 'Mr Charlie, there's two gemmun downstairs waiting to see you.'

'*Two* gentlemen?' I said, soaping freely the parts which I can still reach, 'Two? Nonsense, Jock, I only know three gentlemen altogether; one of them is serving a life-sentence for murdering an unwanted mistress, another deals in rare books in Oxford and the third has gone to the bad . . . publishing, something like that.' He heard me out patiently; he knows the difference between prattle and orders; then he said, 'I di'n't mean *gemmun* when I said gemmun, Mr Charlie, I only said gemmun because you don't like me to say –'

'Quite right, Jock,' I said, raising a soapy hand. 'Are you trying to say that they are art-dealers?' He wagged a regretful head.

'Nar. They're fuzz. Big Brass Fuzz.' I turned the shower to cold; this never fails to make the intellect surge around.

'Have we any tea-bags in the kitchen? We have? *Really?* Well, make them some tea and tell them that I shall be down presently.'

'Ah, Jaggard, Blackwell!' I cried as I bounced into the drawing-room a few moments later, 'Got some tea, eh?' The two men turned and looked at me. They had no tea, nor were they Jaggard and Blackwell. Nor did they get up. They were large, blank-faced, empty-eyed coppers, but for some reason my 'lighthouse' started to flicker a bit. They were almost like coppers but not quite.

'Mr Mortdecai?' asked one of them.

'True,' I said.

'Interpol. Robinson, London.' He pointed to the other chap. 'Hommel, Amsterdam.' That made sense; the lighthouse ceased to flash. Interpol are not like other boys and Dutch fuzz does not look like English fuzz.

'How can I help you?' I asked.

'Get your hat, please.' I thought about that.

'Warrant cards?' I said diffidently. They gave me the world-weary look which policemen give to clients who have read too many thrillers. I strolled about aimlessly until I could get a squint down the Dutchman's jacket. Sure enough, he was wearing a shoulder-holster bursting with what looked like the good old Browning HPM 1935 – a pistol which contains 14 rounds of 9mm Parabellum and weighs a couple of pounds unloaded, a splendid weapon for slapping people on the side of the head with but nevertheless an odd choice of ironmongery for anyone who isn't expecting an invasion.

'I've got one, too,' said the English jack.

'Am I under arrest,' I asked, 'and if so, what for?' The Dutchman allowed himself a sigh, or it may have been a yawn.

'Yost get the hat, Mr Mortdecai,' he said. 'Please.' At that point Johanna entered the room and gave a startled glance at our visitors – a glance of recognition, I'd have said.

'Don't go with these men, Charlie,' she said sharply.

'They are armed,' I explained.

'So am I,' growled Jock from the other doorway, his beefy hand full of Luger.

'Thank you, Jock, but please put it down *now*. The gentleman on the sofa is holding a gun under his mackintosh and I fancy it's pointing at my gut. Also, Mrs Mortdecai is present.' I watched Jock slowly figuring out the odds, praying that he would make the right decision. I often boast that I am not especially afraid of dying but on the other hand I have this heavy addiction to life and I'm told that the withdrawal symptoms are shocking. Finally he placed the Luger on the floor – you do not *drop* automatic pistols – and, at a gesture from the Dutch chap, kicked it across the carpet. He kicked it in such fashion that it slid far under the big break-front bookcase: he is not just an ugly face, you know.

One of them ushered Johanna and Jock into the kitchen and locked them in; the other didn't rip out the telephone cord, he unscrewed the mouthpiece, took out the diaphragm and put it in his pocket.

'Extension?' he asked.

'No.'

'Where is it?'

'In the bedroom.' He walked me there and repeated the procedure. He was *good*. Then we went. Their motor-car was a sensible, Rover-like vehicle and I was made to sit in the front, beside the Dutchman who was driving. The English copper – well, I was still not sure that he wasn't – leaned forward and said that I must not do anything foolish because his pistol was pointed at my left kidney. Now, every schoolboy knows that if a man means to shoot you he does so there and then, without shilly-shallying. Clearly, they wanted me alive, so the threat was idle. I hoped it was idle. I craned over my shoulder for a glimpse of the sidearm in question: he snarled at me to face the front. The pistol was there all right and I had had just enough time to see that it was one of those monstrous US Government Colt.45 automatics which can blow a hole through a brick wall. What was nice about this particular weapon was that it was not wearing a silencer; to let off such a thing in a car would stop the traffic for miles. That was the third mistake they had made. I applied myself to thought.

'Where are you taking me?' I asked idly.

'Home,' said the Dutchman. This was probably meant to be a joke. We sped eastward. As we passed St Paul's I courteously pointed out its beauties to the Dutchman.

'Shot op,' he said.

We sped further eastward, now in parts of London quite unfamiliar to me.

'Where is "home", please?' I asked.

The Englishman answered this time. 'Home's where the heart is,' he said with all the jovial smugness of a large man holding a large pistol. 'We're just taking you somewhere nice and quiet where they can ask you a few questions, then if your lady wife delivers Mr Ree to Gerrard Street within twenty-four hours we let you go, don't we?'

'Shot OP!' said the Dutchman. He seemed to be in charge. Those few words had made my day, however, for it was now clear that they were but the minions of another 'they' who needed to know something that I knew and that I was also a valuable hostage. I was more than ever sure that this was not a time for people to blow holes through the Mortdecai kidneys.

When we came to a complicated road-junction, crammed with traffic and well-populated with uniformed policemen, I murmured to the Dutch chap that we drove on the left in England. He was, as a matter of fact, doing so but it gave him pause and the wheel wobbled. I snatched the ignition keys; the car stalled in the midst of a welter of furious traffic and I sprang out. Sure enough, they didn't shoot at me. I ran over to the nearest 'Old Bill', gabbled that the driver was having a heart attack and where was the nearest telephone. He pointed to a kiosk then stamped majestically towards the car, which was now the centre of a tumult of block traffic.

In the kiosk I frantically dialled my own number and rammed in a wasteful 10p piece. Johanna answered from the dressing-room extension which had not been noticed.

'Look,' I said, 'I'm in a phone-box, corner of . . .' I read off

167

what it said on the instrument '. . . and I've got away from them but not for long. I'll be . . .' I frantically looked out of the kiosk, saw a great, grubby, warehouse-like building opposite with a name on it '. . . Mycock's Farm-cured Bacon,' I read out.

'This is no time for jokes, Charlie dear.'

'Just get Jock here; fast.' I replaced the receiver, did not even spare the time to check the returned coins box. I ran towards the excellent Mr Mycock. Inside the door an elderly slattern, redolent of Jeyes' Fluid, pointed to where the guvnor would be. 'He's probably having his dinner,' she added. 'Out of a bottle.' As soon as she was out of sight I changed direction again and again, diving into the abattoir's labyrinth. The pong of scorched pig became excruciating; I longed for that Jeyes' Fluid. The air was split by an appalling shriek – it was the dinner-time whistle but it gave me a bad moment. I pulled myself together, affecting the arrogant stroll of a Ministry of Health official looking for the germ *Clostridium Botulinum*. The workers who thronged out past me did not even spare me a glance, they were off to chance paratyphoid from beef pies at The Bunch of Grapes; they wouldn't eat *pork* pies, they'd seen them being made. As I stalked proudly through the corridors, turning randomly every now and again in a purposeful sort of way, I was doing feverish sums in mental arithmetic concerned with how quickly Jock could possibly get here. It's all very well being clever and devious, you see, but when you are eyeball-deep in lethal shit you need a thug – a thug who has coped with such situations since his first term in Borstal. Jock is just such a thug – few art-dealers could afford him – and I was confident that he would make all speed to the Mycock *cochonnerie* and would be properly equipped with one pair of brass knuckles, one Luger and, if he had been able to find the key, one Banker's Special Revolver such as I keep in my bedside table. Twenty minutes was how I had the race handicapped. I had to survive for just twenty minutes.

I squeezed past a cluster of bins marked PET-FOOD ONLY: WASH HANDS AFTER HANDLING and was about to thread my way through another lot marked IRELAND AND BELGIUM ONLY when I saw a large chap about thirty feet away, holding a pistol with two hands. He was the Dutchman. The pistol was pointed at me. The two-handed grip was perfectly good procedure according to the book they teach policemen with, but it seemed to me that if he

168

was any good with that thing he would, at that range, have been holding it in one hand, pointing it at the ground a couple of yards in front of his feet. All the same, I froze, as any sensible chap would.

'Comm, Mr Mortdecai,' he said persuasively, 'comm; you have donn the teatricals. Yost comm with the honds behind the head and no one will hort you.' I started to breathe deeply; in, count ten, out – this is supposed to hyperoxygenate the system. Added to the adrenalin which was sloshing around in my blood-vessels, it had a salutary effect: I felt convinced that I could have held Cassius Clay for quite two rounds. Unless he got me against the ropes, of course.

I went on hyperoxygenating; the Dutchman's pistol roved up and down from my privates to my forehead. He was the first to become bored. ·

'Mr Mortdecai,' he said in a dangerous voice, 'are you comming now?' Well, I couldn't resist a straight line like that, could I?

'No,' I said, 'just breathing hard.' While he was thinking about that I feinted a dive to the left, then, for my life, plunged to the right, behind the friendly bins of pig-pieces. 'Rooty-toot-toot-toot' went his shooter. One round went howling off the wall, the others pierced the bins. He was not quite as bad as I had thought but he was not as good as he thought. That two-handed grip, you see, gives you a grand one-off first shot but when you swing to another target you invariably loose off too soon. The good pistol-shooter always lowers his weapon when tracking the second target and only raises it again when he has it cold. Ask anyone. Wyatt Earp, for instance.

I durst not give him time to change his magazine so I shed my jacket and slung it over the bins. 'Rooty-toot-toot' went the Browning. That made seven rounds expended, seven to go; even I could tell that. The floor sloped down in a gentle ramp towards him. I kicked over a couple of bins which rolled down the slope, dripping pig's blood and goodness knows what else. He shot at them, for the Dutch are cleanly folk. Ten rounds gone, four to go. I raised an unoccupied bin-lid and slammed it onto the floor; he fired two more rounds, quite wildly.

Where I had kicked the bins away I saw that there was a monstrous iron door with a lever instead of a handle. It looked like an excellent door to be behind.

'Jackson!' I bellowed – it seemed a plausible sort of name – 'JACKSON! Don't use the bombs: I'm coming out to take him myself.' Hommel can scarcely have believed that, but he must have dithered a bit because I got that great iron door open and scrambled through it without a shot being fired at me. The room inside the door was cold as the tip of an Eskimo's tool: it was, indeed, what the meat-trade calls a Cold Room. The lever on my side of the door had a position marked SECURE in red paint. I made it so. High up on two walls were those rubber-flap kind of entrances you see in hospitals; between them and through them ran an endless belt with large hooks. (Yes, just like a dirty weekend with a shark-fisher.) A pistol roared outside and a bullet spanged against the splendidly solid iron door. I sat with my back to the door and quaked, partly with cold, for I had discarded my jacket in that little *ruse de guerre*, you remember. The secure lever beside my head wagged and clicked but did not allow admission. Then I heard voices, urgent voices: the Dutchman was no longer alone. An unpleasing sort of whirring, grating noise made itself heard: evidently they had got hold of some kind of electrical tool and were working on the door-handle. Had I been a religious man I should probably have offered up a brisk prayer or two, but I am proud, you see: I mean, I never praised Him when I was knee-deep in gravy so it would have seemed shabby to apply for help from a bacon-factory.

The grating noises on the other side of the door increased: I looked about me desperately. On the wall was one of these huge electrical switches such as American Presidents use for starting World War Last. It might well set off an alarum, I thought; it might turn off all the electrical power in Mr Mycock's bacon-factory – certainly, it couldn't make things worse. I heaved with all my might and closed the contacts.

What happened was that pigs started trundling through the room. They were not exactly navigating under their own power, you understand, for they had all crossed The Great Divide or made the Great Change; they were hanging from the hooks on the endless belt, their contents had been neatly scooped out and were doubtless inhabiting the PET-FOOD ONLY: WASH HANDS AFTER HANDLING bin. They were the first truly happy pigs I had ever seen.

The eighth – or it may have been the ninth – pig wasn't really a pig in the strictest sense of the word; it was a large Dutchman,

170

fully-clothed in what would be called a suit in Amsterdam. He was hanging onto a hook with one hand and seemed to have all his entrails. His other hand brandished the Browning HPM 1935, which he fired at me as he dropped to the floor, making his fourth mistake that day. The shot took a little flesh off the side of my belly – a place where I can well afford to lose a little flesh – then he aimed carefully at the pit of my belly and squeezed the trigger again. Nothing happened. As he looked stupidly down at the empty pistol I kicked it out of his hand.

'That was fourteen,' I said kindly. 'Can't you count? Haven't you a spare magazine?' Dazedly, he patted the pocket where the spare magazine nested. Meanwhile, I had picked up the Browning; I clouted him on the side of the head with it. He passed no remarks, he simply subsided like a chap who has earned a night's repose. I took the spare magazine out of his pocket, removed the empty one from the pistol (using my handkerchief to avoid leaving misleading fingerprints) and popped it into his pocket. I cannot perfectly recall what happened then, nor would you care to know. Suffice it to say that the endless belt was still churning along with its dangling hooks and, well, it seemed a good idea at the time.

It was now becoming colder every moment and I was shaking like any aspen, but even cowards derive a little warmth from a handful of Browning HPM with a full magazine. I awaited what might befall, regretting nothing but having wasted a perfectly good jacket. An indistinct voice shouted through the door.

'Eh?' I shouted valiantly.

'Open up, Mr Charlie,' shouted Jock. I opened up. Had I been one of these emotional Continental chaps, I believe I would have clasped him to my bosom.

'We got to get out, Mr Charlie, the place'll be crawling with Old Bill in about ten seconds flat.' We took off at a dog-trot. To my horror, at the turn of the corridor stood Johanna, holding my Banker's Special like a girl who knows how to use Banker's Specials. She gave me one of those smiles which jellify the knees, but the brain remained in gear. From the direction of the entrance there came a sort of crowd-scene noise and, rising above it, the sound of patient exasperation which only policemen can make. Someone came clumping nigh and we ducked into the nearest room. There were no pigs in it. What was in it was bales and bales of newly-laundered white coats and overalls such as those who work in bacon-factories love to wear.

When the legions had thundered past we emerged, white-clad, and I was snapping orders about stretchers at Jock, calling him 'Orderly' and asking 'Nurse' if she knew how to use portable cyclometric infusion apparatus. She said she did, which was not the first time she had lied to me. The policemen at the entrance paid us no heed, they were busy keeping people out. 'Bart's Hospital,' I snapped at the taxi-driver, 'casualty entrance. Emergency: use your horn.' At Bart's we dispersed, shedding white clothing, found the main entrance and took three separate taxis home. I arrived first – I needed that healing drink.

'Well,' I said curtly when the others had assembled, 'first things first.' I still had a residue of hospital-registrar arrogance in my voice. 'Does either of you know what happened to the other chap – the English one?'

'Yeah,' said Jock. 'He's face down in one of them big bins of pigs' guts.'

'Oh dear,' I said, 'poor fellow, how horrid for him. I mean, I don't actually feel any *affection* for him but he must be hideously uncomfortable.'

'I don't fink he's feeling uncomfortable, Mr Charlie.'

'Oh dear,' I said again. 'I suppose that means I've got to send that Luger of yours to Ginge the Gunsmith again? I don't suppose you had time to pick up the used cartridge-cases? No? Ah well.'

(Perhaps a word of explanation to the innocent is called for here. The ballistics wizards, as everyone knows, can infallibly tell which bullet has been fired from which fire-arm – they use comparison-microscopes – and the cartridge-cases are an even greater give-away. Therefore, anyone who has used a fire-arm for a naughty purpose tends to toss it over London Bridge into the Thames where, I fancy, the accumulation of fire-arms so discarded must by now be constituting a hazard to shipping. Jock, however, will no more be persuaded to discard his Luger than to part with his autographed photograph of Shirley Temple. This means that whenever he has 'used up' someone with it I have to pay Ginge a great deal of money to 'tiddly' it. This involves putting in a new striker-pin, buffing up the face of the breech-block and

172

engraving a few new scratches on it and doing some extremely fancy work with a lathe on the chamber and barrel. After Ginge has finished with a pistol the comparison-microscopes get a fit of the sulks and the ballistics wizards go home and beat their wives.)

'Now, Johanna,' I said in a no-nonsense voice, 'you seemed to know those two chaps: who were they? The Englishman and the Dutchman? Eh?'

'They were both Dutchmen, Charlie dear. Deputy Commissioner Rubinstein likes to call himself Robinson because his English is perfect, isn't it?'

'Yes, wasn't it?' I said.

'And they really were both policemen but very, very bent ones. You see, darling, most of the heroin in the world passes through Amsterdam – or do I mean Rotterdam? – and that amounts to a great many millions of pounds, you understand, and you can't really blame an underpaid policeman for kind of not noticing that someone is absent-mindedly dropping ten thousand pounds a year into a West Indies branch of the Bank of Nova Scotia for him, can you? I mean, when it comes to privacy, the Bank of Nova Scotia makes those Swiss banks look like back-numbers of *Playboy*.'

'No,' I agreed, 'I cannot blame them for this. Indeed, I might well suffer a pang or two of temptation myself in the circumstances. What I can – and do – blame them for is for attempting to blow big, painful holes through essential organs of mine which I have not yet finished with.'

'Yes,' she said, 'there is that. But they *got* their blame all right, didn't they, dear?'

'True, true. And now you will please be kind enough to tell me who was employing these sticky-fingered arms of the law. I mean, at the time when they put the old snatcheroo on me.'

'What beautiful American you speak, Charlie!'

'Never mind about that, just tell me who gave them The Notice about me.'

'Is that the same as a "contract" in the States?'

'Oh, burst a bleeding frog!' I bellowed – I believe this was the first time I ever raised my voice to her – 'Forget the semantics, what I want to know is who they were working for.'

'*Pas devant les doméstiques*,' she murmured. Jock left the room in a marked manner; his intellect is second to, well, almost anyone's, but he does know two French sentences. One of them begins with '*Vooly voo cooshey*' and the other is the one Johanna had used. He can be hurt; he has his pride.

'They were working for Mr Lee, silly,' said Johanna.

'And where is Mr Lee now, would you say?' She lifted the telephone, giving me that smile; dialled a number and said something into it in a language I didn't recognize. She listened for perhaps thirty seconds, then said something which sounded like a number. Then she gave me that smile again, the one that softens every bone in my body except one. Hung up. I mean, she hung up the telephone. 'Mr Lee is at present approaching the John F. Kennedy International Airport, Charlie dear. He should be touching down in about fifty minutes. He is in a big, comfy jet and no one else is aboard except a dozen or so of his, uh, naughty friends, six real Interpol agents, half the staff of the US Narcotics Bureau and your friend the Commandant.'

'You mean the dreaded Commandant of that College of yours?' I squeaked. 'Are you trying to tell me that she was on the side of the angels all the time? Next you'll be telling me that she'll draw an MBE for her part in this nonsense!'

'She got her MBE when you were at school, Charlie. Parachuting into Belgium. Her OBE came through when she snitched a boatload of Hungarian scientists out from a little Yugoslav port called Rijeka in the '50s. The least she can draw from this little caper is a DBE – in fact I'm putting her in for a Life Peerage.'

'*You*'re putting . . .'

'Yes, dear.' That seemed to close that subject. Then I thought of another question.

'Just what do *you* expect to draw from this, Johanna?'

'You, dear.' I looked wildly around; there was no one else in the room.

'Me?' I said.

'Yes.' Oh well, I thought, ask a silly question and you'll get a silly answer. Little did she know that Colonel Blucher had offered me a spot of survival in this vale of tears in exchange for infiltrating whatever organization Johanna thought she was running; little did Blucher know how abject a dog's breakfast

174

I had made of it all. I rose and made courteous noises to the effect that I had to go and see a chap in Jule's Bar in Jermyn Street.

'Yes, do go and have a little fun, dear; I know you'll forgive me if I don't join you tonight.' Game, set and match against me, as usual.

22 Mordecai learns the truth, kicks the slats out of a kitchen cupboard and finds solace in bread and jam

Oh selfless man and stainless gentleman!

Merlin and Vivien

It's odd how one drinks different things in different places. For instance, although I hate champagne cocktails, I always accept a couple from one particular mistress because a champagne cocktail, as anyone will tell you, gets to you where you live very fast and two such drinks enable me to ignore the grotesque schnozzle with which this particular lady has been endowed and to concentrate upon her other charms, which are of great distinction. To take other examples, there are some pubs where I just naturally order a scoop of Guiness and a 'half 'un' of Paddy on the side; there is one in Jersey where they always put a large whisky into a split of fresh orange-juice, ignoring the raised eyebrows of the other customers; another place where, even if I have been absent for a year, they draw me a pint of the very best bitter and lay beside it a ball-point pen because they know that I have come there to solve a crossword-puzzle. There is an Italian place in Oxford, which I used to pop into of a morning on my way home, where they are too tactful to greet me, they simply mix a massive brandy and soda and compassionately help me to fold my fingers around it. There is even a place, many miles from anywhere, where I drink something which I think is called Margarita; it comes in a filth-encrusted bottle without a label and seems to be 140-proof tomato ketchup. I could multiply examples but what I am driving at is that, for some reason, when I am in Jule's in Jermyn Street, which is arguably the best pub in the world, I always order Canadian rye whisky with ginger ale. Then I send a glass of wine to the pianist with a courteous message and he flicks a courteous glance at me and plays it. Ingrid Bergman never comes in but a man can dream, can't he?

Having gone through the ritual, and having summoned up the second drink, I made my way to the telephone and dialled Blucher's 'secure' number.

'This is the Home and Colonial Stores,' fluted the familiar voice.

'And my prick's a bloater,' I snarled, for I was in no mood to be paltered with.

'Indeed?' said the voice. 'Then I suggest you get in touch with the Royal College of Surgeons, where you may learn something to your advantage.'

'Grrrr,' I said. She replaced the receiver. I found another coin, dialled again.

'Please may I speak to Daddy?' I grated between clenched teeth.

'Why, sir?' I remembered the rest of the absurd password.

'Mummy's poorly.' There were clicks and scrambler-noises and at last Blucher was on the line.

'I want to speak to you,' I said. 'Now. I've had it up to here.'

'Where's here?' I told him. He was there in rather less than five minutes, which indicated that his Agency, whatever it was, was squandering prodigious sums of US tax-payers' money on addresses far above their station in life. Moreover, he was carrying an umbrella, which did not even begin to make him look like an Englishman.

I ordered a drink for him, although it went against the grain. He was, after all, my guest.

'Just two questions,' I murmured thinly. 'Exactly who have I been working for? And has it finished now? And, if so, do I stay alive?'

'That's *three* questions, Mr Mortdecai.' (You may recall that, early in our acquaintanceship, I had rebuked him for using my Christian name.)

'Very well, three,' I snapped. 'So you can count up to three. I know *women* who can count up to nine. Just start at question one and move gently down the list, using your own words.'

'I have an auto – sorry, a car – outside. Let's drive around a little, hunh? Then I'll take you home.' I thought about that a while, then agreed. I had, after all, telephoned him because I felt that extermination by his Agency would at least be efficient and hygienic; infinitely preferable to being made lethal sport of by female terrorists or Chinese gentlemen bearing grudges.

His car was not one of those great, black limousines that people are taken for rides in; it was a little 'topolino' Fiat with nothing sinister about it but a parking-ticket on the windscreen. He drove, as discreetly as a Rural Dean who has had two helpings of sherry-trifle and dreads being asked to puff into a breathalyser, to Grosvenor Square. To No. 24, Grosvenor Square, to be exact. That's the American Embassy, as if you didn't know.

'I'm not going in there,' I said.

'Neither am I. My desk will be chin-high with paper-work, all marked "Urgent". I'm just stopping here because the cops won't give me a bad time; the number of this car is on the privilege list.'

'How the other half lives, to be sure,' I murmured.

'Now, Mr Mortdecai; your questions. First, you have been working for the United Nations. OK, laugh, enjoy, enjoy. But you have. My own Agency co-operates closely with that particular branch of UNO and I can say most sincerely that in the last few weeks we have achieved some very, very spectacular results.' I probably said something feeble like 'Well done' but he ignored whatever it was and continued.

'Your second question – "has it finished now?" – I can only answer with a kind of qualified "yes". Your third question – the one about whether you get to stay alive – is a little tough. So far as my bosses are concerned I think I can say that there is now no problem.' He turned and looked at me as though trying to puzzle out why anyone like me should want to stay alive. I squared my shoulders and looked as haughty as one can in the passenger-seat of a little Fiat. 'But, Mr Mortdecai, I'm sure you understand that in an operation as complex as this there are many, many loose ends which take a while to sort of mop up and winkle out and we could not of course justify in our budget an expense like protecting, say, you, around the clock for the next few months. I'm sure you see that.'

'I quite see that,' I said, ignoring his garish mixture of metaphors.

'Have you ever thought of the Seychelles?' he asked. 'The Antilles? Samoa? The Virgin Islands?' I turned upon him a stony glare which should have made him think of Easter Island.

'Well, how about the Channel Islands? Your wife has a half-share in a really beautiful mansion there.' I hadn't known that, but there were many things I didn't know about Johanna in those days.

'How do you know that?' I demanded.

He fixed me with that pitying look with which people often fix me when they have decided that I am simple-minded. Often, if the circumstances are propitious, I wipe off the pitying look with what Jock calls a 'bunch of fives', but the passenger-seat of a right-hand drive Topolino is not what I would call a propitious circumstance: the only possible blow would be a round-house left – and the driving-mirror was in the way. Moreover, I was giving away fifteen years, not to mention thirty pounds of self-indulgence.

'I have always longed to visit the Isle of Jersey,' is what I said.

You must guard against hating people or even things: it is easy to become like what you hate. Victory at Entebbe destroys us more surely than defeat at Kursk. I did not hate Blucher at all as he drove me home, although I had to work hard at it.

Johanna was not at home but Jock was, of course. His good eye seemed to look at Blucher almost benignly; had I not been preoccupied with other matters – like life and death – I might have thought this strange, for Jock has never been one to betray a liking for the fuzz. I offered Blucher an assortment of chairs, bade Jock supply him with anything he might long for in the way of drinks or eatables, then melted away apologetically as a host melts when he wishes to put the cat out. What I urgently wanted was to get under the shower and refresh the frame with newly-laundred gents' underwear, half-hose and shirtings as now worn.

I indulged myself, as ever; it must have been quite half an hour before I reappeared, sweet-smelling and freshly clad, in the drawing-room, secure in the expectation that Blucher would have

179

taken his leave. I was wrong, of course. What he had taken was the infernal liberty of sitting next to my wife, Johanna, on the little Louis Quinze sofa which is not designed to support two people unless the two people do not happen to mind a certain intimacy, a certain warm proximity of hip and thigh. They were chuckling, I heard them distinctly. I do not often stand aghast but aghast was what I stood then.

'Charlie dear,' cried Johanna, 'we thought you were never coming. Do sit, darling; have something to drink, you must be tired.' I sat in the least comfortable chair in the room and forced a drink between my unwilling lips. (This was, you understand, only to mask or muffle the grinding of my teeth.)

'Ah, well, Blucher,' I said, 'I see that you have made the acquaintance of my wife. Good, splendid, yes.'

'Darling, we've known each other for ages and ages . . .' Blucher looked at her and nodded knowingly, lovingly. I took another gulp of whisky to disguise the gnashing. No conversational gambit offered itself to me; I merely glowered at the few square inches of carpet between my feet.

'Charlie, dear, you're not being the perfect host tonight – couldn't you sort of tell your guest a funny story or something? I mean, he did save your life, huh?' I lost patience at that point. All bets were off.

'Look,' I rasped, 'this guest of mine – perhaps I should say ours – *sold* me my life. The price was that I married you. I liked being married to you until about five minutes ago, I really did, although the, er, extramarital tasks have been a little trying. But he didn't save my life, he bought and sold it.'

Johanna put onto her face that sweet, tolerant look of a Spock-trained mother whose child has just wet the bed for the third time that night.

'You don't have it quite right, Charlie dear. As a matter of fact, our guest figured that it would be tidiest to sort of terminate you long ago. It was I who bought your life.' My brain started to feel like one of those cages where white mice run happily, mindlessly in a wire treadmill.

'Of course,' I said bitterly, 'of course, of course. You bought my life. I must remember to thank you. No use my asking why, I suppose?'

'Because I loved you, you great, stupid, self-satisfied prig!' she blazed. I never know what to say on occasions like that; I usually just shuffle my feet and look silly.

'Er, was that last word "prig" or "pig"?' I asked, for want of anything better to say. She didn't answer, just sat there with a face of thunder, tapping her foot on the carpet as though there were some small pest there. Like, say, a Mortdecai. I distinctly saw Blucher's hand take hers and squeeze it fondly.

'And how much did you pay for this alleged life of mine?' I asked, my worst fears coming to the forefront of my brain and starting to dance a lewd jig. To my astonishment she giggled – and in the most fetching way. I had never heard her giggle before.

'Please make us some drinks first, Charlie dear.' I did so but with an ill grace, although I softened a little when it came to measuring out my own.

'Now,' she said cosily, 'Franzl will tell you all about it.'

'*Franzl!*' I squeaked. 'Franzl?'

'Hey, that's great, Charlie old boy; I knew you and I'd get onto first-name terms in the end. Now, like I said back there at the beginning, the price of you staying alive was marrying Hänschen here.'

'*Hänschen?*' I squawked.

'Why sure, don't you call her that? No? Well, what I didn't make clear was that it was her idea, not mine. See, she had this crazy idea that you were the only man in the world for her; well, she always had these really weird fantasies, you know?'

'No.'

'Well, she does. Anyway, her organization had penetrated about as far as possible and it was pretty clear that the Chinese guys weren't about to show any more of their cards without the pot being sweetened up with some heavy action. My own Agency, which is more clandestine than, uh, subversive, was also up against a stone wall and the lousy CIA were commencing to sniff around at our fire-hydrants. Uh, lamp-posts?'

'Go on.'

'Well, we'd sort of theoretically ageed that a kind of catalyst was needed, like throwing a new face into the game who might blunder about and get the deer moving . . .'

'He means, Charlie dear, someone resourceful like you but who was not familiar with the scenario . . .'

'You mean,' I said, 'that what I didn't know couldn't be tortured out of me?'

'No, dear, just someone with no preconceived notions which might make you follow . . .'

'. . . the kind of pattern that a trained agent would; we had to puzzle them by throwing into the ball-game someone clearly unprofessional, someone half-smart . . .'

'He means, dear, that it was like suddenly putting an English Rugby International into the Yale-Harvard match. I knew it was desperately dangerous for you – Franzl offered me eleven to two against your surviving the first week – but it was better than having all those awful people in Lancashire quite certainly destroying you in your cave. You do see that, don't you darling?' All I could see was Blucher's hand patting hers and, when I tore my glance away, the whitening of my own knuckles. Blucher took up the story again.

'Also, like I said, the bad guys were looking for some heavy action; really heavy, so we dreamed up this attempted assassination of Her Majesty. We never thought you'd get to first base and gosh, we were worried when it started to look like you'd get away with it. We were a little late getting to you that time – the traffice re-routed and all – it surely was lucky that cartridge jammed in the breech. I guess you'd really have done it, hunh?'

'As a matter of fact, I don't believe I would. Jock wouldn't have liked it, you see; he would have handed in his notice.'

'Well, he wouldn't have needed to do that. You see, there was an Oriental guy in the window right across the street from you with a sniper's rifle and he'd have bipped you right between the eyes one fifth of one second after you fired. To save you from interrogation, you understand.'

'You did wonderfully well, Charlie dear. I have been so proud of you.'

'Yes, you really did, Charlie old boy.' He put an arm about my wife's shoulders and kissed her noisily on the cheek. This was too much. My knuckles were now Whiter-Than-White and I'm confident that any trained observer would have observed that the veins in my forehead were bulging out like firemen's hoses. I rose to my feet, eyeing them dangerously. We Mortdecais do not make a practice of tearing our guests limb from limb, especially when there are ladies present, however base and treacherous the lady. I must confess, however, that I came pretty close to breaking this rule, and indeed might well have done so had I not recalled that it simply is not done to strike a guest whose posture, while embracing one's wife, betrays a shameless bulge under the left armpit, where a large, coarse automatic pistol evidently lurks. I stalked out of the room in a marked manner. I did not trip over anything, nor did I slam the door.

Jock, staunch fellow, was in the kitchen, his great boots propped up on the hygienic working-surface. He peered at me over the top edge of his copy of *Film Fun*. I launched a great kick at the nearest pastel-coloured eezi-slide kitchen-fitment and dented it severely. Jock rummaged in a pocket for his glass eye, moistened it in the mug of tea before him and popped it deftly into its socket.

'You all right, Mr Charlie?'

'I am in splendid form, Jock,' I snarled, 'capital, topping, never better. We cuckolds feel no pain, you know.' He gaped as I delivered a truly mighty kick at the same fitment. This time my foot went through it and was trapped in the ruptured plastic and three-ply. Jock helped me get my shoe off with the aid of the kitchen scissors and I was able to free my foot and limp to the kitchen table.

'Reckon that old kick done you a power of good, Mr Charlie, better than a week at the seaside. Anything else you fancy?'

'How is the canary?' I countered. 'Still sulking?'

'Nah, he's back in lovely voice, a fair treat to listen to him, I had to put a clorth over his cage to shut the little bugger up. What I done was, I give him some hard-boiled egg, a pinch of cayenne in his hempseed and a sup of rum in his drinking water and now, bing-bong, he's ready to take on all comers. Booking for smoking-concerts now.'

'Give me that very cure, Jock,' I said moodily, 'but leaving out the hard-boiled egg, the cayenne, the hempseed and the drinking-water.'

'Right, Mr Charlie; one large Navy rum coming up. Er, will Madam be wanting anythink?'

'I could not say. She seems to be in close conference with Colonel Blucher.'

'Yeah, well, she hasn't seen him for munce, has she?'

'I could not say.'

'Well, he is her bruvver, inne?'

'Jock, what the hell are you talking about?'

'Well, I mean, Mrs M is his *sister*, isn't she? Same thing, innit?'
Many things began to become clear; one of the clearest of these
things was that for once in my life I had behaved like a twit.

'Oh, ah?' I said.

'Yeah,' said Jock. I re-assembled what I like to think of as my
thoughts.

'Jock,' I said, 'unswathe the said canary; I long to hear a few
of its dulcet notes. But in doing so pray do not forget the large
glass of Navy rum which I ordered quite ninety seconds ago.' As
the honest fellow clumped towards the pantry I recalled something
which had been simmering in the back of my mind all the live-long
day: the very crux or pivot of the whole situation, the pin upon
which everything turned.

'Jock!' I cried anguishedly. He stopped in his tracks, span upon
his heel.

'Jock, please add one of your extra-special jam-sandwiches to that
order, if you will be so kind.'

'Right, Mr Charlie; that's one large rum, one jem semwidge.'

'And one canary.'

'Right, Mr Charlie.'

'Right, Jock,' I said.

Leabharlanna Poibli Chathair Bhaile Átha Cliath

Dublin City Public Libraries